P9-AOG-166

the Faelin chronicles

Mage Fire

C. AUBREY HALL

BOOK THREE

SKYSCAPE

SKYSCAPE

Text copyright © 2013 by Deborah Chester

Amazon Publishing
Attn: Amazon Children's Publishing
P.O. Box 400818
Las Vegas, NV 89140
www.amazon.com/amazonchildrenspublishing

Library of Congress Cataloging-in-Publication Date is available upon request.

ISBN-13: 9781477816561 (hardcover)
ISBN-10: 1477816569 (hardcover)
ISBN-13: 9781477866566 (eBook)
ISBN-10: 1477866566 (eBook)

Book design by Alex Ferrari
Map by Megan McNinch
Editor: Robin Benjamin

Printed in The United States of America (R)
First edition
10 9 8 7 6 5 4 3 2 1

Cast of Characters

FAE

Clevn:
mage-chancellor of the Fae, Sheirae's twin brother, commander of wind and lightning

Lwyneth:
mother (deceased) to Diello, Cynthe, and Amalina

Owain:
Lwyneth's twin brother

Penrith:
Queen Sheirae's heir, Owain's daughter

General Rhodri:
commander of the Fae army

Sheirae:
queen of the Fae, mother to Lwyneth and Owain

FAELIN

Amalina:
younger sister to Diello and Cynthe

Cynthe:
Diello's twin sister, gifted magically

Diello:
a thirteen-year-old boy with crystal bones and other magic powers

GOBLINS

Brezog:
ruler of all the goblins

Khuno:
son and heir to Brezog

Scree:
a goblin-boy befriended by Diello and Cynthe

HUMANS

Lord Malques:
the baron of Wodesley Castle

Stephel:
father (deceased) to Diello, Cynthe, and Amalina, a former
Carnethie Knight

TESCORSIANS

Onstri:
the elderly grandfather to Reeshwin and Strieka

Reeshwin:
a shape-shifter girl

Strieka:
sister to Reeshwin

Uruoc:
king of the eagle-folk

WOLVES

Chorl:
a samal wolf, presently in service to Queen Sheirae

Shalla:
Vassou's mother (deceased), formerly in service to Lwyneth

Vassou:
a talking samal wolf pup

ANCESTORS, DEITIES, ORACLES, AND SPIRITS

Afon Heyrn:
the Fae religious council

Ancient Harmonies:
elemental spirits

Batha:
the Wind of the North

Chanda:
the Wind of the South

The Guardian:
the supreme Fae deity

The Knower:
an ancient oracle, appearing in tree form

Qod:
a tomtir spirit

Salmeth:
the legendary First Warrior, creator of the sword Eirian

Thugar:
a deity of Tescorsa

Watchers:
twelve spirits that guard sacred Fae relics in the Cave of Mysteries

Zephyr:
a magical breeze

chapter one

More snow than Diello had ever seen in his life coated the mountain slopes, piling over rock and crevice. The footing was icy slick.

They'd just emerged from a pass overhung with snow and icicles. Sheer cliffs towered above them. The travelers walked single file. Diello had the lead, followed by his twin sister, Cynthe, their friend Scree, and the samal wolf pup Vassou. They were connected to each other by short lengths of leather rope tied around their waists, with a makeshift harness for Vassou.

No one was talking. Vassou had warned them about the dangers of an avalanche, so they were following the trail as quickly and quietly as they could, panting in the thin air.

The worst of the climb lay behind them, and from this point the trail would take them downhill. With luck they'd reach the valley and find a good camping spot before nightfall.

Although Tescorsa—land of the giant eagles—was ruggedly mountainous, they were finding the trek easier now than weeks ago, when they'd struggled to cross their homeland, Antrasia, into the Fae realm of Embarthi. This time, no band of goblins was pursuing them. They could use their magic as they pleased without worrying about leaving a trail for the gorlord to follow. They were now the hunters, for Diello was determined to track down the magical sword, Eirian, and its scabbard. Both had been stolen by enemies of the Fae. Yet the Fae queen, Sheirae, had blamed Diello and his twin—her own grandchildren— and she'd exiled them from Embarthi. Even worse, without Eirian, Diello and Cynthe had no hope of ransoming their kidnapped little sister. Several times lately, Diello had tried to check on Amalina with his Gift of Sight, hoping to conjure up a vision of her, but he'd been unsuccessful. It scared him, not knowing if she was still all right. After Uncle Owain's threats, Diello didn't trust him to treat her well.

The scabbard had last been seen in the talons of a Tescorsian eagle, so Tescorsa was where Diello and his companions were headed first.

Diello glanced back.

"Let's take a rest over there," he said, pointing with his quarterstaff to a flat-topped boulder. "Three swallows of water each, then we'll move on."

The others crowded closer in agreement. Someone stumbled. Diello heard a rock go skittering off the trail.

"Be careful," Diello reminded everyone.

"Watch out!" Cynthe called. As her feet skated on the ice, she bumped into Diello and grabbed his shoulders to steady herself.

"I tripped you, Cynthe," Scree admitted, holding on to

her rope with both hands. "I'm sorry! I was trying not to slide into Vassou."

A rumble shook the ground.

"Run!" Vassou cried.

An enormous sheet of snow, ice, and rocks thundered down behind them, obliterating the trail. Diello stared, stunned by the violence of it.

Cynthe shoved him forward. "Didn't you hear Vassou? Move!"

More snow was coming, breaking free from higher up the mountainside and heading straight for them.

There was nowhere to take cover. On the other side of the trail lay a sheer drop.

It was crazy to run, but they did anyway. Diello's feet skidded on the treacherous path. He was afraid of falling off the trail and dragging everyone with him. But if he didn't hurry, they would all be buried alive. A huge boulder thudded onto the path in front of him.

Diello stopped. *It could have squashed me like a mudskimmer.*

"Break!" Cynthe said in a low, harsh tone, using the power of Voice.

Diello clapped his hands over his face just before the boulder shattered to gravel. Pelted with pebbles and sharp bits of rock, Diello didn't wait for the dust to clear. He hefted his staff and scrambled forward.

"Good job, Cynthe!" he called over his shoulder.

With a yelp, Vassou teetered near the edge, his paws slipping on the ice. Scree yanked him back to safety.

"Keep going!" Cynthe yelled.

Suddenly, the snow engulfed them. It crashed over the top of Diello's head, and he had just enough time to think *It's really heavy!* before he lost his footing and was pushed off the trail.

Deafened, blinded by whiteness, tumbled and bashed—Diello was carried along until his shoulder jammed against a long root sticking out of the ground. He grabbed on to it and closed his eyes, feeling the rope digging into his waist as the avalanche tried to carry Cynthe and the others away.

Don't break, rope. Don't break. Don't break.

Then there was silence.

Diello opened his eyes. He was still surrounded by white. A dome of snow covered him, but a small air pocket had formed around his face. He'd been buried alive, but he could breathe.

"Cynthe?" he called. "Scree? Vassou?"

No one answered.

Diello tried to stay calm. The sensible thing was to dig himself out first, then hunt for the others, but his heart couldn't wait.

He pulled on the rope.

There was a tug back.

Someone's alive! Cynthe?

At that moment, the air pocket collapsed. Snow smothered Diello. He pushed at it with his hands, digging frantically. Some of the snow was soft, some of it icy hard. His lungs were burning cold. *How deep? How deep?*

His left hand broke through the snow. He sucked in a mouthful of ice and sputtered.

A jerk on his rope dragged him deeper into the snow, away from his air hole. He tugged to make Cynthe stop, but it was too late. His air hole was gone. Aware that he might lose his sister forever, he slashed through the rope with his knife and strained upward, pushing his head to the surface.

All around him lay dazzling white snow. The trail had disappeared. He couldn't tell how deep into the ravine the snowslide had pushed him.

He didn't see Cynthe or the others as he climbed out, dragging his pack and quarterstaff with him.

"Come on, Cynthe," he muttered. "You can get out. Hurry!"

The thought of his friends suffocating sent him crawling back to where he thought Cynthe must be. Floundering through drifts, he scooped snow with his hands, digging here, then there, calling her name repeatedly.

Flames shot up through the snow right in front of him. Diello jumped back. Cynthe's head and shoulders poked through the melting snow. She shook the water from her hair as she gulped in several breaths, then slicked the damp strands behind her pointed ears.

"I'm f-freezing," she said, her teeth chattering. "You all right?"

"Yes. You?"

She nodded, lifting her arms. "Help m-me out."

He took hold of her wrists and pulled her free. She

was trembling with cold, but she wouldn't let him brush her off.

"No time. The others," she said.

Diello plucked at the rope still tied around her waist. It was stretched tight. "I thought maybe we could pull Scree to the surface, but the rope won't budge," he said.

"He must be caught somehow. Dig!"

As the twins knelt together to dig, Vassou emerged a few feet away. His muzzle appeared first, then his shoulders, until he was on top of the snow, shaking it from his coat. A broken bit of rope dangled from his harness.

"Come and help us find Scree!" Diello called.

The wolf pup bounded over and sniffed the snow before he turned away and circled a different spot. "Here."

Diello and Cynthe set to work, but Vassou pushed between them.

"I'll dig for you," the pup said to Diello. "You'll lose fingers if you don't warm your hands."

Diello noticed that some of his fingertips were turning white. Hastily he tucked his hands inside his sleeves. The Fae clothing given to him and Cynthe by General Rhodri before they'd left Embarthi was magically warm. Feeling returned almost immediately to his hands, painfully so. He flexed his swollen fingers, wincing, and helped the others by kicking at the snow.

Vassou was digging deep, his head and half of his body inside a big hole, his tail wagging as he sent snow flying. Then he yipped and backed out.

"Scree?" Cynthe called.

"I—I am hurt," Scree said weakly. "I am c-cold."

"Can you make it out?" Diello asked.

"No . . . my leg . . ."

Cynthe dropped to her stomach to crawl inside, but Diello held her back.

"No, it could collapse on you."

So they enlarged the hole until they could reach Scree. He was lying in a jumble of small boulders, his leg pinned by one of the rocks. His eyes were closed.

Cynthe crouched next to the goblin-boy, brushing away more snow. "We're here," she said. "We're going to get you out."

Scree opened his eyes and tried to smile at her.

"We need something to pry him out with." Diello looked around. "A stout stick."

"Your quarterstaff?" Cynthe asked.

Diello shook his head. "It's not long enough."

There were no trees close by. The avalanche had swept them away. Diello lifted his arms and rose up in the air, flying down the slope to the edge of the forest below. The snow had pushed broken timbers and rocks into a pile. Diello climbed swiftly, taking care as the logs shifted under his weight. Most of the branches he found were either too crooked or too short. Finally he came across a stout, straight pine branch.

Flying back with it proved to be a wobbly business, but he managed.

Cynthe guided the branch's tip beneath the edge of the

rock pinning Scree. But when Diello put his weight on the other end, the stick sank into the snow.

"What we need is Pa's digging bar," he said.

"If only we could get it. I'd gladly handle iron right now."

Diello nodded. He and Cynthe had enough Fae blood in their veins to make them break out in itchy welts if they went near that metal. But the digging bar was stout and effective, a perfect tool for the job. Too bad it was leagues away, back on the old farmstead.

"Maybe I can break the rock," Cynthe said.

Diello frowned. "Can you be careful enough? What if you hurt Scree instead?"

"I know." She sighed. "I'm afraid to chance it."

"Let's try the stick again. I'll do the prying, and you pull him free the moment I shift the rock."

"You can't do it alone."

Diello flushed. He was thirteen now, but he never seemed to grow any bigger. *Am I going to be a scrawny weed all my life?*

Vassou stood next to Scree. "I'll pull him free. Then the two of you can work together."

"Can you cast a spell first to block his pain?" Diello asked Vassou. As a samal wolf, Vassou possessed several powers, including the ability to cast spells for shielding and invisibility.

"I'm no healer," Vassou replied.

"Would a *cloigwylie*—if you wrapped that kind of spell around him for protection—would it lift the rock at all?"

Vassou thought for a moment and shook his head. "That's not its purpose. It will not work as you wish."

"Then we have to do this the hard way," Diello said.

"Scree," Cynthe said, touching the goblin-boy's shoulder, "hang on to Vassou's harness and don't let go for any reason. Understand?"

"I will do what you say," Scree whispered. He hooked his fingers around the leather strap.

Together the twins pushed down on the branch.

"Don't bounce it," Diello warned his sister. "Just steady pressure."

"The stick's bending," she said. "It's not strong enough."

"Keep trying anyway."

"The boulder is shifting," Vassou told them. "Just a bit more."

Diello pushed harder. *Don't give up.*

Cynthe gasped. "It's not working."

"It has to!"

A shrill cry nearly made Diello drop the branch.

"Is that Scree?" he asked.

"No," Vassou replied. "Don't stop now. I'm almost able to move him."

The noise came again—more of a moan than a scream this time. It didn't sound like anything Diello had heard before.

"What in the name of Thugar are you doing to my children?"

Before Diello could look around, there was a loud snap, and the branch broke in his hands. Cynthe lost her balance, sprawling in the snow. Diello landed on top of her.

As the boulder rocked back into place, Scree yelped loudly, then was silent.

chapter two

After the twins helped each other up, Diello saw that Scree had been dragged clear.

"I did not mean to bite his shoulder when I pulled him free," Vassou said. "He's fainted."

In the past, Vassou probably would have made some comment about how awful goblins tasted; but ever since he and Scree had been imprisoned together in the Fae palace, the wolf had shown Scree more respect. Neither Vassou nor Scree had talked much about how they'd been treated, but Diello knew that the Fae had been unkind to them.

Cynthe pulled a blanket from her pack to wrap around Scree. "He's awfully cold. Help me, Diello. I think his leg's broken."

Diello was distracted, looking around. "Did you hear someone speak just before we fell?"

"No." Cynthe was busy breaking two bits of wood to the same length. "Are these long enough for splints?"

"Let me find something better." Diello turned around and almost stumbled over a round stone about the size of his foot. He started to kick it aside, but before he touched the stone, it rolled away from his toe and stopped just out of reach. Diello crouched to look at the stone more closely and found a pair of dark eyes staring up at him.

He sprang back. "What is that?"

The wolf pup approached the stone, sniffing; but the rock lobbed itself up in the air, coming down about ten steps away.

"Diello!" Cynthe called. "Get busy and help me."

Not taking his eyes off the rock, Diello gestured to his sister. "Cynthe, look at this."

"What?" She joined him. "Why are you tossing rocks around when Scree's hurt?"

"I didn't throw anything."

She stared farther up the mountain. "Is another avalanche going to come down?"

Diello saw the rock move slightly. He grabbed Cynthe's arm. "Look!"

Suddenly, the rock grew, expanding into a short, squat creature reaching as high as Diello's knees. Bits of lichen clung to its lumpy surface. It had no arms or legs, no ears or feet. Its round, dark eyes met Diello's with reproach.

"What a vexing Fae-boy you are," the creature said. "You aren't civil at all. First you disturb my children, then you ignore a perfectly reasonable question, and now you try to kick me. Really, I find your behavior most displeasing."

Before Diello could find his voice, the creature came sliding toward them, plowing a furrow through the snow.

"Mind your feet!" it roared, making Diello and Cynthe

jump apart. It sailed past them and stopped next to the boulder they'd shifted off Scree.

Cynthe shrugged her bow from her shoulder and readied it. "What in the name of the Ancient Harmonies *is* that?"

Diello could only shake his head.

"I think," Vassou answered quietly, "that it must be a tomtir. I've heard of them, but I've never seen one."

"Now you have," said the tomtir. "Don't just stand there staring, Fae-boy. Kindly give me assistance. Gawking never gets a day's work done."

Diello glanced at his twin. "Can you hear it speaking now?"

She nodded, her eyes wide.

"Good. I didn't want to be the only one."

"So," Cynthe said, "a tomtir is a talking rock?"

"Not exactly." Vassou didn't explain further. He was staring at the tomtir with as much puzzlement as the twins.

Diello could have sworn that the tomtir didn't move, but the next thing he knew he was looking at the creature's lumpy back while the tomtir studied Cynthe instead. Diello squinted, using Sight. Now—instead of a blur of amazing speed, he could see the tomtir turning around to face him. It blinked up at Diello.

"If you'd be good enough to remove this stick from beneath my child," the tomtir said, "I should be much obliged to you."

"Sorry, but what child?" Diello asked.

"Look how you've left it tilted and exposed to the air!"

the tomtir said impatiently. "Freezing, thawing, letting snow and ice build up underneath. Such weathering can cause fissures far too early. Bad enough that you've brought an avalanche down over the nest. I suppose you couldn't help that, being what you are. But no need to add injury to accident."

"Excuse me," Diello said as politely as possible. He rested his hand on the boulder that had pinned Scree. As far as he could tell, it was just a lifeless stone. "Are you saying that your child is inside this?"

"Certainly not. What a ridiculous question."

"Tomtirs," Vassou explained, "are usually tree spirits. Sometimes they appear as rocks, but—"

"Are you a scholar?" interrupted the tomtir. "Are you an authority? No, you most certainly are not. Please hush like a good fellow."

Vassou's ears drooped.

"Are all these rocks alive?" Cynthe asked, gesturing at the mountain slope.

"Not in the way you mean," Vassou told her. "They—"

"The air!" the tomtir yelled, spinning around on its base so that Diello had to move back to avoid a collision. "Do you want the stone to crumble before its time? For ice to work its way into every crack and crevice until the boulder splits apart? It's much too young for that. Someone here simply has to be responsible and put a stop to it."

"I don't think we hurt it," Diello said.

"Tilted like that? With its base exposed to the elements?

Why, in five hundred years it might not even be recognizable."

Cynthe gurgled as she tried to swallow a laugh. She clapped her hand over her mouth.

Diello didn't dare meet her gaze. "Then there's no actual hurry," he said slowly.

"Wrongs should be righted before damage is done. No reason to be slack about it."

That sounded oddly like Pa. Diello and Cynthe exchanged a look and then strained to shift the boulder back into place.

"This is a daft business," Cynthe grumbled. "Scree needs our attention, not this—this—"

"Too far!" the tomtir said, eyeing the rock critically. "More to the left. That's it. Ah. That'll do nicely."

"Why can't, uh, your child move around like you do?" Diello asked.

"Yes, that's an excellent position for it. Thank you, Fae-boy. Thank you, Fae-girl."

Cynthe rolled her eyes at Diello before wiping her face with her sleeve and returning to the search for Scree's splints.

"Actually, we're Faelin, only half Fae," Diello explained to the tomtir, realizing it wasn't going to answer his question. "My name is—"

"No names, please, not out here on the open slopes," the tomtir said in alarm. "That would be most unwise. Don't you realize you're in the land of shape-shifters?"

Diello glanced around but didn't see any other living

creatures, unless more tomtirs were hiding under the snow.

"If they have your name, they can assume your shape," the tomtir said.

"Who?" Diello asked.

"The creepers. The peepers. The crawlers. The hiders."

"Are all Tescorsians shape-shifters?"

"Caution is best."

"Thanks for the warning. If you don't mind, we'd better be going. It's a long way to the valley," said Diello.

"I don't think we'll get there before dark," Cynthe added. "Diello, help me set Scree's leg before he wakes up."

Diello hesitated. He'd held a young calf while Pa splinted its front leg, and he and Cynthe had tried once to set a duck's broken wing. The calf always limped, and the duck never flew again. Diello knew they had to do something, but he was afraid for Scree.

Cynthe's eyes flashed up at him. "Well?"

"Do you want me to pull or place the splints?"

"You pull. I'll bind."

Drawing a deep breath, Diello took hold of Scree's ankle.

Cynthe hooked her blond hair behind her ears as she always did when she was nervous. "Ready?" she asked.

Vassou moved back, and the tomtir rolled a short distance away.

Gently but firmly, Diello pulled Scree's leg straight and held it while Cynthe bound the splints in place.

When they finished, Diello wiped the perspiration from his forehead and helped Cynthe to her feet.

"I'm glad he didn't feel any of that," she said.

Scree opened his eyes. They were huge with pain. "I felt everything," he whispered. "I did not think you would like it if I screamed, but I wanted to scream loud enough to make more of the mountain fall."

"I'm sorry," Diello said. "It—it had to be done."

"You are good friends to me. Now you must leave me behind."

"Don't be daft," Cynthe said.

"You must go on. I am of no use to you. I cannot do my share. I do not think I can walk."

"No one expects you to," Diello assured him. "We'll make a travois to carry you."

"We aren't leaving you behind," Cynthe said, kneeling to give Scree a drink of water from their supplies.

Diello stopped himself from protesting. They'd been eating snow on their journey to conserve as much water as possible, but this was no time to be strict.

When they'd left Embarthi, they'd absolved Scree for his betrayal in "giving" the sword Eirian to Brezog, ruler of the goblin horde. Eirian could not be taken by force. Its possessor had to surrender it. They had been shocked to learn that the gorlord was Scree's father. With his magical powers, Brezog had coerced Scree to obey him and then fled, abandoning his son. Even though Diello and Cynthe had forgiven Scree, he couldn't seem to forgive himself.

Vassou circled them restlessly, nosing first Cynthe, then Diello before climbing atop an outcropping to keep watch.

"He still feels cold," Diello said, holding one of Scree's thin hands between his to warm it. He tried to be gentle, for both of Scree's palms had been seriously burned from handling Eirian's blade. The healing skin was tender, and Scree would have scars for life. "Maybe we should camp here for the night and continue tomorrow."

"Here?" the tomtir cried, unexpectedly shrinking to the size of Diello's fist. "In the open? On the mountain? All night?"

"Yes." Diello pointed toward the forest. "Or maybe over there. We'll need some cover if the wind picks up."

"No, no, no," the tomtir said. "This is most inadvisable. I strongly urge you to reconsider."

"Why?" Cynthe asked.

"There are many dangers in the mountains. You need shelter for the night. I would offer you the protection of my hole, but I don't think it will hold all of you." The tomtir shrank to the size of a pebble. "Can you make yourself smaller?" it asked in a very tiny voice.

"No," Cynthe said.

The tomtir expanded to the size of a small dog. "How untalented you are. What is the good of being only one size?"

Diello had crystal bones, which usually tingled when magic was used nearby, but they weren't even reacting as the tomtir changed its appearance.

He couldn't waste time wondering about that. A biting wind began to blow. Dark clouds covered the sun. He thought of the logistics of moving Scree safely. Scree was tough, but he was also the most accident-prone creature Diello had ever known. *What if he has more injuries besides the broken leg? We could really hurt him.*

Vassou's soft yip caught Diello's attention. Diello climbed up next to the wolf and raised his hood against the wind.

"Look that way, toward the valley," Vassou said, pointing with his muzzle.

Diello stared hard. "I'm not sure what I'm supposed to see."

Cynthe joined them. "Trouble?" she asked.

"Your eyes are keener than mine," Diello said. "Look at the valley."

"What about it?" Cynthe said.

"Look *toward* the valley," Vassou corrected.

She stiffened. "Is that a hut in the trees?"

"I think so," the wolf said.

"A hut?" Diello tried to spot it in the undergrowth. Maybe—just maybe—he could make out a corner of the roof.

"Red?" he asked.

Cynthe nodded. "If we can get to it before this storm hits—"

"Stop talking and get moving," Diello said.

chapter three

the wind strengthened, whipping snow flurries into Diello's eyes. He didn't like how swiftly the weather had changed. Pellets of sleet hit him as he lashed some of their rope between two long sticks and spread a blanket across it. With Cynthe's help, he lifted Scree onto the travois.

The tomtir—now as round and smooth as a river stone—rolled here and there, getting under Diello's feet. "Where are you going? The valley is too far away. You need to take shelter now. Perhaps I could dig a tunnel for each of you to lie in."

It would be like sleeping in a grave. Diello tried to remain polite. "Look," he said, "I'm grateful for the offer, but no. We're moving on."

"I insist on offering you my hospitality. I've had no visitors for quite some time. Have you not heard of tomtir hospitality?"

"It's legendary," Vassou said.

"Legendary good or legendary dangerous?" Diello muttered.

"I can offer you three varieties of cake," the tomtir said. Diello paused a moment before he shook his head.

"I like cake," Scree spoke up from the travois. "If I had cake to eat, I think I would soon feel much better."

The tomtir increased its size, rocking from side to side. "Splendid! Do you prefer mud, lichen with a frozen-worm garnish, or rock cake made of shale, flaked very fine?"

Scree blinked. "Do you have grubs?"

"No, but I serve warm mud tea."

"We can't eat those things," Cynthe said, gathering up their packs.

"None of them?"

"Nothing," Diello said firmly.

"Flesh and grain eaters, I suppose."

"That's right." Diello glanced at his sister. "Ready?"

"Shall I come with you?" the tomtir asked eagerly. "I'm happy to oblige."

"Sorry, no," Diello answered. He was growing suspicious. He wondered why the tomtir didn't go away. *Is it trying to distract us until something else shows up?*

Fog closed in around them, shrinking visibility to a few feet. Diello looked around, but he had no bearings. "Let's tie ourselves together," he said. "Vassou, can you guide us through this?"

"I think so."

Cynthe got busy tying rope to their waists as before. She laid Diello's quarterstaff next to Scree and secured it. "Want me to help you drag Scree?"

"Let's take turns," Diello said. "Lead off, Vassou."

As they set out, Diello looked around for the tomtir, intending to bid it farewell; but the creature had vanished.

"Good-bye, tomtir," Diello called.

The mountain was steep and long. The going was especially difficult, thanks to deep, powdery snow reaching to about midthigh. Among the trees and brush, the drifts piled taller. Past the edge of the avalanche, the snow's surface had developed a wind-scoured crust; but it proved too thin and brittle to support their weight. Vassou and Cynthe did their best to break a trail for Diello to follow, but it was slow and tiring work. Scree's travois seemed to snag on every bush and bump.

"Let's stop!" Cynthe said, breathing hard.

Diello lowered the travois gladly. Although his clothing kept him warm and dry, he wasn't sure he could feel his toes anymore; and his cheeks felt raw from the constant sting of wind. He'd pulled his sleeves over his hands to protect his fingers as much as possible, but they were stiff. His shoulders were aching from dragging the travois, and Scree grew heavier with every passing moment. Diello worried about the goblin-boy. Every jolt must be agony, but Scree—squinting against the weather—hadn't uttered a single whimper.

The wind gusted, making Diello stumble. It cleared the fog away, but snow was falling now, cutting their visibility further.

"We're thinking like humans," Cynthe said. "Why don't we fly? We're good enough at it now."

"Can we handle Scree's weight?"

"Let's try."

They picked up the travois like a stretcher.

"*Up!*" Cynthe cried.

Diello tried to relax as he lifted gently in the air. Cynthe rose faster than he did, making the travois wobble; but they leveled it. A squawking bird flew off its perch in a tree, nearly colliding with Diello.

Vassou yelped as the rope pulled him onto his hind legs.

"Untie me!" he cried, snapping at the rope.

"Sorry, Vassou," Cynthe called to him.

"We'll fly lower," Diello said.

They sank down until they were hovering just slightly above the top of the snow. *A few weeks ago, I'd have fallen on my face,* Diello thought. It wasn't just practice that had improved their flying skills. His and Cynthe's powers— their Gifts—were growing a little stronger every day. The twins never knew when a new Gift might manifest itself. Having been told by their mother that they would possess almost no magic because they were Faelin, they were still amazed by all they could do.

They quickly got the hang of flying in tandem. At first they tried floating and letting Vassou tow them, but even if samals were larger and stronger than ordinary wolves, the pup had to bound through the drifts and then rest, making their progress too jerky.

Scree still hadn't made a sound, but Diello saw his mouth drawing tighter at the corners. The goblin-boy was clutching the sides of the travois.

The twins flew as slowly as they could, staying close to Vassou's heels. Holding the travois between them grew increasingly difficult. Diello's arms and shoulders trembled from the strain, but he kept on, knowing this had to be equally difficult for Cynthe. *I'll never call Scree a runt again,* Diello thought.

Sometimes wind gusts swatted him sideways. He managed to keep his end of the travois level, so Scree didn't fall off.

"Let's stop," Cynthe said at last, sinking down. Her chest was heaving, her face red.

Diello knelt, wishing the air wasn't so thin. The shadows were lengthening under the trees. He heard an eagle's cry in the distance but paid it no heed.

"Have . . . to keep . . . going," he panted.

"I—I don't know if I can," Cynthe said. "The wind's getting too strong."

"Vassou," Diello asked, "how much farther?"

"Untie me, and I'll scout."

Cynthe unfastened the rope from Vassou's harness, and the wolf shook himself.

"Wait here," he said, and headed into the snowy brush. His pale coat blended in with the surroundings, making it impossible to watch where he went.

Diello pulled his hands farther inside his sleeves and turned his back to the icy blast.

"How's Scree doing?" he asked.

Cynthe finished tucking a corner of Scree's blanket around him. "I can't tell. Stand over here beside me, and we'll block some of the wind from him."

Scree's eyes remained closed.

They ate snow and a few mouthfuls of their dried rations. Diello knew they couldn't afford to rest here very long. It was getting colder all the time. His hands and feet were freezing. He let his eyes close for a moment before he shook off his sleepiness.

Dangerous, he told himself, stamping his feet. *Must keep moving.*

"It will be dark soon. C-Come on," he said through chattering teeth. "We'll follow Vassou's tracks."

"We can't fly through that thick undergrowth," Cynthe protested.

"Then you break a trail like you did before, and I'll drag the travois."

"It's my turn this time."

"Let me start," Diello said. "Every twenty strides we'll switch."

She took the lead. Over the wind's howl Diello could hear her counting. When she stopped to take the travois from him, he was happy to hand it over. He stepped in front, concerned at how fast the snow was filling Vassou's tracks. Soon they'd be gone.

Then we'll really be in trouble.

Stamping down the snow to make it easier for Cynthe to follow, Diello had reached his twentieth stride and was turning back to take his turn when he tripped over something under the snow. He landed hard on his hands and knees, grunting.

"Are you all right?" Cynthe asked.

Diello picked up a brown cloak, shaking it out. Parts

of it were still dry. There was a long tear. He saw spots of fresh blood.

He dropped it, looking around cautiously.

Cynthe came over. "What is it?"

"Hush a moment. I want to listen."

She stayed quiet, giving him a chance to use his newest Gift. At first Diello heard nothing but the wind and creaking trees, but then those sounds faded. He ignored the faint, sleepy thoughts of the forest's denizens, hibernating in snug dens, and reached beyond them for . . .

Help me! Help me! Don't let me die!

The thought hit him with such intensity that he swayed. Cynthe grabbed his arm, steadying him.

"Someone—a girl, I think—is in danger." Diello pointed. "That way!"

"Wait! What kind of danger?" Cynthe piled all their gear next to Scree and strung her bow. "Is it something we can fight?"

"Let's hope so. She's really scared."

Cynthe pulled out three arrows and held them ready between her fingers. "Let's go."

chapter four

iello took his quarterstaff from the travois and touched Scree's shoulder. The goblin-boy roused.

"We'll be back as soon as we can," Diello said. He felt guilty about leaving Scree alone. "Keep brushing the snow off your blanket while we're gone."

Then he ran after Cynthe. When he caught up, she said, "I thought I heard a shout ahead. A man's voice."

Diello drew his knife and cut a mark in a tree. "The snow's going to fill our tracks fast. Remember, this notch is where we should turn to retrace our way to Scree."

Cynthe nodded impatiently. "I'll do the cutting. Head that way."

A few strides later, Diello almost ran into Vassou, who had appeared through the swirling curtain of snow.

The wolf nosed his hand. "There's trouble ahead."

"We know."

A scream tore through the forest. The three of them ran toward the sound. The falling snow blurred everything. Twilight was gathering fast now.

Another scream—abruptly ended—made Diello's

knuckles whiten on his quarterstaff. They ran until they reached a clearing. Diello dropped to his knees in the brush. Cynthe crouched next to Vassou. Keeping their heads down, the twins crawled forward.

Diello couldn't tell what was going on in the clearing. He edged closer through a thicket of vines and pine saplings and made out four burly men—Antrasins—in heavy cloaks and wool jerkins. One was holding the arms of a girl dressed in a shapeless robe. Her long, dark hair was streaming in the wind. She struggled, crying out something in a language Diello didn't recognize.

The other three men were kneeling around what looked to be one of the giant eagles. The creature was lying on the ground. The snow was trampled and blood splattered, as though there had been a struggle. Diello couldn't see exactly what the men were doing with their knives. *Are they butchering that creature?*

"No! No!" the girl protested, trying to twist free. She was speaking Antrasin now. "Have mercy. Have pity. Stop!"

"Got it!" a bearded man cried, holding up something gray and spherical.

Diello thought it must be the bird's heart. The men laughed, slapping one another on the back. Sickened, Diello averted his gaze.

Beside him, Cynthe whispered, "Look."

A shimmer passed along the length of the dead eagle. Diello assumed it was a trick of the wind-swirled snow, but then he realized the body was changing shape. The outspread wings were shrinking to a more slender form, the feathers becoming fingers and a hand.

"A girl," he said, horrified. "They murdered a girl for her *heart*?"

"Strieka!" The other girl was sobbing. "Oh, Strieka, *no!*"

"It's not a heart," Vassou murmured. "But this is an evil thing they do."

The sphere was glowing now, casting an eerie orange light over the men's faces.

"We're rich! We're rich!" they sang.

"One *stona*, now ours." The bearded Antrasin pocketed the sphere. As his companions shoved the crying girl to her knees in front of him, he raised his knife. "And one more to go."

The girl spit at him, twisting this way and that.

"Hold her still! If I botch the killing blow, she'll change too soon."

"Then let me do it." A blond man shoved the bearded one aside. "This will be *my* kill."

Another one gripped the girl by her hair, pulling back her head.

"Now," Diello told his sister.

Cynthe rose to her feet, drawing her bow smoothly. She released an arrow, and it struck the blond man's back.

He yelled, dropping his knife and staggering. He grabbed frantically at the arrow. "Get it out!" he screamed before collapsing on the ground.

The others spun around, spreading apart just as Cynthe's second arrow hit the shoulder of the man holding the girl.

He stumbled, sitting down in a heap and blinking in shock.

The girl scrambled to one side, trying to flee, but the bearded Antrasin jerked her roughly to her feet.

"No you don't!" he snarled, and whirled around to face the twins' hiding place. His knife point pressed against the girl's throat. "You see this, Huldair? Eh? She's *our* catch! You've no right to come sneaking around, trying to take what's rightfully ours."

Diello noted that the fourth man was slipping off into the trees while his bearded friend talked. Diello tapped his sister's arm and nodded in that direction. She drew another handful of arrows, nocking one to her bowstring. This time she missed. Meanwhile, Vassou had melted into the woods like smoke.

Holding his quarterstaff tightly across his chest, Diello crept in a circle until he positioned himself behind the bearded man. The Antrasin was still nervously shouting at the attacker he thought was Huldair. *What kind of barbarians are these knaves?* Diello wondered. The girl had stopped struggling and hung limply in her captor's grasp.

Diello knew he and Cynthe had one chance to save the girl's life. *If I mess up and make a sound . . . Don't think. Just act.*

Diello rose in the air and flew against the buffeting wind, swooping at his target's back. His quarterstaff thudded off the bearded man's skull, and the Antrasin dropped, landing on the girl.

Dragging the girl free, Diello tried to revive her. There was a gash on her forehead, oozing blood.

"Wake up," he urged her. "You're safe now. Wake up!"

Cynthe emerged from the trees with her bow over her shoulder. "I missed the fourth one when he ran," she said. "My aim is off in this wind."

"As long as he's gone," Diello replied, rubbing snow on the girl's cheeks. She had no color at all, but when he touched her throat, he felt her pulse beating strongly. "I can't rouse her."

A soft yip warned them before Vassou came back. "The coward outran me," he said. "He's heading east. He won't be coming back for his friends."

"What should we do for the—the other girl?" Cynthe asked.

"I'll cover her," Diello said.

Taking the bearded man's cloak, Diello spread it over Strieka, averting his gaze from what had been done to her. Close up, he could see that she hadn't completely changed to human form when she died. She had feathers instead of hair, and a downy tuft grew at the base of her throat. When Diello closed her staring eyes, images of Sight flashed through his mind: soaring high and free, diving for prey so quickly the sky was a blur, then a stunned sense of panic at being tangled in a net and unable to fight clear of it.

"I'm sorry, Strieka," Diello whispered. "May your soul fly in peace."

His crystal bones were tingling in the familiar response to someone else's magic. *Whose?* Diello surveyed the wounded Antrasins before staring at the unconscious girl lying in the snow.

"What is it?" Cynthe asked.

"There's magic here."

His twin rolled her eyes. "Obviously. We just saw an eagle transform into a girl."

"Not that. Something else." Diello's gaze went to the man he'd knocked out. He hesitated, then swiftly searched the bearded man's pockets.

"Careful," Cynthe said.

Diello brought out the *stona*. He was reluctant to handle it. The sphere felt smooth, warm, and surprisingly heavy. Magic pulsed inside it, and the glow grew brighter as though responding to Diello's presence. Then it was suddenly *aware*. The anger pouring out nearly made Diello drop it.

"What is this?" he asked.

Cynthe crowded close to look. He expected her to pluck it from him, but she didn't touch it. "Does the *stona* make them change shapes?"

"I think there's more to it than that," Diello said.

"That's right," Vassou agreed. "They have—"

"You dirty little thieves!" shouted the Antrasin with the wounded shoulder. He snapped off the arrow and flung it aside, gasping. "That *stona*'s ours! We got it fairly."

"You murdered a Tescorsian for it," Cynthe said.

"'Course we did. Worth a fortune, ain't it? Caught this pair in our trap. It'll bring us enough gold to live on all winter."

"What's so valuable about it?" she asked.

The man smirked. "Like you don't know."

"We don't," Cynthe insisted. "Why is it worth so much?"

"Makes you live longer if you eat it. We sell by the slice and make a tidy profit. There's some I could name that dry 'em and grind 'em to powder, but that's a thieves' game, that is. More often than not, that powder's mixed with filler and is too weak to do a body good."

"Don't speak with him, Cynthe," Diello said. "You're wasting your breath."

"Give it back!" the man called out, groaning. "Law of the woods says what we catch is ours."

Diello wasn't trying to look on the *stona* with Sight, but it came to him anyway. Inside the sphere, Strieka's face appeared through a mist. Her eyes were fierce.

You saw my murder, she said in his mind. *Avenge me.*

I'm sorry, but I can't, he told her. *I have another task I must do. My duty lies with it.*

Then take my stona *to the eyrie. Let the temple have it so that our people do not lose its power.*

I don't know where my quest will take me. Can this other girl be trusted with it?

Reeshwin is my sister, but my spirit speaks to you, not her. Stona *cannot hold* stona. *Your bones are crystal. They feel. They make you kind. And you have held Eirian. Because of that I entrust you with this task. Take my* stona *to the eyrie. Let the temple have it. No one else.*

The vision fell away. Diello became aware of the snowy clearing again.

Cynthe and Vassou were watching him.

"What did your vision tell you?" Cynthe asked. "What does this thing do?"

"It holds her spirit," Vassou said softly.

"Yes." Diello placed the sphere carefully inside his belt pouch. He told them what Strieka had asked for.

"You mean you spoke to her soul? Truly?" Cynthe touched his arm. "What is it like, speaking to the dead? What if you—"

"I can't summon the dead," Diello broke in. "I can't bring Mamee and Pa back to us."

He pulled Reeshwin to a sitting position and shifted her across his shoulder.

"Can you manage?" Cynthe asked.

He nodded. "If you can handle Scree."

"I can do it." Cynthe turned away from the Antrasins in disgust. "Let's get out of here."

"Faelin pigs! That's all you are!"

Cynthe spun around and said, *"Break."*

The sapling the man was sitting against shattered. He yelped and scooted aside as sawdust and splinters rained down on him.

"She could just as easily have done that to your skull," Diello said. "Stay away from us."

The man clutched his injured shoulder and said nothing. The bearded Antrasin mumbled and began to stir. Cynthe picked up a stick and knocked him out again. She poked at the blond man, but he remained unconscious.

Diello, Cynthe, and Vassou turned into the wind and left the clearing.

chapter five

Cynthe kept glancing over her shoulder to make sure no one followed them. She raked across their tracks with a stick, and the fast-falling snow obliterated her marks.

Carrying the girl made for very slow going, but Diello trudged on. With dusk closing in, it was hard to find the notches Cynthe had made in the tree trunks.

"The men may follow these," Diello said worriedly.

"Maybe the dark and this blizzard will discourage them."

When they reached Scree, he was sitting upright on the travois, shivering. His relief at seeing them was so obvious that Diello clasped his shoulder in apology.

"I'm sorry it took us so long," Diello said.

"You are here. You are well. You came back for me," Scree said gratefully.

Diello sank to his knees, easing the girl to the ground.

"Were you lost?" Scree asked.

Cynthe tossed the rucksack to Diello and gathered up the rest of their bundles. "When am *I* ever lost?" she replied. She pulled out the waterskin and drank before handing it to Diello.

"It's nearly empty," he said, shaking it. "Vassou, do you want some?"

The wolf pup was eating snow. "This will serve me."

Diello scooped snow into the waterskin before handing it back to Cynthe.

"That won't melt down to much," she said. "But it's all we have time for. We need shelter soon."

"Who is this girl?" Scree asked. "Is she hurt? Is she the one who was screaming?"

Cynthe explained to Scree. He did not often make goblin sounds, but now he hissed. "Those are bad men, evil men. They serve those who work dark magic. I think you cannot scare them enough to stop chasing us."

"I should have killed them," Cynthe said grimly. "Not left them wounded and angry."

"No," Diello told her. "You did what was needed. You did what was right."

She was staring into the woods as though she hadn't heard him. All she said was "Have you rested enough?"

"Yes," Diello lied, lifting Reeshwin once more. He grunted with the effort.

"Still heading for the hut?" Cynthe asked, coaxing Scree to lie down while she tucked the blanket around him. "What if the hunters head there, too?"

"It's protected," Vassou said.

"Protected how?" Diello asked. "Magically?"

"Yes."

"With a *cymunffyl*? No, that can't be right. We wouldn't be able to see it then."

"This magic is different from mine," Vassou said. "But the effect is similar for the Antrasins."

Cynthe frowned. "If someone has a protection spell on the hut, then—"

"—it's being lived in," Diello finished.

"Will Tescorsians be friendly to us?" Cynthe asked.

Diello was too worn-out and cold to care. "I'll give anything to sit at someone's hearth fire."

"Tescorsians will *not* show us welcome," Vassou warned. "I doubt we'll be asked inside."

Diello tightened his arm around Reeshwin. "Maybe they'll grant us hospitality for this girl's sake. Surely they won't turn away strangers in need."

"I thought you'd learned to be less trusting," Vassou said.

"If you've found anything else we can camp in, I'll agree to it," Diello replied.

"There's nothing, not even a hollow log or an old animal den."

"This girl could die if we don't get her warm and dry soon," Diello said. "The same for us."

"We have to take the chance, Vassou," Cynthe added.

She fastened a rope to Vassou's harness, then tied the other end around Diello's waist before linking herself to Diello. He was sorry she had to pull Scree the whole way, but he wasn't sure she could carry the girl.

It was dark and bitterly cold by the time they reached the hut. The wind had become a fierce, howling beast that tore at their clothing and battered their faces. Bushes grew against the walls, and bare vines snaked over the roof. A dim light showed around the edge of the stout door. Laying the girl on the ground next to Cynthe and Scree, Diello ventured forward alone. Before he reached the step, Diello could feel the repellent effect of iron hinges. Despite his urgency, he faltered.

Although Diello could force himself to go near iron when necessary, at the moment he couldn't cope with one more problem.

The wind whipped past the corner of the building, driving chimney smoke down around them. The warm and homey smell gave Diello fresh motivation. *It's only a pair of hinges.* Standing on the slab of rock that formed a step, he hammered his fist on the door in three hard blows, then backed away.

Vassou positioned himself protectively next to Cynthe and Scree.

No one came to the door.

Diello knocked again. This time he thought he heard a sound from inside.

Slowly the door creaked open, spilling a narrow rectangle of light.

"*Caw ti, mu vereek?*" a gruff voice called. "*Sik! Sik!*"

"Please, sir," Diello began in Antrasin.

A beady eye appeared in the crack, glaring at them. "What d'you want?"

"Shelter for the night."

"Not an inn. Begone!"

"There are two of us who are injured and need tending. We're not asking for food. Just the warmth of your fire."

"Haven't a fire," the gruff voice lied. "Haven't warmth to share. Go!"

"Do you know two girls named Reeshwin and Strieka?"

"Why do you speak these names? What trick do you play?"

"There's no trick. We found them under attack. Reeshwin is hurt. Her sister—Strieka is dead."

"You did this? You attacked them?"

"No. There were Antrasins trying to—"

"Reeshwin!" The man hobbled outside. He was old, with white hair flowing to his shoulders. Peering at the girl, he grunted something and tenderly pushed back her hair from her face.

"Bring her!" he said, gesturing for Diello to carry her inside.

As soon as Diello stepped into the gloomy interior, the old man slammed the door shut.

"Let the others in, too," Diello demanded.

The old man ignored him, moving stiffly over to a bed in the corner. He stooped and pulled out a trundle.

"There. Be gentle."

Diello lowered the girl and stepped back. The old man pulled off her snow-crusted cloak and tucked a plump eiderdown over her. He held her slender hands between his gnarled ones.

"Reeshwin, *vereek*," he whispered. He was speaking a mixture of Antrasin and Tescorsian. "Reeshwin, can you hear me?"

Diello looked around. The house was lit only by

a meager fire on the hearth. Bits of bone, clusters of feathers, and pieces of metal were tied to long strings hanging from the rafters. Diello supposed they were charms. The furnishings were sparse, mainly a small table, three stools, and a shelf that held three bowls and mugs. A cooking pot hung from a hook at the fireplace. *Our family wasn't rich,* Diello thought, *but we had a lot more than this.*

The old man turned his head. "By the hearth, a pail of water. Bring!"

Diello obeyed. By now the door was easing open, letting in gusts of snow and wind. Vassou entered first, followed by Cynthe supporting a limping, half-conscious Scree.

"Quick!" Cynthe said.

Diello hurried to help her, kicking the door shut on the snarling weather. Together they lowered Scree to the floor by the fire, wrapping him more securely in his blanket.

"No!" the old man called out. "Not welcome here. Wolf is enemy. Begone!"

"You can't turn us away," Cynthe said indignantly, but Diello signaled for her silence.

He carried the pail of water to the old man and handed him the dipper.

The old man lifted Reeshwin's head and held the brimming dipper to her lips. Making a soft, trilling sound, he coaxed her to drink. Her eyes fluttered and opened. She drank again, then sighed and slept while the old man stroked her hair.

Getting up, he gave Diello a grudging nod. "You saw the attack?"

"Yes."

"How many hunters?"

"Four," Cynthe answered. "Three are injured. One ran away."

Diello expected him to ask about the fight, to demand details about Strieka; but instead the man dropped a heavy bar across the door. Diello touched his belt pouch but did not mention the *stona* in his possession.

"Sleep upstairs," the old man said, pointing at a crude ladder.

"Thank you," Diello said, but the man had turned back to Reeshwin.

It was chilly in the hut. Diello looked around for firewood, hoping to build up the blaze, but he saw nothing. *I'm not going back outside to gather wood.*

"I'm worried about Scree," Cynthe murmured. "He seemed better for a while, but now he's . . . Aren't goblins cold-blooded? He doesn't feel hot, but how do you tell if he's feverish?"

"I'm not sure," Diello admitted, stretching out his hands to the small fire. As soon as his fingers were warm, he rubbed the half-frozen tips of his ears, trying to bring back some feeling in them. "If we keep him warm and let him rest, perhaps he will get better."

"Goblins heal quickly," Vassou said. "It's his human blood that will keep him from recovering fast."

The old man came toward them. Even with stooped

shoulders, he was tall and rangy. His face was weather-beaten, with a hook of a nose. There was an odd odor to him that Diello couldn't identify.

"Not at fire," the old man insisted. "Upstairs! Or go."

"Can our friend lie here at the hearth?" Diello asked. "His leg is broken. We need to keep him warm."

The man peered at Scree with no change of expression. "Goblin."

"Half," Cynthe said.

"Goblin is goblin. Upstairs, or go."

"I left the travois outside," Cynthe said. "It's propped by the door."

Sighing, Diello started to get it, but the man blocked his path.

"Door is barred for all night," he said.

"But we need—"

"If you go out, you do not return."

Cynthe pulled Diello aside. "How does that old coot expect Scree to climb a ladder with a broken leg?"

"We'll fly him up there," Diello said. "He can sit on our linked arms."

She fumed a moment more but nodded. Rousing Scree gently, she asked, "Can you sit up and stay awake?"

"I'm cold," Scree said in a small voice.

"I know. But we have to take you upstairs now."

If Diello and Cynthe hadn't been so tired, it would have been easy. Instead, it took them three tries to ascend to the ledge at the top of the ladder. When they finally got there and carefully set Scree down, Diello's whole body was trembling. Cynthe looked so pale that Diello was afraid she'd pass out. He insisted they rest before they brought up Vassou.

"I'm all right," Cynthe protested, but she sat there until both she and Diello had caught their breaths.

Then the twins went down the ladder to where Vassou was standing with his front paws on the bottom rung. The wolf pup had grown long and lanky in the last months. He weighed a lot more than Scree. Diello tied another rope to Vassou's harness. "We're hoisting you up the human way," he said.

Flying back to the ledge, the twins stretched the rope over the top of the railing and pulled together. Legs dangling, Vassou spun slowly in a circle. When the pup was level with the landing, Cynthe braced her feet and held him in place while Diello maneuvered him onto the ledge.

"Whew!" Cynthe sat down and wiped her face with her sleeve while Diello unfastened Vassou's harness. The pup bounded through the short doorway.

Diello peered into the room beyond, but it was so dark he couldn't see much. Vassou emerged from the shadows to press his cold nose to Diello's hand.

"Safe," he said.

Almost no light filtered through the open doorway. Inside, Diello bumped around, exploring the room. As his eyes gradually adjusted to the dimness, he estimated that this upstairs room was half the size of the one below. Diello could feel a draft blowing from one of the outside corners. The place smelled of mouse droppings and something else.

"Remember that owl's nest we found last year?" he said to Cynthe. "Remember how it stank?"

"The same as this." Cynthe sneezed. "Some kind of bird's been roosting up here."

"Or shape-shifter," Diello said.

"And there must be years of dust."

Diello heard a furtive sound behind him. He turned, just as a panel slid closed across the doorway.

Shouting, Diello ran to it, but he heard the thump of a bar being dropped into place. Try as he might, Diello couldn't budge it.

"Locked in!" he yelled, giving the panel a kick.

The room was completely dark until Cynthe flicked fire.

"There's a window," Diello said as her light faded. "Behind those closed shutters."

"Don't open it." Cynthe's voice came out of the dark. "You'll let in the storm."

A gust of wind shook the rafters, and the icy draft made Diello shiver. "I think it's already inside."

"Stop grumbling. As long as it doesn't start snowing through the roof, we'll be fine."

Diello flicked fire, illuminating the room long enough for him to spy a stub of a candle on a shelf. He flicked fire again, but Cynthe was quicker. Her magic lit the candle first.

She grinned at him cockily, blowing on her fingertips.

By the candle's feeble glow, they could see exposed rafters and a battered wooden floor. There was no bed and no table. Instead, they had a rickety stool and a storage box containing some musty blankets and what looked like a pile of old feathers.

Cynthe sneezed and slammed the box shut. "That's awful!"

"But at least it's not snowing in here," Diello said with forced cheer.

She made a face at him. "What can we use for a fire? It would serve the old man right if we built one on the floor."

"Until the fire burned through the floor and fell on our gracious host's head."

Cynthe looked hopeful. "I wouldn't mind."

Although she sounded more than half serious, Diello laughed. "Not yet."

"When? After we turn blue and lose our ears to frost-bite?"

"Let's keep busy."

They shook out bedrolls and divided their food. A few withered apples. A piece of leathery dried meat. A handful of autumn nuts. Cynthe gave Vassou the meat. She and Diello shared the fruit and nuts. It wasn't very satisfying.

Vassou lay next to Scree to keep him warm. The wolf licked his paws.

"Are they sore?" Diello asked, munching his tasteless apple. "Do you need some of our healing salve?"

"It's better that you save it," Vassou told him. "I'm all right."

From below, Diello could hear the faint murmur of two voices, but the floor was too thick for him to make out any words. He was too tired to extend his magical senses to eavesdrop. "Sounds like Reeshwin woke up," he noted.

The old man uttered a hoarse cry, and then the girl screeched. Even muffled, the sounds held unmistakable grief. *Strieka,* Diello thought.

"Maybe in the morning we can talk to Reeshwin," he said. "She might be grateful enough to help us search for the scabbard."

Vassou glanced up. "Grateful? Unlikely."

"Then maybe I can bargain for help," Diello said. "The *stona* for—"

"Take care," Vassou said. "A promise made to a person's soul is not one to be broken."

"I've got to think about Amalina. If we don't get the sword and scabbard back—"

"No need to remind us of that," Vassou replied.

"Should I rouse Scree again?" Cynthe asked worriedly. "He needs to eat something."

Diello looked at the goblin-boy. Scree was shivering in his blanket. There were gaunt hollows in his face.

"Maybe it's better if he sleeps."

"Now I wish that we'd stayed in the tomtir's hole," Cynthe said. "It would have been better than this."

"Why, thank you!" said a voice. "How very kind of you to say so."

Diello felt a shifting in his pocket.

"No," he breathed.

"That sounded like—but that's impossible!" Cynthe said.

A pebble fell out of Diello's pocket and went bouncing

across the floor. In the next moment, it swelled to the size of a bucket and sat there blinking at them.

"Isn't it thrilling to have adventures?" the tomtir asked. "I quite enjoy them, don't you?"

chapter six

The twins stared at the tomtir.

"How did you— Why— What do you want from us?" Diello sputtered.

"I made a wish," Cynthe said. "Is that why you appeared? Are you a spirit that grants wishes?"

"All in good time," the tomtir said cheerfully. "As shelters go, this is much bigger than my hole. Are you truly wishing yourself elsewhere?"

"Yes!"

"No!"

Cynthe and Diello looked at each other.

"Now, now. No need to make quite so much noise."

"No thank you, tomtir." Diello fixed his eyes fiercely on Cynthe to keep her quiet. "This place will do."

"As you prefer. The dust here looks scrumptious! May I eat some?"

"Of course," said Diello.

"Thank you. Much obliged."

The tomtir headed for one of the shadowy corners, bumping into the wall.

Diello turned to Vassou. "Do tomtirs grant wishes?" he whispered.

"I'm not sure. The friendly ones are said to be helpful, so perhaps they do."

"At what price?" Diello murmured. He glanced at Cynthe. "Be careful what you say."

"Don't be so bossy," she told him. But she lowered her voice. "What are we going to do with it?"

"I don't think we can get rid of it, if it doesn't want to go. Besides, we're locked in together."

"Unless I break the door."

"Let's not do that until we need to," Diello cautioned her. "If the old man's afraid we might kill him and Reeshwin for their *stonas*, then he has a reason for locking us in."

"Reeshwin should tell him that we saved her." Cynthe paused while the cries from below swelled louder. "It doesn't sound like they're talking right now. I hope they don't grieve this way all night."

"They have a right to mourn," Diello said.

Cynthe looked down. Her eyes welled with tears. "Do you still miss Mamee and Pa? I catch myself saving up things to tell her, and then I remember."

"I do that, too," Diello admitted. "And when we hunt or camp, I keep expecting Pa to show up and tell me how to do it better. I guess we'll always miss them."

Sniffing, Cynthe rubbed her face dry. "Vassou, is the tomtir dangerous?"

The wolf's eyes reflected the candlelight. "Possibly not.

It seems to like you both. But a tomtir can have very strong powers."

"Like what?" Diello asked.

"Excuse me," said the tomtir.

Diello found it next to his foot. He jumped back.

"I'd rather you didn't discuss me as though I weren't here. Awfully rude of you, I must say."

"I'm sorry," Diello said. "It's just—well, we aren't used to you. Vassou usually explains whatever we don't understand."

"We haven't introduced ourselves properly," Cynthe said. "We're Cynthe and Diello." She pointed. "And that's Vassou and Scree. What should we call you?"

"Ah, this silly insistence on names," the tomtir said. "I do admire good manners, but must we go into such details at the moment?"

"We can give you a name if you don't want to tell us," Cynthe said. "How about Knobby? Or Mossy? I know! Bouncer!"

Diello shook his head to tell her she was being rude.

"You may call me Qod," the tomtir said. "It isn't precisely my name, but it's something you can pronounce."

"Glad to meet you, Qod," Diello said.

"We're good at languages," Cynthe boasted. "Please tell us your real name."

The tomtir uttered a screech far worse than the Tescorsian noises downstairs. Diello clapped his hands over his ears. Scree sat upright. Vassou howled in anguish. Cynthe looked stunned.

"As you can see," Qod said, "it would be quite a challenge for you to say that properly."

"We're more than happy to call you Qod," Diello agreed. "Satisfied?" he hissed at Cynthe.

She crossed her eyes at him.

"Now that that's settled"—Qod rolled away—"some warmth, don't you think?"

First the room began to glow. Then that icy draft stopped blowing.

Cynthe smiled. "This is much better," she said. "Thank you."

"You're welcome," Qod replied. "I have to say, it's intriguing to be somewhere new. It's been years since I've traveled so far."

"We're just partway down the mountain where you live," Cynthe said.

"True. You didn't go very fast. I expected you to fly."

"Scree and Vassou can't fly," Diello explained.

"A samal wolf unable to fly? How extraordinary."

Both Diello and Cynthe stared at Vassou.

"Can you?" she asked.

"I'm too young," the pup said. "Later perhaps, when I've reached my full growth."

"Why didn't you tell us?" Cynthe pressed.

"Because I cannot do it yet."

"Why didn't your mother fly when she came to Antrasia to warn us about the goblin attack?" Diello asked. "Why did she run when it took her so much longer?"

"Our females don't fly. And my sibling and I were too

young to wean when she left Embarthi. We slowed her." Vassou's blue eyes met Diello's. "Shalla did her best."

"I wasn't criticizing," Diello said quickly. "It was just a question."

"A tactless one," Cynthe murmured, popping the last of the nuts into her mouth.

"What is it that you intend to steal from the Tescorsians?" the tomtir asked.

Cynthe choked on a nut, and Diello had to pound her back.

"What makes you think we're thieves?" he asked.

"A duel of questions! How exciting! Why else would Fae younglings venture so deep into Tescorsa? You aren't the first to come on a quest, hoping to gather enough feathers to make yourselves magic coats and other ridiculous things. You won't be the last. But you are the most unusual assortment of companions. Fae and goblin. Goblin and samal. Extraordinary!"

"We're Faelin," Diello said. "We told you before. And Scree is only half-goblin."

"You really are concerned with the lesser details, aren't you? Now, where have I heard about such a combination of companions? Was it a legend? No. A saying? No, no. A prophecy? Hmm. I don't care for those, you know. They tend to be too gloomy."

"Maybe you've met the Knower?" Cynthe asked.

"Ah, the Knower!" the tomtir said excitedly. It blinked. "Who's that?"

"Never mind," Diello said. He didn't want to talk about

old legends and broken destinies. The Knower—an ancient tree they'd encountered in the Westering Hills near the border of Embarthi—had told them they were supposed to rule Embarthi one day.

This creature's awfully curious about our business. I think all the silliness is just a ruse to distract us so we'll talk. It's a good thing Pa and Mamee taught us not to discuss our affairs with strangers. But why does Qod want to know our quest? Does it know about Eirian? Maybe by now every magical creature in existence knows that Brezog has dragged it back to his lair in the Barrens.

"Looking for gold, are you?" the tomtir asked, interrupting Diello's thoughts.

"No."

"Just as well. It's the wrong time of year. If you're seeking magic eagle feathers, I should warn you that the Tescorsians won't look kindly on that."

"We're not after feathers," Cynthe said.

"Then you're *stona* hunters, the worst of the lowest of the most despicable."

"We aren't," Diello said.

"There's something in your belt pouch, something you shouldn't have. Take it out. Throw it away! You've no right to it." Qod's tone was suddenly urgent.

"You've been in my pocket all day," Diello countered. "You overheard everything that was said, so you know we didn't kill that girl."

"No, but you've kept her *stona*," the tomtir said. "It belongs to her family."

An odd sensation stole over Diello, as though he'd been pushed underwater and held there. "*Stona* cannot hold *stona*," he whispered.

"Diello," Cynthe asked, "what are you hearing? Are you having another vision?"

He shook his head, but Strieka's words seemed burned into his mind. He could hear her voice again, murmuring to him.

"I must take it to the eyrie," he said.

"We've no time for that," said Cynthe. "Amalina comes first. Maybe later we can help with other people's problems."

Vassou licked Diello's hand, pulling his attention from the voice in his head. "Tie your belt pouch to my harness," the wolf said. "Let me carry the *stona*. It's not good for you to be near this magic."

A shudder passed through Diello. He felt invisible creatures crawling up his arms. He wanted to fling open the wooden shutters and fly out into the storm toward the tallest mountains. "There's a temple. I must go to it."

As he spoke, he levitated off the floor, rising toward the rafters. Cynthe pulled him down and clamped her arms around his waist. Hardly aware of her, Diello struggled to reach the window. His bones felt as if they were on fire. He yearned to plunge outside into the cold, to feel the wind lift him and carry him away.

"Diello!" Cynthe shouted.

Strieka's voice was calling him. He pushed Cynthe away and lifted off the floor. "I must go to the temple *now!*"

chapter seven

Pain exploded in Diello's jaw. His head rang. He hit the floor with a jolting thud. The fog in his mind cleared enough for him to see Cynthe standing over him with a clenched fist.

Drawing her knife, she cut his pouch strings, opened a shutter, and flung the *stona*—pouch and all—into the darkness.

"No!" he shouted, trying to scramble after it.

Cynthe shoved him back and closed the shutter. "And good riddance to it!"

The pressure inside Diello vanished. Strieka's voice stopped talking inside his head. He sank to the floor, and Vassou nuzzled his face.

"What happened?" Diello asked.

"That *stona* took over your mind." Cynthe knelt in front of him. "I had to hit you to keep you from flying away. Do you understand?"

Diello nodded. He could feel the *stona*'s magic faintly. It was still reaching for him, trying to control him; but the distance helped him to resist it. He would rather Cynthe had destroyed it.

"Are you listening to me?" Cynthe said. "Diello, pay attention."

"But I promised her—"

"I don't care what you promised. You owe that girl nothing. And if her spirit is trying to hurt you now, then I don't even feel sorry for what happened to her."

"Come and sit next to Scree," Vassou said. "The room is warmest there."

Another shiver passed through Diello as he allowed them to lead him over to Scree. "I'm not cold," he said, anxious that they should understand. "It's just my bones."

"Your crystal bones made the *stona* more powerful than usual," Vassou told him.

Diello sat down. He was so tired and weak that he could barely lift his head. He felt a thousand years old.

"Is your leg still hurting?" he asked Scree.

The goblin-boy nodded. His lack of chatter worried Diello.

The tomtir rolled closer to Diello. "Take heart, Fae-boy. Don't let a little brush with magic upset you."

"I can't help it sometimes," Diello said, embarrassed. He wasn't sure Qod should know about his ability. The tomtir might want to make use of it.

"How splendid that you have crystal bones! You remind me of a boy who came into these mountains many years ago. Now what was that Fae-boy's name? Clute? Callun? Clevn! Yes, Clevn. He grew up to be rather important, I believe."

"Important!" Cynthe echoed. "He's mage-chancellor to the queen."

"Which one?"

"The present one," Cynthe said.

"Nolandra?"

Cynthe exchanged a glance with Diello.

"Sheirae," she said.

"Oh, the *child*."

"Queen Sheirae is not a child," Cynthe said. "She's old."

"Nolandra is the old queen," Qod corrected her.

"You've been on this mountain a long time," Cynthe said. "Queen Sheirae rules the Fae now."

Diello lost interest in the argument. Clevn was their great-uncle, and he governed Embarthi jointly with their grandmother, the queen. Clevn was strict and unforgiving. He had made sure their mother's exile was permanent. Even after death, her body couldn't return to Embarthi. Now Diello and Cynthe were banished, too. *For something we didn't do.* After all their efforts to bring the sword Eirian back to Embarthi to atone for their parents having stolen it years ago, the queen blamed Diello and Cynthe for letting the goblins capture it. Now, the gorlord Brezog could wield Eirian's power against the Fae, and the twins had no way to meet their little sister's ransom. *We have to get the sword and scabbard back. We just have to.*

"Don't look so serious, Fae-boy," Qod said. "I daresay you'll become important someday as well, provided you live long enough. I do recommend that you stay away from dangerous things like *stonas*, but any boy who smells of Eirian can surely fend off a ghost."

"What do you know about Eirian?" Diello asked.

"Quite a bit. Eirian and I have known each other a long time."

"You're talking about Eirian like it's a person," Cynthe said, kneeling beside Scree.

"Isn't it?"

Diello was signaling to her to be careful, but she was too smart to be caught by the tomtir's games.

"I don't think we mean the same Eirian," she said. "Why don't you talk about the one you know?"

"I love telling stories!" the tomtir said, shifting back and forth. "Let's see . . . back in the mists of time, there was a— No! How rude of me. What you all need first is a good, hot dinner. Everyone, mind your feet!"

The tomtir began to spin faster and faster until it became a blur.

A golden stream of light circled the room. When Qod stopped whirling, a white cloth lay on the floor before them with a feast spread across it. There was a pink ham, a bowl of steaming taties, buttered marrows, purple peppers, yeast buns, and a cake glazed with camelary sauce and bitty seeds. Diello stared at it all, his nose twitching at the scents.

"How do you know our favorite things?" he said.

"I just do."

"Is it real?" Cynthe asked.

"Of course it's real," the tomtir told them.

Scree leaned over to prod the ham. "It is warm. It smells good."

Cynthe pulled out their assortment of wooden spoons and bowls that Diello had whittled during evenings around the campfire. She dished up food for each of them.

Diello ate three lavish helpings.

"It is very tasty, this magic food," Scree declared. "May I gnaw the ham bone? To heal bone, you must eat bone."

"Who told you that?" Cynthe asked.

Scree looked away. "It is an old saying."

A goblin saying? Diello thought. He glanced at Vassou. "Do you want to gnaw the bone, too? I can spin my knife—winner takes the prize."

Vassou rolled over onto his side. "I've eaten enough. Let the goblin have it."

"That is kind, very kind." Scree clapped his hands, reaching eagerly for the bone.

"Now I shall tell Eirian's story," the tomtir said. "Back in the dim reaches of antiquity, there was one who came to be known as the First Warrior."

"What was his name?" Diello asked.

"Ah, names again . . . Salmeth."

"Go on," Cynthe said.

"Salmeth wandered through the Land Now Lost—"

"The Sinking Lands?" Cynthe asked.

"Really! Is this my story or yours?"

"Hush, Cynthe," Diello said. "Let's hear Qod's tale."

"Salmeth wandered through the Land Now Lost until

he came to a forest of large, ancient trees. Among them was a tree taller and wider than the rest."

"The Knower," Cynthe murmured.

Diello shook his head. The Knower was on a mountaintop. He remembered the skeletal trunks of the underwater forest he'd seen when Clevn had taken him and Cynthe to the Isle of Woe. Diello edged away from Cynthe, trying to listen.

"This was the Sacred Tree," Qod went on. "Its fruit was as round as the Sun and made of light. To eat this fruit was to become immortal, but immortality was not what Salmeth wanted. Instead, he gathered all the fruit and smelted it into ore like no other. As he worked, he pulled radiance from the Sun and strength from the mountains and ferocity from the sky. He used the weight of air and the clarity of water. At last he added one drop of his blood. From this ore he hammered out a sword, and he gave it the name Eirian."

Eirian. Just thinking about the sword brought Diello a rush of longing.

"As for the bits and scraps and scrapings that were left after Eirian was finished, Salmeth tossed them away, and they became the stones of *this* mountain. And the tomtirs grew from those stones. Thus ends my tale."

Diello applauded. "A good story."

"How kind." Qod rolled to the far side of the room.

"I feel better," Scree announced, crunching up the last of his bone. He grinned at them. "Much better."

"You don't look feverish anymore," Cynthe said. "Is your leg still hurting?"

"Very little."

"And I'm not as tired as before. Are you, Diello?"

"No," Diello replied. *There was more magic to our food than we thought.*

A thump caught his attention. He saw Qod moving back and forth across the floor, cleaning the dust. "Why do you suppose it's helping us?" Diello asked his twin softly. "What does it want?"

"It must have a reason for coming along. Do you think it wants us to lead it to Eirian?"

"Who knows? But there's more to Qod than what we've seen so far."

There was a loud rapping on the door.

"Quickly!" Qod spun itself into a blur.

The door panel slid open just as the remains of the feast, the light, and the warmth all vanished.

Qod had disappeared again. Diello felt his pockets, but the tomtir—however small—didn't seem to be there.

A dim figure crouched in the doorway, peering at them. It was Reeshwin.

"The boy is to come with me," she said. "The boy who carried me here. The boy who guards my sister's *stona.*"

Diello swallowed.

"What about the rest of us?" Cynthe asked.

"Only the boy," Reeshwin said. "Come."

chapter eight

As Diello ducked through the low doorway, Cynthe scooted out with him.

"I'm coming, too," she said to Reeshwin. "I don't care what you say."

"We go together," Diello added, glad of Cynthe's support, "or not at all."

Angrily, Reeshwin shut the panel behind Cynthe and dropped the bar across it.

"You don't have to lock my friends in," Diello said. "You must realize by now that we mean you no harm."

Reeshwin just pointed at the ladder, and Diello and Cynthe climbed down it.

The old man was sitting on a stool near his hearth. The fire was much bigger now. Its warmth filled the room. A candle burned on the table, where used bowls and mugs had not yet been cleared away. Diello saw bread crumbs; but the cooking pot still hung, unused, on its hook.

Did these folk have only stale bread for supper? He felt guilty about the feast he'd just eaten.

"Come here," the old man said.

Reeshwin nudged Diello. "My grandfather is called Onstri. Obey him."

This time when Cynthe stepped forward, Reeshwin held her back.

Cynthe batted her hand away. "We told you we're in this together."

"Did you find me together?" Reeshwin countered. "Did you carry me together?"

"Yes." Diello looked over his shoulder. "My sister's arrows saved you."

Reeshwin bowed her head and stepped aside, letting Cynthe pass.

Onstri's gaze seemed even more hostile than before.

Does he blame us for what happened to Strieka? Diello wondered.

"Faelin do not often travel through our mountains," Onstri said. "Your kind are not welcome here."

Clearly no thanks were coming for helping Reeshwin.

"We're just passing through. We have no quarrel with you," Diello said.

"Faelin live in Antrasia. You speak like Antrasins. You hunt us!"

"No, we don't," Cynthe said. "We aren't barbarians."

Onstri's gaze barely flickered in her direction. "You do not belong here. Faelin are not welcome. Goblins are not welcome. Samal wolves belong to Fae, and Fae are not welcome. You smell of magic strange to us. That is not welcome."

Onstri glanced up at his granddaughter. She rested her hand on his shoulder.

"Reeshwin will now speak," Onstri said, nodding at her.

Diello noticed that her brown skin and hair were the same color as her shapeless robe. Everything about her seemed drab except for her eyes, which were an intense shade of gold. When she focused on Diello, he felt as though she could see all his thoughts, maybe even his feelings.

"Thank you for bringing me to my grandfather's home," she said. "You are a stranger. You owed me nothing, yet you were kind." She paused, her gaze darting to Cynthe. "You were *both* kind."

Diello relaxed slightly. *This is more like it.*

"You needed help," he replied. "I'm sorry about your sister."

"Sorry?" Reeshwin frowned as though she didn't understand.

"We honor your dead. We—uh—we offer you our sympathy for your loss."

Both Tescorsians stared at him without comprehension. *Maybe they don't believe me.*

"We're sorry we couldn't save Strieka," Cynthe said.

Diello fought the urge to look away from their unnerving stares.

"Ah. You speak from kindness. Our grieving is done," Reeshwin announced. "What are your names?"

Diello remembered Qod's warning against giving his real name to a shape-shifter.

"I'm Del and this is Cynnie," he said, using Amalina's nicknames for them.

"Del." Reeshwin sank to one knee with her head bowed and her palm held up. She rose, then repeated the gesture to Cynthe. "Cynnie. You saved my life. You tried to save Strieka. This, I will not forget. This, I will repay."

"We've repaid that debt with shelter tonight," Onstri said. "It is enough."

Only because I shamed you into letting us stay. Diello gave Reeshwin a smile, which she didn't return.

"We need to stay here for several days and rest up," Diello said. "Our friend has a broken leg."

"No! Not for days," Onstri argued. "Tonight is enough."

"Grandfather," Reeshwin said. The old man fell silent.

We need to stall them, Diello thought, *at least until Cynthe and Vassou can find the* stona. *The Tescorsians mustn't know it's out in the snow.*

"We will give you shelter," Reeshwin said. "We cannot feed you."

"We can hunt for ourselves," Cynthe told her.

The old man spoke sharply, uttering words that Diello couldn't understand.

"It's unsafe to hunt," Reeshwin said. "My grandfather is concerned that you will lead the Antrasins here."

"This hut's visible from—"

"No," Reeshwin said. "The hut cannot be seen. It is protected."

"Then your protective spell has worn off," Diello told her. He hadn't sensed a *cymunffyl* around the structure, but perhaps the Tescorsians used a different kind of invisibility spell. "We saw it from farther up the mountain. That's why we headed in this direction."

"You're not fully human. Our protections safeguard us from human eyes."

"Strieka!" the old man yelled. "What of Strieka?"

"You took Strieka's *stona* back from the hunter," Reeshwin said.

"How do you know that?" Diello asked. "You were unconscious."

"The *stona* is sacred to us. Surrender it now."

What if we can't find it?

Reeshwin extended her hand to Diello. "We must have her *stona*."

"I can't give it to you. I was asked to take it to the temple."

Reeshwin's mouth opened without sound. The old man rose to his feet. Both of them stared at Diello. Cynthe edged closer to Diello with her hand on her bow.

"How is this possible?" Onstri whispered. "You mock us?"

"No. Strieka said, '*Stona* cannot hold *stona*.' And she—"

The old man attacked, slamming Diello against the wall. He gripped Diello's throat. "Demon! You will not work dark magic on Strieka!"

Diello gasped, tugging at the man's fingers. Onstri's hands tightened. Diello kicked and fought, but there was no air, *no air*. . . .

"OFF!" Cynthe shouted, using the power of Voice. Her magic sent the old man skidding across the floor.

Diello dragged in a breath. His throat was aching, his chest in agony.

Reeshwin crouched beside her grandfather. The man sat up. He seemed dazed.

Cynthe put her arm across Diello's shoulders to steady him.

"My bones made your magic stronger," Diello said, after gathering enough breath to talk. "You could have killed him."

"I don't care. He was trying to kill *you*. Come on. We're getting out of here."

"The storm hasn't let up. We can't leave." Diello rubbed his throat. "We have to make them understand."

"How?"

"I don't know. Tell them the truth about the *stona*, I guess."

"What truth?" Reeshwin demanded. "What are you hiding?"

"I threw the *stona* out in the snow," Cynthe admitted.

Reeshwin brought both hands to her mouth in horror.

Onstri crouched like an animal about to do combat. Feathers had appeared in his white hair. The rest of his body looked less distinct in the gloom.

"Is he changing shape?" Cynthe whispered.

"It looks like it." Diello tried to imagine an enormous eagle attacking them in this room—and wished he hadn't. He and Cynthe backed away.

Reeshwin took her grandfather's arm, talking to him

too softly for Diello to hear. She glanced nervously at the twins.

A harsh eagle's cry came from Onstri's throat. Feathers covered his face now.

"We're sorry," Diello said. "We meant no disrespect."

"My brother has crystal—he's sensitive," Cynthe explained awkwardly. "The *stona* was hurting him."

Both Tescorsians muttered in disbelief.

"It's true!" Cynthe said. "Diel—Del doesn't want the *stona* for himself. The magic makes him sick. He was trying to do what Strieka's spirit asked of him, but—"

"Who can believe you?" Reeshwin interrupted. "Strieka's spirit would not speak to a Faelin. You're lying!"

"Look, you can have the *stona*," Diello said. "In the morning, if the storm's over, I'll help you look for it."

An angry screech came from Onstri. His head and upper body had now completely transformed into an eagle.

"Fools!" Reeshwin said. "A *stona* must be kept warm. It must be kept alive."

"I'm truly sorry," Cynthe said. "We didn't know."

Reeshwin pounced on Diello, grabbing his arm. She had a grip as powerful as the old man's. "We must find it now."

"Now?" Diello echoed, unable to twist free.

"If you freeze, I do not care. But the *stona* must be saved."

Reeshwin marched Diello to the door.

"Wait!" Cynthe hurried after them. "I'll go out there.

I'm responsible. I threw it away, not him."

"But he hears it speak. Or so you claim."

"He mustn't go near it. Don't you understand?"

"No," Reeshwin said. "Only that you have lied and tricked us, like all your kind." Unbarring the door, she opened it to a howling gust of snow.

Diello tried to shield his face with his hands.

"Find it," she said, "or don't come back."

Diello turned around. "But—"

"Find it." Reeshwin shoved him out into the blizzard and slammed the door in his face.

chapter nine

The bitter cold knifed through Diello's clothing despite their magic. He pulled up his hood and tucked his hands inside his sleeves. Cynthe hadn't followed him, which meant Reeshwin must be restraining his twin.

If he didn't find the *stona* quickly, he would freeze to death.

Stumbling off the step, he struggled through the hip-deep snow to the back of the hut. No light shone from any window. The storm had obliterated even the starlight. Bending double against the wind, Diello blundered into the low-hanging boughs of a tree and was buried in a cascade of snow. By the time he fought clear, he'd lost his bearings.

Forcing himself to focus, he turned around and took ten steps back toward the dwelling.

It wasn't there.

Retracing his steps, he changed his direction and counted off another ten steps. His outstretched hand touched wood planks. Diello hugged the wall in relief and resumed his search, keeping one hand on the building.

When he came to a chest-high drift, he tried to push through without luck. Then he tried to climb but sank deep into the snow instead. His floundering caused more snow to cave in on top of him.

Like falling into a trog den, he thought, recalling the day when he was picking berries and the ground had dropped from under him.

Only this time the cold was his enemy.

He caught himself yawning and fought off his drowsiness. The energy from Qod's meal had worn off. Diello tried digging the snow with his hands, but soon he couldn't feel his fingers. He blew on them to warm them. He knew he wasn't making much progress.

And more snow was falling rapidly.

Listen to the stona, he told himself. *Use it as a guide.*

Only he'd lost contact with it. The howling wind drowned out everything else. Instead of Strieka's voice, Diello heard a different sound, something in the wind itself. It seemed to be several voices babbling at the same time. They reminded him of the night before his thirteenth birthday, when a rainstorm had awakened him and he'd heard the wind calling his mother's name.

Diello concentrated. He could sense the wind as an entity now—with a will and spirit of its own. Its wild nature appealed to him. He wanted to be one with it.

Let me fly with you to the far reaches of the world, he thought.

Suddenly he was sucked out of the snowdrift and tossed

high in the air. The wind lifted him higher than the treetops and swirled him around until the mountain and the forest disappeared.

Diello laughed in exhilaration. *I'm the wind! I can race across the world. I can destroy . . .*

"Stop!" he called aloud. "Take me back."

But he was swept on, higher and faster. The babbling voices grew louder. Diello had no idea where he was going or how he could get back.

"No!" he shouted. "Release me now!"

It was like being caught up in Clevn's whirlwind, the one that had taken him and Cynthe from the Isle of Woe back to Queen Sheirae's palace. But this time no one was in control.

I can't match the wind's strength. I have to be smarter. Diello drew the wind's power into himself. He dropped a few feet without warning but stayed calm as he continued channeling the wind's fury.

Easy. Steady, he thought. He pulled in more of the wind, taking its strength for his own.

He stopped falling, stopped moving. He was floating far above the ground. Although he could feel air currents flowing around him, he was no longer flying with them. Shadow and mist surrounded him.

The many voices within the wind grew even louder, deafening him before they faded to silence.

A shifting form appeared before him. It was fog gray and twirled like a cyclone with miniature forks of lightning. Then it grew dark.

I am Batha, Wind of the North. Who dares to direct me and my legions?

I'm Diello, son of Lwyneth and Stephel. Take me back to where you found me.

What is 'found'?

I was at the home of Onstri, in the mountains of Tescorsa. Return me there.

I am what I am. My legions blow as they must. Breeze, zephyr, hurricane, cyclone—all move according to what they are.

Just take me back.

I am the Wind of the North. I blow in this direction only.

Diello remembered a rainy afternoon when he was small and Mamee had gathered him and Cynthe onto her lap and told them stories about the elements of weather.

You're one of the Brother Winds, Diello said. *Tell me how to find the Wind of the South.*

Chanda? Batha seemed surprised. *No. It is not Chanda's time.*

I'll make it Chanda's time, Diello said. *I have to go back.*

You would dare to summon Chanda? When it is my season? Of the Fae mages, you are unknown. I will not be mastered by you.

I'm not trying to master you. You abducted me.

You called to me, and I answered.

Return me to where you found me.

I blow in this direction only.

Chanda! Diello called with all his might. *Chanda, Wind of the South, I summon you!*

The shadowy mists around Diello lightened. The air grew warmer and fragrant. Birds twittered. A shape made of rainbow colors appeared some distance away from Batha. Lightning flickered in both entities. Diello heard the rumble of thunder, and his skin prickled. He could feel the building pressure in the air.

I blow elsewhere, a soft voice said. *Why have you summoned me, mage? What do you want of me?*

Take me back to the mountain in Tescorsa where Batha—

This is not my season.

Diello was tired of them both. *I don't care. Obey me!*

And if I refuse?

Then I—I'll fight you.

Laughter tickled his mind. *So fierce, little mage! Give me a reason why I should serve you.*

Diello was too exhausted and cold to explain. *I ask in Eirian's name.*

Eirian will I serve, Chanda said.

Am I released? Batha growled.

Yes, Diello replied.

Batha's dark shape vanished, and Chanda's warmth engulfed Diello. He was moving gently. The mist cleared, and he could look down at the snow-covered ground rushing past far, far below him. The mountain loomed tall against the night sky, and Diello found himself descending.

Thank you, Chanda!

Without a reply, Chanda was gone.

Diello landed on his back in a pile of snow. He lay there, trying to catch his breath.

The blizzard had stopped. Not a breath of wind stirred the forest. Above him, the stars had come out.

It was tempting to lie there longer, but Diello forced himself to his feet. He didn't know how long he'd been with Batha and Chanda—a few moments or half the night? He wanted to get this task done.

Now that it was quiet, he should have been able to sense the *stona*'s presence easily. But there was nothing. His bones weren't tingling. Had the *stona* been damaged by the cold?

He tried to judge where the pouch landed when Cynthe threw it. He chose a likely spot and began to dig.

At last his half-frozen fingers brushed fur. He scooped snow aside and pulled out his belt pouch, which Cynthe had made for him from animal skins. He held it aloft before clutching it to his chest.

"Hurry," he muttered to himself, struggling back through the heavy drifts to the front of the hut.

He pounded on the door, too weary to care about the iron. No one came.

Diello knocked again. "I have it! Let me in!"

A hand grabbed him from behind. Diello was yanked backward against a burly chest. A powerful arm clamped him tight despite his squirming, and the stink of liquor, garlic, and unwashed clothing engulfed him.

"Told you I'd get you, Faelin rat," the hunter said, and plucked the belt pouch from Diello's hand.

chapter ten

Before he could react, Diello felt a small *cymunffyl* close around him, rendering him invisible. *Thank you, Vassou,* he thought.

The Antrasin's grip loosened in surprise, and Diello jerked free.

The man spun around. He was the one Cynthe had shot in the shoulder. "Where are you, brat?" he shouted. "Where'd you go?"

Dodging, Diello kicked him in the shins as hard as he could. The hunter swore, hopping on one leg, and Diello wrenched the belt pouch from his grasp.

"Give that back, you little—"

Diello danced out of reach, then moved in from the side and clouted the man hard on one ear. The Antrasin struck back. It was a wild blow but too quick for Diello to duck. The pain made him dizzy. He wobbled, unable to stand straight.

Don't fall! he told himself, but he was already crashing to the snow. Everything seemed to be happening very slowly. He sucked in air to shout for Cynthe, but no sound came from his throat. When the hunter accidentally stepped on his hand, Diello could not move fast enough to get away.

"There you are!" The man kicked him in the leg.

Diello crawled to one side, finding it hard to make his arms and legs move as he wanted. The man kicked at him again but missed.

"Where are you? Show yourself, you Faelin piglet!"

The door to the hut burst open, shining light across the trampled snow. The Antrasin whirled around with a frightened yelp. He drew the sign of the crumix on his chest.

"What in the name of the Holy Circle is this?" he yelled, gaping at the hut that was now revealed. "How many more of you magic-wielding brats are there?"

Reeshwin emerged into view, her face a pale oval in the shadows. Cynthe stood beside her, holding her bow ready.

The man grinned. "Well, now. That's better. I'll gut you both."

Drawing his knife, he advanced on the two girls. As he passed by, Diello grabbed him by his knees and knocked him off balance.

Kicking and swearing, the man struggled to regain his feet. As Cynthe raised her bow, Reeshwin stopped her.

"No," she said, walking forward. "Now he is *my* prey."

A screech drowned out Cynthe's protest. An eagle flew through the doorway and opened enormous wings, flapping them hard and fast to gain height. Talons tore the Antrasin's shoulder, injuring it further.

Screaming, the man cringed back. The big eagle soared as high as the treetops and banked, diving fast to strike the man again.

"Get inside," Reeshwin said to Cynthe. Her cold, curt voice permitted no disobedience.

"Diello?" Cynthe called, looking around. "Are you there? Do you need help?"

Still dizzy, Diello staggered toward her.

"Drop the spell, Vassou!" Cynthe shouted.

The *cymunffyl* faded. Diello weaved toward his twin, seeing two of her, and she ran to steady him.

Reeshwin took the belt pouch from Diello and pushed him and Cynthe toward the door. "Stay in your room upstairs and don't come out until morning. No matter what you hear." Her gold eyes were stern. "For your own safety, do as I ask."

Silently, both twins nodded. They headed for the door. As they crossed the threshold, the Antrasin screamed again—a piercing cry.

Diello glanced back and saw the giant eagle's fatal strike.

"Don't look," Cynthe said.

"Too late." Diello shook his head, then sagged from another wave of dizziness.

The door closed behind them.

Cynthe helped Diello to the loft ladder. "Up!" she said, prodding him. "Onstri wants revenge, and he'll attack anything as prey. Hurry, Diello!"

Diello tried to cooperate. He got one foot on the bottom rung before he passed out.

• • •

"Mind you," Qod was saying as Diello floated up to consciousness, "I don't think it's a *bad* thing to steal from King Uruoc, provided you're clever enough. The trick, of course, is to *succeed*."

Still groggy, Diello flopped around in an effort to sit up. "What—what are you doing?" he asked wildly.

Cynthe hurried over to him. "You're better! No, don't get up. Just lie back and rest."

Diello gripped her sleeve. "When did Qod come back? What have you been saying? How does it know what we're—"

She pinched him hard to shut him up. "Nobody tells Qod anything. It just knows."

"But—"

"It's all right."

Confused, Diello put a hand to his head. His jaw was aching. His left shoulder felt as though someone had wrenched it from its socket and put it back in wrong. The rest of him was stiff and tired. He looked around, realizing he was in the upstairs room.

"How'd you get me up here?" he asked.

"It wasn't easy," Cynthe said. She poked his arm and chest with a finger. "Are you growing muscle or something? You're heavier than you used to be."

A raucous screech came from downstairs.

"Don't worry." Cynthe patted his shoulder. "We're locked in again."

"I don't understand."

"You've been asleep. You were worn-out, and no wonder. Are you hungry? Qod has your breakfast ready."

"Here it is!" Scree said, shoving a bowl at Diello. The goblin-boy was bright eyed and smiling.

He was also walking without a limp.

"Your leg," Diello said, holding his serving of steaming food. "It's healed? How?"

"I have been eating many bones," Scree replied.

"Don't be silly!" Cynthe said. "Tell Diello what really happened."

"Qod spun magic around me," Scree said. "It tickled until I wanted to laugh. Cynthe would not let me. She said I had to stay very still. But I did laugh. Then the pain went away. And now I can walk."

"I'm glad," Diello said. "Where's Qod now?"

Cynthe waved vaguely. "Over there, eating dust. You should be eating, too."

Diello sniffed the food. It was porridge mixed with bits of crisp sausage, with honey and cream poured over the top. "But—"

"Diello, you need the nourishment," Vassou said. "You used too much magic for one day."

"I have to know what's been going on."

"I will explain while you eat."

Diello dug into the porridge. It tasted even more delicious than it smelled. With every bite, he felt better.

"Two days have passed," Vassou told him. "Until this morning, there's been no sign of the Tescorsians, but the girl has returned."

"Why are we still locked in?" Diello asked.

Cynthe shrugged.

Vassou continued, "Qod has kept us supplied with food and water. Scree should be fit for travel by tomorrow. Qod has given us a map of the mountains and told us which peak the palace is located on."

"And I still say," Qod added, rolling over to Diello and blinking up at him, "that you should leave King Uruoc alone. He doesn't usually attack Fae, but it would be foolish to antagonize him. He's capable of being very fierce."

"We're Faelin," Diello said. "Not Fae."

"Gracious, such a stubborn insistence! If you're capable of weaving winds together, Fae-boy, then you're far more Fae than human. Might as well accept the fact and go forward."

Diello looked at Cynthe.

"Qod told us what you were doing while you were out in the blizzard," she explained. "Qod said that summoning winds is very risky."

They were all staring at Diello.

"I didn't choose to do it. It just happened," he said.

"What's dangerous," Qod said, "is trying to ride a wind. The summoning and so forth is a part of any young mage's education. However, usually it's done under supervision. You really are rather reckless, aren't you?"

Diello wasn't going to answer that. He put down his empty bowl. "Thanks for breakfast."

Going over to the window, he pushed open the shutters and squinted at the dazzling radiance of sunlight reflecting off a snow-covered world. The drifts reached almost up to the windowsill, and the trees wore white coats. The sky was cloudless, and although the air was sharp with cold, there wasn't even a breeze. He saw the tracks where Cynthe and Vassou had gone outside, using the biggest drift as a slide.

Cynthe joined Diello. "We've been scouting," she said. "Found a few bones, picked clean . . . all that's left of the hunter who attacked you."

Diello shivered. He didn't want to think about it.

"And Vassou caught a fat snow hare yesterday," Cynthe went on.

"I thought Qod was providing the food."

"Mostly, but the tomtir's good for one big meal a day before it shrinks down to pebble size and rests."

"Can we really go tomorrow?" Diello asked.

"Yes. I think we should." Cynthe paused. "I should've gone with you, wherever you went. If Reeshwin hadn't stopped me, I would have been with you."

"I know. It's all right. I came back."

"Vassou and Qod both say that mages have to be trained. It's too risky to try the serious magic on your own. Our Gifts of Sight and flying and Voice—what we've been learning to do so far—are minor compared to what we might be capable of."

"There's no might," Diello said. "We *can* do serious magic. The real, very powerful kind. I suspected it before we met Uncle Owain, and after I fought him with mage fire, I knew. Mamee was wrong about us. All her talk about how we'd never be able to do more than flick fire was just—"

"—a way to keep us safe," Cynthe said. "She *did* know. She had to. She just didn't want us trying to do things we shouldn't."

"She should have prepared us better," Diello insisted. "She should have told us the truth."

"She didn't have visions of the future," Cynthe said. "She couldn't know that her brother was going to betray her to the goblins or that Brezog would kill her and Pa. . . ."

"I think our powers will make us strong enough to rule Embarthi one day," Diello said quietly, glancing over his shoulder. Scree and Qod were huddled with Vassou, talking about something else. "I think we can take the realm away from Uncle Owain and Cousin Penrith, if we ever want that."

Cynthe's eyes widened. "*Do* you want that? What about Amalina?"

"We're going to save her—but if I ever get my hands on Eirian again, I'm not giving it to anyone," Diello vowed.

Cynthe stayed silent for a long moment. Then she said, "I guess I never really believed that someday we'd go back to the farm. We've changed too much, haven't we?"

Diello nodded.

"Queen," Cynthe whispered, then straightened her shoulders. "But Amalina first."

"Absolutely. Do you think Qod could train me in stronger magic?"

"I don't know. Vassou says that Qod's really old. It's a

funny creature. It's given us wonderful help, but I still don't know what it really wants."

"Eirian. Just like the rest of us."

"What could a rock do with a sword?"

"I have no idea. But Eirian's what it's after, just the same." Diello pushed the shutter closed. "I've got to be a better fighter the next time I meet Owain."

"You did all right before."

"I was lucky. Pa always said to know your opponent in order to outthink him, and that's what I intend to do."

"Owain's smart," Cynthe said. "He knows what you're capable of now."

"That means I've got to become as powerful as Clevn. He's stronger than Owain."

"But what if you can't do that? As a Faelin, you might not be able to grow as strong as you want to be."

Diello curled his hands into fists. "We have to stop doubting ourselves. I've always been more cautious than you, but I can't be cautious now. We have to push ourselves to be as strong as possible. Eirian will be our biggest advantage."

"*If* we can get it back."

"We'll get it."

"And if it takes possession of you?"

"I don't care."

"Diello!"

"I don't," he said. "I'm not going to let Owain get away with what he's done—to Mamee and Pa, to Amalina, to all of us. Whatever the price, I'll pay it."

"And if we don't recover Eirian in time to save Amie?" Cynthe asked. "If Owain hurts her or if he really does sell her to the goblins like he said, what then?"

"Then we make *him* pay."

chapter eleven

At that moment, the door to their room slid open and Reeshwin peered inside. There were dark smudges of fatigue beneath her eyes. Her robe was torn. Small brown feathers and bits of down clung to her hair.

"Come quickly," she said. "My grandfather is injured. I need your help."

"What's happened?" Cynthe asked. "Is he downstairs?"

"No. We must climb into the ravine. Hurry!"

Diello reached for his quarterstaff. "Vassou, go out the window and meet us. Scree, you stay here with— Stay here and rest that leg."

Cynthe had already put her arrows in her quiver and was slinging her bow over her shoulder. She followed Reeshwin down the ladder while Diello boosted Vassou through the window.

"I could be useful," Scree protested. "I want to help, too, Diello!"

"I know you do," Diello said. "But we can't risk hurting your leg. Close the shutter after me, will you?"

"Yes, I will do that. But I do not like missing everything."

Diello patted the goblin-boy's shoulder. "Qod will keep you company. We'll be back soon."

Crouching on the windowsill, Diello jumped into the pile of snow and went sliding and tumbling down its slope with more speed than grace. He landed sprawled on his stomach at Cynthe's feet.

She helped him up. "Impressive."

Diello brushed himself off, not responding. He fetched their travois from the other side of the hut.

"This way," Reeshwin said, leading them into the woods.

Reeshwin set a quick pace. She was so light she could walk on the snow's crusty surface, but Diello and Cynthe couldn't. Soon Diello was flying, ducking beneath low branches and hampered by carrying the unwieldy travois. Cynthe flew beside him, her breath streaming white.

Vassou bounded along, keeping up easily.

The ravine was steep and narrow, its bottom choked with boulders. Landing next to Reeshwin, Diello dropped the travois on a snowdrift and craned his neck to look up at the tall, sheer cliffs towering high. Icicles hung off rocks and crevices. About halfway up one side, a figure lay crumpled on a ledge.

Cynthe touched down and shrugged off her bow and quiver. "Not even a goat could climb up there."

"I would not have asked you," Reeshwin said, "but if I shift form to fly, I cannot carry him."

"Don't worry," Diello assured her. "We can handle this."

"Flying will be difficult," Vassou warned them.

Cynthe ascended, her slim form silhouetted against the sunlight. Diello dropped his quarterstaff and followed, rising fast as he flew.

Inside the ravine, the walls blocked out the sunlight. Treacherous air currents buffeted Diello. Cynthe suddenly plummeted in a downdraft, her arms flailing. Diello grabbed her before she smashed on the rocks below. They paused to rest on a short ledge, hugging the cliff face.

"Thanks for that," she said. "Too bad you can't control this wind."

"Maybe I can. . . ."

"Hurry!" Reeshwin called from the bottom of the ravine.

Ignoring her, Diello closed his eyes and concentrated. After a moment, he could hear faint murmurs around him. He wasn't interested in the sighing of snow or the grumble of stones. He ignored the tiny murmurs of hibernating insects in crevices and holes. And then . . . *there* was the voice of the wind. Several voices, as though each eddy and gust was an entity of its own.

Batha? Diello called in his mind. *Chanda?*

Who calls two of the Brother Winds? a voice responded in his thoughts. *We are but little sisters to them.*

Hear me, Diello commanded. *Do not flow down this ravine. Go elsewhere on the mountain.*

The response was a violent gust that almost blew him off the ledge.

"You're not doing it right!" Cynthe shouted.

Sister Winds, I command you! Diello cried out in his mind. *Be elsewhere. Leave these rocks and this ravine. Let the air be still.*

A gentler breeze swirled around his face. *Who? Who? Who?*

Diello . . . son of Lwyneth and Stephel.

The breeze blew through his heavy clothing, numbing his hands where he clung desperately to the rock. *Master of Eirian?*

Diello wasn't sure how to answer. *Eirian is mine no longer,* he admitted.

The air went still.

"You did it," Cynthe said, grinning.

Diello pushed off the ledge in relief. Honesty had been the right answer. *Someday I'll hold Eirian again. . . .*

Cynthe flew past him to the ledge where Onstri lay. The Tescorsian was in human form, although no man could have climbed to this point. Diello figured that Onstri had been flying when the dangerous wind currents had driven him onto this ledge.

The twins hovered in midair next to the old man.

"Is he alive?" Cynthe asked. "Should I touch him?"

"I can see his chest moving. We'll have to fly him down between us."

"As long as he doesn't wake up and attack us," Cynthe said.

Blood trickled from a gash on the old man's forehead. His eyes were shut.

"I don't think he's in any condition to fight," Diello said. "If he's like Reeshwin, he'll weigh less than a human."

"He's still big," Cynthe said. "I'll pull him off, and you catch him. Lightweight or not, he's going to push you down fast, so be ready."

Gripping Onstri's arm with both hands, Cynthe tugged him off the ledge. Diello caught him. But it was as Cynthe had predicted: Diello found himself sinking through the air. His foot glanced off the ravine wall, making him wobble. He nearly dropped Onstri, but Cynthe was quick to help.

Together they descended until they brought the old man safely to the ground.

Winded, they flopped back on their elbows while Reeshwin bent over her grandfather. She took off her cloak and wrapped him in it.

"He lives," she said, straightening. "But he's very weak. We must get him to shelter."

Cynthe shoved her hair from her eyes. "Can't we have a chance to catch our breath?" she muttered in Diello's ear.

A yip from Vassou kept him from answering. Diello saw the wolf pup approaching with a rope in his mouth, dragging their makeshift travois over the snow.

"Good job, Vassou!" Diello called.

With Reeshwin's help, they managed to lift the old man onto the travois. But he was twice Scree's height and much broader. He didn't fit. They used the cloak to keep his arms from dangling, but his long legs stretched out past the end.

"Flying will be the quickest way back," Reeshwin said.

Groaning, Cynthe tried to ascend. She rose only a foot off the ground before she came down. "Can't do it," she said.

Diello tugged experimentally on the rope. "Dragging him will be even harder."

"So you fly and pull, and I'll push from the ground," Cynthe said.

Diello found he couldn't keep himself in the air either. He knelt a moment, breathing hard, and ate some snow to slake his thirst.

"We'll have to do it the hard way again," he decided. "Come on!"

He and Cynthe tugged on the rope. Reeshwin pushed from behind. Vassou ran ahead of them, breaking a wider trail through the snow. By the time they reached the hut, Diello's legs were aching. He couldn't remember when he'd been so tired.

Reeshwin barred the door behind them, plunging them into gloom. Cynthe wearily flicked fire at a candle on the table, giving them a tiny glow.

"Where's your ax?" Diello asked Reeshwin, although he wasn't eager to use an iron-headed tool. "I'll cut some firewood."

"No need. We have wood stored in that box."

Diello built a fire and sat back on his heels with his hands stretched to the warmth. Reeshwin and Cynthe had lifted Onstri onto the bed and covered him. Cynthe joined Diello and Vassou at the fire.

"Commanding the wind exhausted you," Cynthe noted.

"Don't fuss. You know how hard it is to use a new Gift at first."

She nodded. "But you have to get used to it."

A loud moan from the old man made them both look over.

Reeshwin settled her grandfather, tucking him firmly beneath his covers, and said to the twins, "Come. Sit at my table."

Diello and Cynthe sat with her while Vassou stayed close to the fire.

"Will your grandfather be all right?" Diello asked.

"Yes. Now that he is safely indoors, he will recover."

"Was he hurt in the fight?"

Reeshwin looked puzzled. "Fight?"

"With the hunter," Cynthe said.

"That was an execution, not a fight," Reeshwin said grimly. "No, Onstri stayed in his other form too long. At his age, he no longer has the strength to fly as fast and as far as he wishes. In his heart, he is still young and strong. But his *stona* is old. The blizzard taxed him too much; and for the old ones, it is harder to control shifting, especially when they feel the wind. When the storms end and the winds die down, it's as if we lose something." She hesitated, pressing her hand to her chest.

"Reeshwin," Diello said carefully, "I'm sorry about Strieka's *stona*. We honestly didn't know the snow would hurt it."

"I was very angry," she admitted. "Now I understand that you acted in ignorance. You would not have rescued me, nor would you have worked so hard today to save my grandfather, had you intended Strieka harm."

"We'll be leaving in the morning," Diello said.

"Back to Embarthi or Antrasia?"

Diello wasn't expecting her show of interest. He didn't have a lie ready.

"Or neither," Reeshwin said, studying each of them in turn. "Chance did not bring you to us. Onstri was the eagle that followed you weeks ago when you came down from the Westering Hills. He reported to our king, who has had you watched for a long time."

Diello remembered the eagle circling overhead when he fought the sprites at the Embarthi border. Later, when Queen Sheirae's Fae army faced Brezog's goblin horde, an eagle had seemed to come out of nowhere, stealing Eirian's scabbard and flying off with it.

"Was it your grandfather or you that caught the scabbard when I threw it?" Diello asked.

Reeshwin almost smiled. "Neither of us had that honor. Onstri was once the best of King Uruoc's fighters. He was fearless in battle. Now that he's old, the king lets him serve as a spy but no longer permits him to come to the royal eyrie. He likes only the company of those who are vigorous and quick or those who will flatter him. Even if my grandfather had caught the scabbard, he would have been forced to surrender it to one of the king's favorites."

"Are you going to take us prisoner for your king?" Cynthe asked warily.

"No," Reeshwin said. "Now that you have saved my

grandfather's life, again I am in your debt. What payment do you ask now?"

"Guide us to King Uruoc's palace," Diello said. "Get us inside."

Reeshwin threw back her head and laughed. "You are bold, little Faelin. You expect me to commit treason for you? You are more than bold."

Diello's face grew hot, but he didn't back down. "Then Onstri's life isn't worth as much to you as you said."

Reeshwin lunged at him across the table, slapping him before he could duck. Diello's ears roared from the blow. He wanted to walk out of there and never return. But he couldn't.

"Don't insult me again!" Reeshwin said, striding away from the table. She kicked dust at the fire, then swung toward Diello and Cynthe. "What do you know of Tescorsian honor? Of Tescorsian ways? Nothing! Yet you dare judge me."

"We have a good reason for what we're asking from you," Cynthe said.

"Who does not seek to touch the power of Eirian?" Reeshwin responded. "Our king thinks only of that. He doesn't consider how many enemies will flock to our lands."

"We aren't your enemy," Diello said. "But the scabbard doesn't belong here."

"Eirian was forged in these mountains. It is *of* these mountains."

"That doesn't mean it should belong to King Uruoc."

"Why not? The Fae want all the magic for themselves."

"We aren't acting for the Fae," Diello said.

"Aren't you? Your clothing is wrought of Fae magic. You are served by a talking wolf that only the Fae queen can direct. You have even tamed a goblin into a pet. You have enough Fae magic at your command to do what I've never seen another Faelin do. You are spies in the queen's service. You want one thing: to take Eirian's scabbard from us."

"Yes," Diello admitted. There was no point in lying or trying to explain. "That's what we're here for."

"We have a younger sister, only four years old," Cynthe said. "She's being held hostage. We need Eirian to save her."

"Eirian is not here. Only the scabbard is in King Uruoc's possession."

"We know," Diello said. "But we need that, too."

"Surely the scabbard is not important to you. It cannot serve your purpose."

"Well, it does," Cynthe snapped.

"Tescorsa is a poor land," Reeshwin said. "We are few in number, and the Antrasin hunters further diminish our population. The scabbard's presence here should make the land more fertile, the game more plentiful. We are not greedy. We do not seek to possess the mighty Eirian. The scabbard is enough."

Cynthe rubbed her fingers over the scarred tabletop. "But you've already said you know it will bring your people trouble."

"It will. You are the first, and more will come. But not until spring. Until then, the magic can work for us."

"I wish it could," Diello said. "But we need it."

Reeshwin hesitated, then said, "I'll pay your price if you'll pay mine."

What now? Diello wondered.

"Strieka's *stona* is damaged, but you can keep her spirit alive, perhaps even heal the injury."

"No," Cynthe said. "He mustn't be near it. It's dangerous for him."

"You are the only one among us who can keep it alive," Reeshwin said to Diello. "You will do that. You will give it the nourishment it needs. And if Strieka is delivered safely to the temple, I will help you steal the scabbard."

"And escape," Diello added.

"And escape," she agreed.

"No!" Cynthe said, plucking at Diello's sleeve. "You mustn't connect with that thing again. It tried to control your mind. We'll find another way."

"What remains of Strieka still responds to you," Reeshwin said. "There is still a chance for her."

Diello thought of his vow to Cynthe, that he'd pay any price to regain both pieces of Eirian and save Amalina.

"Are you listening to me?" Cynthe yelled at him. "Strieka tried to possess you. What if she succeeds this time? What if she drives you mad?"

"It's the only way."

"No. We can't trust—"

"We have to," Diello said.

Tears filled Cynthe's eyes. She looked from Reeshwin to Diello.

"Reeshwin will help her sister," Diello said. "And we'll save ours."

"But what if we lose you?" Cynthe whispered.

He had no answer for her.

chapter twelve

hey prepared to leave shortly after dawn. Pale gray washed the sky above the bare treetops. Coral and red streaked the horizon.

Diello hadn't slept well. Now his eyes felt gritty, and his head seemed to be stuffed with wool. But the sharp bite of the winter morning helped clear his mind.

"Scree, are you up to this?" he asked.

The goblin-boy hopped on one leg and then the other, grinning. "I am well," he said. "I feel ready to climb six mountains."

Vassou and Cynthe were play-fighting in the snow. And Qod, shrunk to the size of Diello's palm and as light as pumice stone, nestled in his pocket. The tomtir had insisted on coming with them. Diello tried to tell Qod that they didn't need two guides, but Qod would not be left behind. The tomtir also wanted its presence kept a secret from the Tescorsians but would not explain why.

Reeshwin emerged from the hut to join them. Onstri peered out, muttering something, and slammed the door, only to reopen it almost immediately with an object cradled in his hand. He limped partway to the group and stopped, scowling.

"Del!" Reeshwin called, still using the nickname Diello had told her.

Diello warily joined her and the old man.

Onstri held out the wad of rags. "You guard," he said. "You save."

Diello took the *stona* and peered beneath the layers of cloth where it lay dark and shriveled to half its original size. Fresh guilt washed over him. *Did the night in the snow damage it this much, or is it dying without Strieka's body?*

"Help. You help," Onstri said as though unsure Diello understood him. "Please," he added.

"I'll do my best," Diello promised. He tucked the *stona* in his belt pouch, afraid to handle it more. A cool sensation spread over him as Vassou wrapped him in a *cloigwylie*.

Onstri turned to Reeshwin. "Fly swiftly on your journey. Return safe." He touched her cheek before hobbling back inside the hut.

"Not even a thank-you for yesterday," Cynthe grumbled, coming up to Diello. "The old buzzard could at least—"

"Hush," Diello whispered. "She'll hear you."

"I already did," Reeshwin said. "My grandfather is angry about our bargain."

"You told him the *truth*?" Cynthe said. "If he sends word to the king ahead of us, we'll be captured as soon as we arrive."

"Onstri will not do that. Family matters most. Come!"

• • •

All day, they hiked higher into the mountains. That night, they camped beneath a jutting rock that sheltered them from a light snowfall. Crouched by the campfire, Diello unwrapped the *stona* to check on it.

"Touch it," Reeshwin said. "Give it some of your strength."

When he tried to press a fingertip to it, the *cloigwylie* shot off sparks. Tumbling back, Diello nearly dropped the *stona*.

"Careful!" Reeshwin said, taking it from him, rewrapping it, and placing it on the ground next to the fire. "Your fear is killing it."

"You hold it," Cynthe said to her. "Give it *your* strength."

"I wish I could," Reeshwin replied. "How many times must it be explained to you? *Stona* cannot hold *stona*. If I touch it, I drain life from it. My *stona* must take. It cannot give. But your brother can give it life. He must!" Her eyes pleaded with Diello.

"Remove the *cloigwylie*," Diello said to Vassou.

The wolf hesitated.

"No!" Cynthe cried.

"Do it."

Vassou dropped the protection spell. Diello forced himself to pick up the *stona*. At once he felt a pulse from inside it, even through the rags.

"More," Reeshwin said.

Reluctantly, Diello shook off the rags and curled his fingers around the wizened sphere. It was about the size of a duck egg and heavy. It seemed to be covered with skin. He couldn't tell what it was made of. The *stona* grew warm in his grasp. Its color lightened to gray, and its surface became smooth instead of puckered. Strieka's voice touched his thoughts: *You are back with me. Thank you.*

I'll help you, but only if you don't hurt me like before.

Forgive me. It was not my intention to do you harm.

Reeshwin crowded closer, peering over his shoulder. "It looks better already. You are doing well."

"That's enough," Cynthe said.

"No, a bit longer," Reeshwin insisted.

Diello felt dizzy and sluggish. He couldn't seem to move.

Cynthe plucked the *stona* from his hand and put it inside the belt pouch.

"That's too soon!" Reeshwin cried. "Strieka wasn't finished."

"Doing what? Draining all his strength?" Cynthe asked.

"He's agreed to share."

"Agreement fulfilled," Cynthe said. "For tonight." She took the pouch from Diello's belt and placed it near the fire again. Scree edged away from it. Cynthe glared at Reeshwin as though daring the shape-shifter to protest.

"I must hunt," Reeshwin said, and vanished into the darkness.

"Diello," Cynthe said, "come and sit down."

His knees buckled beneath him. Cynthe caught him. With Scree's help, she eased Diello to the ground as far away from the *stona* as their small campsite would permit.

Scree fetched the waterskin, and Cynthe coaxed Diello to drink.

When he'd managed a few swallows, he dredged up a smile for her and found enough strength to clutch at the blanket she'd wrapped around his shoulders.

"I hate this weakness," Diello muttered. "I'm no better than a sickly baby."

"You're tired and hungry. That's all," Cynthe said. "You're not weak, and you're not a baby."

Diello made a face. "Just sickly."

"Not even that. You're the strongest person I know."

"Liar."

"I mean it." Sitting down beside him, she fished Qod from Diello's pocket and put the tomtir on the ground.

"You've stood up to Brezog," Cynthe continued, "matched wits with Clevn, and fought Owain with mage fire. You solved the riddle that led us to Eirian's hiding place on the farm, and you broke Mamee's protection spell there. Now you seem to be the only one who keeps this *stona* thing going. There's nothing weak about you, unless it's your wits."

The feeble joke lifted Diello's spirits. He pretended to punch her arm, and she gave him a mock push back.

"We should eat," Scree said. "Diello will feel better, and I am hungry, too."

"Qod," Cynthe said, "I wish you to provide us with supper."

"Certainly." Qod swelled to the size of a large melon and began to spin. "Mind your feet!"

Moments later, a bowl heaped with food appeared before each of them.

"Grubs!" Scree cried in delight.

Vassou had sizzling hot venison.

"Eggs with cheese," Cynthe said, pulling out her spoon.

Diello also had eggs and cheese. He ate hungrily, finding his energy returning with each bite.

Qod rolled here and there, bumping gently into their legs as it explored. Then the tomtir spoke: "Before the shape-shifter returns, there is much I need to say. Kindly heed me and do not interrupt."

"We're listening," Cynthe said as she shook out their bedrolls. "What is it you want to tell us?"

"Tomorrow, the shape-shifter is going to divide you," Qod said, speaking faster. "No, please don't bother me with questions. Once you ascend to an open meadow-like place where it's impossible to climb farther, you will have to fly the rest of the way to King Uruoc's eyrie. Which means that the samal, the goblin, and I must all remain behind."

"I can carry you," Diello said. "Like I did today. As for Scree and Vassou . . ."

His voice trailed off in dismay. "What can we do? I'm not leaving anyone."

"Vassou," Cynthe asked, "do you think you might try to fly if we—"

"The power is not yet within me," Vassou said. "How long will Diello and Cynthe be with this shape-shifter, tomtir? How far away will they be?"

"I am trying to acquaint you with all the pertinent

knowledge," Qod said impatiently. "If you will kindly *listen* instead of chattering. I wish to prepare you as much as possible without being overheard by the shape-shifter."

"You don't trust her," Cynthe said.

"Never trust a shape-shifter."

"But you're one."

"I," Qod said with dignity, "am a size-shifter. It is not at all the same thing."

"Will Diello be too far away for me to guard with a *cloigwylie*?" Vassou asked.

"Probably."

"I don't like this," Vassou said to Diello. "How can I protect you—either of you—so far inside the enemy's territory? We must think of a better plan."

"Then think of it," Qod said. "Now, I hope you realize that while Reeshwin may get you into the eyrie, the theft will be up to you; and you will have to escape entirely on your own."

"She agreed to help us escape," Diello said.

"An oath of blood?"

Cynthe glanced at Diello. He shrugged.

"Her idea of what she's agreed to won't necessarily match with yours," Qod said. "Especially once you're in the eyrie. Rules differ there, as they do in any royal court. Don't count on Reeshwin. As for the scabbard—"

"Quick! She's coming," Vassou said.

Qod nudged closer to Diello's foot. "The best way past the king is to make yourself invisible."

"We need Vassou for that spell," Diello said. "I've tried,

but I can't make a *cymunffyl*."

"Draw on the scabbard's power. Remember that! Don't confront Uruoc directly."

Qod shrank down, and Diello shoved it into his pocket, wishing he could have asked more questions.

Reeshwin stepped into the firelight. She crouched to check on the *stona*. Diello smelled the wind and forest on her. Her hair hung tangled around her shoulders, and there was a faint smear of blood at the corner of her mouth.

"Any success?" Cynthe asked.

"Yes, I have fed. And you?"

"We can fend for ourselves just fine," Cynthe said. "We're ready to turn in now, only you don't have a bedroll or a blanket, do you? We should have thought of that earlier."

Reeshwin seemed unconcerned. "I'll manage. Who will take the first watch?"

"Against what?" Diello asked.

"There are many dangers here. Perhaps more *stona* hunters. We are never done with them." Reeshwin sighed. "There are also other predators—"

"The creepers," Scree recited. "The peepers. The crawlers. The hiders."

Reeshwin gave him a startled look. "Where did you hear that?"

"It's hard to say," Diello said hastily, nudging Scree's ankle. "He overhears all sorts of odd things."

"I'll take first watch," Cynthe announced. "Then you and you." She pointed first at Scree, then Vassou.

"What about me and Reeshwin?" Diello asked.

"Not you," Cynthe told him. "You need a full night's rest. Reeshwin can take the last watch if she wants."

"But I should do my share," Diello said.

"No, I agree with your sister for once," Reeshwin told him. "It is best that you sleep."

They all settled down around the dying fire while Cynthe wrapped herself in a blanket and climbed atop the ledge of rock over their heads.

"It's too cold up there for you," Diello said.

"The cold air will keep me awake," she replied. "Go to sleep."

Diello rolled himself in his blanket and stretched out on the hard ground. Qod's warning had worried him more than he wanted to admit. Splitting up the group might be necessary, but he didn't like it. He saw no reason why Qod couldn't remain in his pocket.

Maybe the tomtir just doesn't want to take the risk with us, Diello thought, closing his eyes.

A dream clouded his sleep—a nightmare of suffocating heat and a panting struggle to breathe. Each beat of his heart brought a stab of agony.

Diello tried to fight his way awake without success.

Then he found himself in a cave-like room, dimly lit by torches. He could hear guttural chanting all around: goblin chanting. He strained to see them, but his body was frozen in place.

"You!" a hoarse voice said.

A pair of red eyes appeared in the gloom.

Brezog's face came into focus. His features had grown haggard and wasted. Droplets of sweat beaded his brow. "You have no place here, Faelin morsel," he said in a voice so weak it was almost inaudible. "Begone from my dreams!"

"You're dying," Diello said. "I'm glad."

A blow from nowhere rocked Diello backward.

He jerked awake and sat up, clutching his chest where the pain still reached him. *I can't be linked with him,* Diello thought. *I don't deserve to suffer his agony.*

Shuddering, he smoothed back his hair and rubbed his face.

"What's wrong?" Cynthe whispered next to him.

It was all he could do not to yell and wake the others.

"Is the *stona* bothering you?" she asked.

Looking down, Diello saw it lying on his blanket, as though Reeshwin had placed it on top of him while he was asleep. He fought the urge to bat it into the fire and instead put the pouch on the ground.

"It was a nightmare. That's all." Diello tugged a lock of Cynthe's hair. "I'm fine."

She looked skeptical but moved away. Diello drew his blanket over his shoulders, but he couldn't go back to sleep. Mind Walking in Brezog's dreams was dangerous. He feared he might do it again.

Eirian is linking us together, Diello thought. *Why?*

chapter thirteen

In the morning, they hiked until their trail disappeared completely. Ahead lay a jumble of boulders and rock formations that looked impassible. Reeshwin scrambled on top of a vast boulder and paused there.

"Come," she said.

Cynthe grumbled as Diello gave her a boost.

Diello and Scree heaved Vassou up, and Cynthe grabbed the pup's forelegs. They managed to get him beside her.

Diello started to give Scree a helping hand, but the goblin-boy shook his head.

"I will push you," he said. "I do not need help climbing rocks."

By the time they reached the top of the first giant boulder, Reeshwin was high above them and still climbing steadily. She didn't look back to see if they could follow.

"Do you suppose she's really taking us to the eyrie?" Cynthe asked. "Or is she just leading us to the middle of nowhere?"

"Stop complaining and let's catch up," Diello said.

By midafternoon, the ground leveled off.

We must be at the top, Diello thought. He ducked through a narrow fissure between two leaning slabs of rock and came out into the open. *Is this Qod's meadow?* Diello wondered. A gust of wind made him stagger. Turning around, Diello saw dizzying views in all directions.

"It's beautiful," Cynthe said in wonder.

"Yes," Vassou agreed. "Very beautiful."

Scree moaned and sank down, clutching his head. "I cannot look. I am dizzy. I am going to fall."

Cynthe laughed. "You can't fall. You're on solid ground."

"There is a spell on me," Scree insisted. "Everything is spinning."

"Not everyone can manage the great heights," Reeshwin said.

"Put your head between your knees," Cynthe instructed Scree. "Keep your eyes closed and rest a moment."

Diello was gazing up at an immense crag. It had to be twice the height of the mountain they were on. Clouds obscured its top.

He joined Reeshwin a short distance from the others and pointed. "Is that where the eyrie is?"

She nodded.

Diello's spirits dropped a little. That mountain was black, its sides so sheer they looked artificial, as though the gods of antiquity had carved an obsidian column. Its summit rose well above the tree line. Not even a weed grew on it.

"Are you afraid?" Reeshwin asked.

Diello wanted to shout, *Of course I am!* But he shook his head.

"You are kind and good of heart. Your courage is strong. I wish to say . . . it was wrong of me not to trust you sooner. I should have known that Strieka's *stona* would not misjudge you."

"We aren't there yet," Diello said.

"It is not easy to reach the eyrie. You must be clever and quick. The king has many who guard the skies. I will draw as many as I can away from you, but that might be all I can do. I may have to pretend to turn on you or they will attack me. It will not be a true betrayal. Do you understand?"

"Yes."

"Then . . . until we reach the summit, may we fly as friends?"

Meeting her eyes, Diello felt a blush rising to his hairline. "Sure," he managed.

She handed him a slender brown feather and smiled as he took it.

"It has no magic. It is for luck," Reeshwin said. "It is our custom to share feathers between friends."

"Uh, what do I give you?"

Reeshwin didn't answer.

Looking around, Diello plucked several strands of dried grass and twisted them into a knot. It seemed silly, but he had nothing else. With his face on fire, he handed the gift to her.

Reeshwin seemed very pleased by it. "Thank you."

Cynthe came over to them. "Where now?"

Tucking away the feather, Diello pointed at the black

peak and watched Cynthe's expression change from curious to horrified.

"You're daft!" she said. "Nothing can live that high."

"I'm not quitting now," Diello muttered.

"How strong is your magic?" Reeshwin asked Cynthe. "Can you fly that high, featherless one?"

"Why do you think we can't?" Cynthe countered.

"All fledglings fear falling."

"We don't," Cynthe said. "And we're not fledglings."

Reeshwin seemed about to respond, but then she turned to Diello instead. "How fares the *stona*?"

He pulled it out and showed her.

"Alive, but not as well as I would wish," Reeshwin said. "Strieka's time grows short. We should go now."

"In the morning," Diello said.

"Now is better. If you fly swiftly, we can just reach the top before dark."

"And what if we can't go as fast as you?" Cynthe asked. "What happens if it gets dark before we arrive? Where will we shelter?"

"What about them?" Diello added, pointing at Scree and Vassou. He was glad that Qod had warned him about Reeshwin's plans. "How are we going to get them up there?"

Scree squinted at the tall peak and shuddered. "I do not wish to go."

Reeshwin gave the goblin-boy a scornful look. "Only the twins will go. As soon as I return—"

"Where are you going?" Diello asked.

"To shift into my other form. Be ready." She gave him a fleeting smile. "Please."

Before Diello could reply, Reeshwin clambered down into the rocks out of sight.

Cynthe opened the rucksack and started pulling out its contents. "Hurry! I don't think she'll wait for us. I wish we had food rations to take."

There was a wiggling in Diello's pocket, and Qod bounced out, rolling over to Cynthe. The tomtir swelled in size.

"What do you prefer? Dried fruit? Frozen bits of worm and mica? A tasty nibble of pyrite?"

"Don't be silly." Cynthe flung a spare blanket on the ground. "Just the fruit, please."

Qod blinked at Diello. "Feet out of the way?"

Diello motioned Scree back. "All clear."

The tomtir spun, magic sparkled in the air, and packets of paper tied with twine appeared before Diello and Cynthe. Qod stopped abruptly.

"It doesn't seem adequate. You need something much more filling. I do wish you consumed shale."

"This is enough," Cynthe said. She scooped up the fruit packets and tossed them in the rucksack. "We're grateful for this and—and all you've done for us."

"Why can't you just come with us?" Diello asked.

"I'm of the ground, not the sky," Qod replied.

"That's no answer," Cynthe said. "You've been in Diello's pocket while he was flying."

"I'm of this mountain, not that one," Qod said. "I will not explain further."

Scree filled the waterskin with snow and handed it to Cynthe. "I am worried," he said, glancing at both twins. "I do not like thinking of you up there. I cannot even look at it without growing dizzy. You need my help, and I will not be there."

"We'll be as quick as possible," Diello promised, patting Scree's shoulder.

Vassou came over to Diello. "I will watch with all my senses," the wolf pup said. "If I can, I will assist you with my magic. Call to me with your thoughts, and I will hear."

Scree was wringing his hands. "I think they will eat you. I think the bird king will have you served to him for dinner."

No one responded to that.

Cynthe tied her quiver shut, slung her bow over her shoulder, and handed Diello the rucksack. As he shrugged its strap across his chest, he saw a large, brown eagle soar over them.

"Reeshwin's back," he said. His throat felt suddenly scratchy, and swallowing didn't help. "Vassou, you and Scree be careful. If we don't come back—"

"Bad luck to say that!" Scree cried. "We will wait for you. We will not leave."

"Vassou," Diello went on, "if we're not back in a few days—"

"Give us three days," Cynthe said. "That's all."

Diello nodded. "You and Scree are to leave."

"We'll wait," Vassou said. His blue eyes held Diello's gaze without wavering. "We'll wait as long as it takes."

Diello found he couldn't protest. He could only say, "Thank you." He turned to the tomtir. "Qod—"

But the tomtir had vanished.

Is it back in my pocket? Is it going with us after all?

"Diello!" Cynthe called. She was already rising in the air. "Come on!"

The eagle uttered a cry, wheeling overhead before flying away. Cynthe followed Reeshwin. There was no more time.

"Good-bye," Diello said to his friends.

He flew after his sister. Within a few moments, Cynthe vanished inside one of Vassou's *cymunffyls*. Diello felt Vassou trying to wrap an invisibility spell around him, too, but it slid away.

What's wrong? Diello wondered. *Vassou!*

But the wolf didn't answer.

Strieka's voice filled Diello's mind: *Fly faster. Faster! Hurry!*

She was blocking Vassou's magic. Diello felt heavy and lethargic. The *stona* was draining him at the worst possible time. He started to sink.

Stop! he shouted at Strieka.

Her voice faded from his thoughts, but he went on sinking. Reeshwin was a brown speck in the sky, and he assumed Cynthe was close behind her.

Diello was about to shout to his twin when a shadow passed over him. He saw a black eagle high overhead. It flew on, ignoring him, but he dared not call more attention to himself. And all the while, his energy was failing. Strieka's *stona* was like a millstone weighing him down.

I'm going to fall.

Then he felt a breeze blowing from beneath him, lifting him up. It was fragrant and gentle. *Take hold of my back,* the breeze said. *Cling tight. You will not fall.*

There was nothing tangible to grasp. But Diello dug his fingers deep into the currents of air flowing around him. His fear faded.

The breeze strengthened, moving faster and faster until his hair whipped back from his face and the cold air stung his skin. Even his uncle's flying chariot had not gone at this speed.

I'm riding the wind!

Diello wobbled a bit, but he hung on. Using Sight, he looked for Cynthe and found her. The *cymunffyl* looked like a rainbow wrapped around her. She was flying steadily while checking over her shoulder for him.

Diello whistled as he passed her. He waved. "Ride the breeze!" he shouted.

She said something he couldn't hear and reached out, but she was too slow. Diello swept onward, catching up with Reeshwin's broad wings before zipping ahead of her.

He heard her eagle cry but couldn't tell if it was a greeting or a warning. The breeze was lifting him to the top of the mountain. He passed through cloud wisps and then thick fog, before breaking through to clear skies. Before him was a large structure perched precariously at the summit. Part of the structure jutted out over thin air. Eagles of all sizes were flying in and out of the expansive windows, while others wheeled slowly about. Some sat on the roof.

Diello had expected the palace to be rich and exotic. Instead, it had a ramshackle aspect, as though it had been tossed together haphazardly. Some of it was made of timber. Another section was made of stone. It looked very old. The tall entrance was arched and had no door. Diello saw a sculpture of an eagle head chiseled into the arch's keystone. The stone beak was chipped, and a large crack ran up through one eye. Other parts of the wall were also cracked. Diello could see no evidence of any repairs.

The wind took him close to a projecting corner, startling several eagles about his size. They flew after him.

Please, Sister Wind! Diello called. *Don't let them catch me.*

The wind veered to the left and then dived fast. Hanging on, Diello squeezed his eyes shut.

When he dared to peek, he saw that the birds had dropped back, abandoning the chase.

Grinning in relief, Diello saw a huge eagle—the largest one yet—pass perilously close over his head. It tried to snag him with its talons, but Diello ducked in time.

The eyrie's too well guarded, he said to the wind. *Take me to the temple, please.*

They worship my kind there, the wind replied. *You are wise, young Master of Eirian.*

Diello was whisked past the palace and away from the striking talons of more eagles. Gritting his teeth, Diello felt the breeze shifting from side to side, surging up and plunging down. His stomach flipped over, and he struggled to hang on.

The breeze soared straight up, higher and higher, until Diello couldn't breathe. Little dots flickered across his vision, and he heard himself wheezing. Then the breeze dropped him so quickly, he thought that he'd fallen off. The world was a twirling kaleidoscope beneath him. He couldn't watch.

Mercifully the wind slowed down as it circled a domed hut made of baked mud. Diello wasn't sure that this little tumbledown structure could be a temple, but the wind deposited him on top of it just the same.

Be well, young mage, the wind said softly.

Diello clung to the curved roof. He was gasping for breath and still dizzy. *Thank you, Sister Wind. I'm grateful.*

Laughter rippled through his thoughts. *I'm only a small zephyr without a name. But it is proper and good for you to thank me. May you succeed in your quest. Remember that the power of Eirian is yours to command if needed.*

Wait, please! Diello called. *My twin—*

The zephyr was gone.

Diello knew he couldn't linger on the roof. He crawled to the edge and lowered himself down the wall by cautious degrees. When he landed on solid ground, his knees almost buckled under him.

The air was so thin he struggled to breathe. Cynthe wasn't in sight. But whether she joined him or not, he had a job to finish.

Diello staggered with every step, clutching his belt pouch with both hands. The *stona* weighed more than the treasure of gold coins he'd once taken from that trog den.

He circled the building twice. He couldn't find an entrance.

Look again. Look again. Hurry! Strieka shouted at him.

He heard a sound and saw two eagles flying toward him. They weren't close yet, but they were moving fast. *Think!* he told himself.

Diello remembered how Onstri's hut had been invisible to the hunters. Maybe the door to this building was also concealed.

Drawing a breath to help him focus, Diello concentrated on summoning Sight. The building wavered and changed. Instead of a squalid mud structure, he saw a finely wrought edifice of stone and brick. The whole front was carved with rows of stylized birds. Some held their wings outstretched; others pointed one wing forward. To Diello, it looked more like writing than art. He still couldn't see a door, though.

The eagles flew closer, black with snowy heads, their beaks held open.

Diello studied the wall of carved birds. The answer had to be here somewhere . . . and then he noticed the edges of a panel. It was masterfully constructed, but in a few places the carvings didn't exactly match.

Diello pushed along the edge. A portion of the panel slid away, revealing a shadowy interior.

He smelled an unpleasant odor, like blood left to dry. It didn't matter. Swiftly he ducked inside. The panel closed behind him, and for a moment he was blind.

Then he flicked fire.

Guide me, Strieka, he thought.

Do not touch the altar, she replied. *Walk forward four steps, then turn right for eight steps, then left for two steps.*

"Forward four, right eight, left two," Diello muttered.

Each time he flicked fire, he caught a glimpse of walls painted with squares and squiggles in muddy colors. Then he bumped into something large and solid. A hideous face loomed from the shadows. Diello cringed back, but it was only a statue.

He caught his breath and wiped the sweat from his face with an unsteady hand. The statue towered above him, carved with a human face, a bird's head, and a lion's body.

Place my stona *between the paws of Thugar, great and powerful deity,* Strieka directed.

Fumbling slightly, Diello drew out the *stona* and laid it by the massive stone paws.

He heard a grating noise of stone rubbing against stone. The statue moved, curling its claws around the small *stona* and tucking it out of sight.

Light flashed, dazzling Diello. He stumbled back, shielding his eyes.

"Diello, look at me."

Lowering his hand, Diello saw a ghostly shape shimmering between him and the statue. It was neither girl nor bird, but rather something ethereal and lovely, suspended there in continuous, fluid motion. Its face—the features almost indistinguishable—peered down at him.

"You have done well." The voice spoke to him aloud in Antrasin, yet with a precision and an accent Diello had never heard before. He wasn't sure if this was Strieka or possibly Thugar. "You have honored your promise," the voice went on. "You have saved this torn and damaged spirit, even at cost to yourself. We thank you."

Diello couldn't stop staring at it. *What do I say to a spirit?* He'd hated every moment of carrying the *stona*. It had nearly gotten him killed. It had driven him out of his wits at times. He hoped he never encountered another one. But he knew he couldn't just stand there in silence.

"I hope Strieka can have peace," he said.

"What remains of her knowledge will not be lost from the collective. We will tend to her and enable her to rest. You came into Tescorsa as a stranger, but you will not go unrewarded for your service. Thugar will grant you one wish."

"I wish for my sister Amalina to be safely out of my uncle's control," Diello said.

"You have made a hasty wish, one that benefits another rather than yourself."

"Then I wish for Eirian's scabbard so Cynthe and I can—"

"No," the spirit said. "You do not understand. This reward is for *you*. You must wish on your own behalf."

"But I—" Diello stopped, frowning. *What do I wish for? To be stronger? To be a warrior?* For some reason, he thought of Pa and the things his father had talked about when they were at work in the barn. *I should have listened to him more. I shouldn't have been so impatient when he lectured about honor and responsibility.*

"I wish," Diello said, "to—to always do the right thing."

It sounded a bit silly when said aloud. He hoped this spirit understood what he meant. *Oh, Pa, wherever you are, please don't be disappointed in me.*

"You have asked for wisdom," the spirit said. "Your wish shall be granted. Touch Thugar's foot once."

Diello extended his hand gingerly, afraid the statue would move again. It could grab him or crush him. He brushed his fingertips across a stone paw.

Sinew and bone shifted in response. Diello jerked his hand away. He didn't feel any different. There was no flash of magic, no evidence that his wish had been granted.

I should have asked to be taller, he thought glumly.

When he looked around, the spirit had vanished. The dim light that had surrounded it was fading.

"May I go?" Diello called out.

Nothing answered him. He gave the statue a quick bow just in case and retraced his steps. The carved panel slid open, and he stumbled outside, squinting against the sunlight.

Three eagles were circling above the temple. Crouching low, Diello tried to retreat inside, but the panel had closed soundlessly. This time he couldn't open it.

A bird's shadow moved across the ground in front of him. There was no place to hide.

chapter fourteen

Vassou, help me! Diello thought with all his strength.

Just as an eagle dived for him with outstretched talons, Vassou's *cymunffyl* slid around Diello, turning him invisible. He ducked, and the talons grabbed only air. Diello hurried across the open ground, making sure he walked where the wind had swept the snow away so he left no tracks.

Another bird struck at the temple door, followed by the third. Screaming, the frustrated creatures flew back and forth.

Diello reached the edge of the swept ground and halted. *Fly!* he told himself.

Without the *stona* to hinder him, he lifted up in the air easily, as light as one of Reeshwin's feathers. He needed to go higher to get his bearings and locate the eyrie. But doing so put him in the path of the birds. Almost colliding with one made him drop swiftly. Although he'd made no sound, the eagle's head swiveled in his direction. The shape-shifter banked in a tight turn and came back, angling down to Diello's level. Diello could see the keen eyes searching.

Even if the eagle couldn't see him, it obviously sensed his presence.

Its big wings extended, beating so hard Diello was buffeted away, and the claws struck at nothing.

Cynthe's whistle was Diello's only warning before her arrow thudded into the attacking eagle. The bird cried out and faltered. One wing hung limp while the other beat twice as hard. It couldn't stay aloft. Spiraling toward the ground, the creature shifted into human form and landed awkwardly, revealing a man with an arrow in his shoulder.

The other two eagles came at once to join their fallen comrade. They didn't shift, but their anger and distress could be heard in their loud cries.

Diello wasted no time flying away while the birds were distracted. He stayed on the lookout for more Tescorsians. Using Sight, he spotted Cynthe. Her *cymunffyl* was shining around her. She was heading back to the eyrie, and Diello followed.

Soon he caught up with her. Not wanting to startle her, since she couldn't see him, he whistled before he touched her arm.

Cynthe jerked, tilting to one side and flailing her arms.

"It's me," Diello whispered.

She'd righted herself. She was scowling. "I knew that."

Diello grinned, not believing her for a moment. It took Sight to see actual magic in use, and Cynthe didn't have that Gift.

"We can't talk much," she said softly. "They hear everything."

"I know. Where's Reeshwin?"

"She drew most of the eagles after her, and I kept going. Did you get rid of the *stona*?"

"Yes. I'll tell you about it later."

Cynthe nodded. "We need to split up before we reach the royal shack."

"The palace," Diello corrected her. "Nothing's really what it looks like here. The temple appeared to be made of mud, but truly it was carved stone with columns and statues."

"If you say so. Look! More guards."

Diello saw five eagles flying toward them in formation. He tapped Cynthe's shoulder. "Good luck. I'll meet you inside the eyrie."

She fumbled blindly until she caught his hand in hers, then dropped below him. Diello veered sharply to the right, angling higher than the oncoming birds. They flew directly to where he and Cynthe had been talking and circled with cries of frustration.

They must have heard us, Diello thought.

As he soared onward, Diello discovered that this mountain was as deceptive as everything else in Tescorsa. On the eyrie side it was sheer; but on the opposite side, where the temple stood, it was much more rugged, with deep, narrow ravines and short cliffs and ledges. At least it provided places to hide while more eagle guards passed him.

Can they hear the air when I fly? he wondered.

Approaching the back of the eyrie, Diello flew over a crevasse stained with offal, bits of rotting fur, and bird droppings. The stench was horrific. Stifling the urge to gag, Diello landed quietly.

He crept beneath the undergrowth at the base of the building and pressed his back against the timbered wall. As he caught his breath, he noticed that his *cymunffyl* was fading. At first his body was just a shadow, then it solidified, and Diello was visible again. He pulled himself deeper into the bushes, grateful for the cover they offered.

He heard a faint rustle, then Cynthe crept up beside him. Her top half was visible; the rest of her remained unseen. It was a very strange sight that made Diello rub his eyes.

"What's happening to the spell?" he whispered as low as he could. He pulled out the waterskin from his rucksack to share. "You look like you've been beheaded."

She tilted her head, crossed her eyes, and stuck out her tongue. "Vassou must be tiring."

"Or something's interfering with his magic."

Cynthe drank thirstily before handing back the waterskin. "If you'd been invisible to start with, they'd never have noticed our arrival. They move around a lot, but unless they're after something—"

"—like us," Diello interjected.

"—they don't seem all that alert." She untwisted her packet of fruit. "Want some?"

Diello munched on the dried bits. They held more flavor than he expected, and Qod's food immediately restored his flagging energy.

"So how did you know I needed help at the temple?" he asked.

Cynthe rolled her eyes. "When *don't* you need help?"

He sighed. "Go on."

"After I got separated from Reeshwin," Cynthe said, "I noticed the mud building and headed for it. And when I saw those eagles attacking thin air, I knew I'd found you."

Diello smiled. "Just in time."

"So what do we try next?" Cynthe asked. "This place looks like it has passages in all directions. Without Reeshwin to guide us, our chances of finding the scabbard quickly are next to impossible."

"This is where we need Scree. He could locate it."

"He said once that the best way to steal is to keep close to the walls and stay down."

"Like a mouse," Diello said. "Unnoticed."

Cynthe rested her chin in her hand. "I don't think it's helpful advice for us."

"If only the *cymunffyls* weren't wearing off."

Cynthe looked at herself. "I can see my waist now. Can you let Vassou know there's a problem?"

Diello tried. *Vassou! We need your help.*

He waited while Cynthe's *cymunffyl* faded entirely. "No response from Vassou," Diello said worriedly.

"They can handle themselves," Cynthe replied, but she didn't sound as though she believed it. "What about us? No one I've seen is in human form, so we can't blend in. Reeshwin should have done more. Or do you think she led us into a trap?"

"No. She tried to warn me that we couldn't stay together."

"Is that all the help we're going to get from her?"

Diello shrugged. "We haven't been caught yet. I'm going to see if I can sense where the scabbard is. I was able to find Eirian's hilt when the sprites took it, so I should be attuned to the scabbard, too."

"That sounds good," Cynthe agreed. "What then? If only I could have learned a disguising spell from Vassou. Mamee could do them. Why can't we?"

"Maybe we've been going about it wrong. Vassou uses samal magic. Mamee used Fae."

"We should've thought of that before," Cynthe said. "Figure out the Fae spell. Right now!"

"If I've never been able to do it before, why should now be different?"

"Desperation?"

Diello grinned. "One thing at a time. Let me see if I can sense the scabbard first."

"Well, hurry!"

Diello closed his eyes and tried to block out everything from his mind but the scabbard. He envisioned how it looked the last time he saw it: the vivid jewels set in a patterned design along its length.

The pattern . . . it wavered in his memory and blurred. Frowning, he concentrated harder. *Eirian,* he thought, *guide me.*

The colors of the jewels were blending together, swirling. His thoughts were filled with ripples of varying hues. He couldn't focus. There was something he should understand, something he should *see.* . . .

Then he realized that the design was changing into symbols. He couldn't decipher them. They looked very old, like runes. And looking at them too long hurt his eyes. It occurred to Diello that he'd seen marks similar to these before, but where?

On Clevn's staff.

Diello's eyes snapped open. Drawing his knife, he picked up his quarterstaff and began carving the characters down its length.

"What're you doing?" Cynthe asked. "We've no time for whittling."

"Hush."

He'd finished the first symbol. The quarterstaff vibrated slightly in his hands. He went to work on the second symbol, then the third. With each mark, the wood came alive. He could feel a warmth pulsing through it and hear a faint hum. *Eirian's power,* he thought. *No—something else, something older.*

"Diello," Cynthe whispered, crowding so close she almost jostled his arm. "Your quarterstaff's giving off light."

Irritated by the interruption, he looked up at her.

She gasped. "Your eyes! They're glowing like your staff. Be careful!"

He didn't want to be careful. He didn't want to stop what he was doing. But he realized that Cynthe's warning was justified. The more symbols he carved, the more power ran through his staff. *Don't conjure up more than you can handle,* he told himself.

With a shaking hand, he put down his knife. But his

other hand gripped his staff tighter than ever. He remembered how he couldn't let go of Eirian's hilt the first time he held the sword.

If I strike the ground with the tip of my staff, will I create lightning and thunder the way Clevn does?

A shadow swooped down. Diello rolled to one side, eluding the claws that reached for him. *Becoming invisible is like flying,* he thought as he dodged another strike. *I don't have to strain to do it. I just have to let it happen.*

The eagle's startled squawk made him glance down at himself. There was nothing there.

I've done it!

Cynthe screamed.

Diello whirled around and saw talons grip her shoulders and lift her, struggling, up in the air.

He didn't take time to think. He grasped the end of his quarterstaff with both hands and swung it like a club. There was an explosion of fire, ashes, and feathers. Cynthe went tumbling to the ground.

Diello ran to her. "Are you all right?"

Her tunic was ripped, and she was gasping and shuddering. Her gaze shifted around. "I—I think so. Where are you?"

"Here." He clasped her hand. "Come on!"

More eagles came at them, and Diello fended them off with his staff. Cynthe knelt at his feet, clutching her bloodstained shoulder.

"Tell me how!" she cried while he struck another attacker and blew it to bits like the first.

The other eagles soared over them, circling and screaming, but they didn't attack.

"Diello!"

"Not now," he said. "The king will know we're here—and what we're after. Here's my hand. Don't let go, no matter what happens."

She tightened her fingers around his, and Diello let the invisibility spell flow down his arm and across their clasped hands, extending over her.

"Oh! That tickles," she said as she disappeared.

An eagle dived at them, and Diello jerked Cynthe to one side. They hurried away, keeping close to the building.

The whole eyrie came alert. Birds streamed out the open windows. More were circling the mountaintop. Not just eagles, but also smaller birds flew back and forth, squawking in alarm.

Taking cover behind some bushes, Diello dropped the spell and bandaged Cynthe's shoulder, using snow to stop the bleeding. She had three deep scratches, painful looking but not serious.

"I'm all right," she whispered.

"You were lucky."

Diello made them invisible again. When the exodus from the eyrie slowed down, he waited for a gap and climbed through one of the tall windows. Cynthe followed him, steadying herself with her free hand. The sill was coated with mud and droppings, and snow had drifted inside the corners. Cold wind whistled through soaring, wide passages. Diello saw signs of neglect everywhere. The timbers were rotting. Pieces of the ceiling had fallen. The whole place looked dingy. It smelled worse than the poultry house back at the farmstead. Diello didn't bother to use Sight. There was no disguising spell at work here.

Silently, still holding hands, Diello and Cynthe explored. When they met a trio of men coming up the passageway, the twins pressed themselves against the wall. But the shape-shifters didn't sense their presence. On tiptoe, holding his breath, Diello went on. Cynthe crowded his heels. Her hand gripped his so tightly his fingers were going numb.

Diello realized that his spell seemed to be a *cymunffyl* and *cloigwylie* combined. It was more effective than Vassou's protection. None of the palace's inhabitants had detected them so far.

Maybe it's stronger magic, Diello thought with pride. At the moment, as long as it worked, he didn't care.

The deeper they ventured into the eyrie, the more deserted it became. The place was a maze, with rooms leading to other rooms or passages coming to dead ends. All Diello could sense was that the scabbard was here, but he couldn't determine its exact location.

Where would the king keep it? Is he wearing it the way Pa used to wear the deed seal of our farm, to keep it safe?

Diello wished he had Vassou and Scree here to help. The prospect of searching this entire building was daunting.

A flock of swifts flew by, arcing through a doorway and

almost brushing Diello's face with their wingtips. He jerked back, squashing Cynthe against the wall.

She uttered a muffled squeak of protest, and the swifts reversed direction to flash past them again. Four more times the swifts flew back and forth. Diello didn't dare move.

Finally, the swifts left. Diello waited, but they didn't return. Cynthe poked him in the back.

Cautiously, he eased forward. She gave him an impatient push, dropping his hand in the process. At once her head, shoulders, and arms appeared. Diello pounced on her, fumbling for her hand, and she vanished from sight. He sagged against the wall, wiping the sweat from his face.

"Sorry," she murmured into his ear.

He couldn't bring himself to answer her. They'd been lucky again. They couldn't count on it a third time.

"What's wrong?" Cynthe asked. "I said I'm sorry. Go on!"

"Hush. I'm listening."

With his inner senses fanned out, Diello heard the babbling of the breezes blowing through the halls. The timbers creaked and complained.

Faster! Faster! Find the nest, trilled the swifts.

Grain! Grain! Grain! Cold, chattered the sparrows.

My straw. Mine! squabbled the crested jikkits.

Someone's fear pricked Diello. He gasped, fighting to withdraw from the contact even as he recognized the source.

"Reeshwin's in trouble," he told Cynthe.

Cynthe dug in her feet. "She's not in trouble. We are."

Diello looked over his shoulder and saw three Tescorsians in human form blocking the hall behind them. They looked like the same three males who'd passed by before. They stood side by side. They stared straight ahead, at nothing.

Diello swallowed. There was no choice but to go forward.

Except that now men were blocking the other end of the passage.

Diello and Cynthe were trapped.

chapter fifteen

"This is my fault," Cynthe hissed. "I gave us away."

"It doesn't matter now," Diello told her.

"So we fight . . ."

Before Diello could respond, a portion of the wall slid aside, revealing another passageway. Two young boys emerged. Both had fluffy down on their heads instead of hair. They wore long tabards of woven leather. Both carried tall poles with enormous, curling plumes attached to the tips. Behind them marched guards, also in human form, clad in leather. The guards wore short, straight swords at their hips, and each held a weapon that looked like a mace—except that instead of a bludgeon on the end there were sharp metal talons.

Keeping formation, the guards turned sharply to pass Diello and Cynthe, who were still invisible and pressed against the wall. The men blocking the corridor stepped aside to let the newcomers pass. Another pair of young pole-bearers appeared. Their plumes were even bigger, waving in the air. The poles were encrusted with gold and rubies.

Diello's eyes widened as a tall figure came out of the side passage. He stood upright on two legs like a man, but he was certainly no human. From head to foot, he glittered and shone. His skin appeared to be encrusted with diamonds. His eyes were like uncut emeralds that glowed from within. Feathers wrought of gold covered his arms and body.

"The king," Diello breathed.

Looking closer, he realized that it was just a costume, including a gold, diamond-covered mask that covered the king's head and face.

Eirian's jeweled scabbard dangled from Uruoc's belt.

Hastily Diello averted his eyes from the patterns made by the colored stones, but he wasn't quick enough. He could feel the stirring of power within the scabbard. It was responding to his presence and making the magic inside his staff hum. Diello's crystal bones grew so hot he wanted to run or fly to release some of the building tension. He tightened his grip on the staff, trying to keep control.

Uruoc didn't walk. He was borne along on a low, wheeled platform drawn by sweating Tescorsians. More guards followed him before the door slid closed.

Cynthe gave Diello a pinch. He could feel her breath on his ear. "He was wearing the scabbard," she murmured. "Did you see it?"

Diello pressed his hand to her mouth to silence her.

Uruoc and his entourage were already out of sight. Diello and Cynthe followed on tiptoe. The passage turned to the right. Diello slowed down, easing around the corner.

Ahead, through an archway, a square chamber stretched all the way to open windows overlooking a breathtaking vista of purple-smudged hills with a silver ribbon of river winding through the canyons.

The chamber walls were slabs of marble—once white but now darkened with grime. The floor was covered with countless rugs overlapping one another. The rugs were faded and dirty as well. The only piece of furniture was a chair carved from stone. Worn smooth from years of use, it stood atop a platform as tall as Diello's head.

The king perched on the stone chair, his gold-covered arms motionless. The scabbard hung empty from his waist.

"I'll bet he can't move under all that gold," Cynthe whispered. "So once we reach him, it should be easy to take the scabbard away."

One of the guards turned his head in their direction.

Diello squeezed Cynthe's hand. Then he led her past the guards at the doorway and slipped into the throne room.

It was filled mostly with Tescorsians in human form. All were clad in the loose, shapeless robes favored by Reeshwin and Onstri but made of finer fabrics. *These must be the courtiers.*

Diello thought of the poverty in Reeshwin's home and looked again at the cracks in the timber and stone, the signs of filth and neglect.

A lazy man fails to keep his house and barns in good order, Pa always said. *If he won't take care of his own, he won't take care of you in a time of need.*

Then Diello stared at King Uruoc's gold feathers and diamonds.

Uruoc won't use Eirian's scabbard to help his people. A handful of his diamonds would pay for a year's supply of food for those like Reeshwin and her family. No, he wants the scabbard for himself. He's no better than an old, greedy trog stashing a hoard of gold in its den.

The courtiers were talking to one another in the rapid clicks and whistles of their language. Small sparrows flitted in and out through the windows, landing on shoulders to convey messages. Diello and Cynthe found it hard to thread through the crowd without giving away their presence. People kept moving around. They seemed angry and excited. Ducking a man who was shouting and waving his arms, Diello managed to reach the base of Uruoc's platform. Cynthe pressed close against him, trampling one of his feet.

The king seemed oblivious. He spoke to no one, making no effort to control the chaos.

Wincing, Diello worked his way toward the back of the platform, where steps led to the top. Diello hesitated. The steps were narrow. It would be best if he climbed them alone and grabbed the scabbard, but that would break the spell on Cynthe and leave her exposed.

Before he could take action, a scream sliced through the din. The crowd parted to make way for a pair of guards who approached the platform, half shoving, half dragging Reeshwin between them.

She looked hurt. Her face was drawn and pale beneath

her tangled hair. One sleeve of her robe was torn. When they pushed her to the floor in front of the king's platform, she curled up tightly, clutching her stomach as though in pain.

"Traitor!" Uruoc spoke in sharp, cruel tones. Diello read his thoughts to translate. "Why did you guide our enemies here? Where are they hiding now?"

Reeshwin bowed her head and mumbled a plea.

Uruoc gestured, and one of the guards pulled Reeshwin to her feet and struck her.

"That's enough!" Diello shouted.

Stunned silence filled the room before the crowd started looking in all directions. The king lifted both hands high.

"Spirit!" he called out in Antrasin. "What has summoned you? How can we appease you?"

Diello grinned to himself. He made his voice stern. "Release your prisoner."

"How can this lowly creature—this traitor—interest one such as you?" Uruoc countered.

Diello struck his quarterstaff on the floor, and thunder rumbled. "Release your prisoner!"

Several courtiers cried out. Uruoc gave the guards a command, and they cut Reeshwin's bonds. She scrambled back toward the windows.

"Were you successful?" she called out, her gaze darting everywhere. "Is Strieka well?"

"Strieka is well," Diello replied. "Thugar has received her."

Joy lit up Reeshwin's face. She opened her mouth and sang a trill of pure emotion.

"Stop!" the king shouted. "Silence her."

But Reeshwin kept singing as she dodged the guards. She skipped up onto the windowsill and stretched out her arms toward the sky. The music pouring from her throat was like nothing Diello had ever heard. It wasn't birdsong. It had no words, and yet he understood her elation and relief. Suddenly he wanted to sing with her, but he held back. *This is the perfect distraction,* Diello thought. *I mustn't waste this opportunity.*

He eased onto the lowest step of the platform, tugging at Cynthe to follow him.

One of the guards snagged Reeshwin's ankle and pulled her away from the window. She was shoved, sprawling, onto the floor. The other guard planted his foot on her neck. Still smiling, Reeshwin didn't struggle. People murmured, edging away from Uruoc's throne as they stared and pointed at her.

Now! Diello thought, keeping his gaze on the scabbard. He dropped Cynthe's hand. She became immediately visible, but Diello had to take the risk.

As soon as he put his weight on the second step, the boards collapsed beneath his feet. Diello was falling, plunging straight down through a trapdoor that had opened in the floor.

He tried to catch his quarterstaff across the hole, but it all happened too quickly. His fingers slipped on the staff and lost it. He went hurtling down into a dark shaft.

chapter sixteen

iello bounced along the stone sides of the shaft like a pebble dropped into a well. He heard Cynthe yelling as she fell after him.

He tried to control his panic. *Fly!*

His wild impetus slowed and then stopped. He forced himself to relax, floating in the narrow space, and let himself become visible.

"Cynthe," he called, "slow down—"

She tumbled into him, knocking him to the bottom of the shaft. The impact shook every bone in his body. He whooped and wheezed, squirming to get out from under her.

"Sorry," she said, kneeing him in the stomach and then stepping on his hand as she tried to get off.

"Could you try not to trample me completely?" He pushed her away and scrambled to his feet. They barely had room to stand in the shaft. The merest glimmer of light trickled down from cracks in the floorboards high above them. Diello heard a knocking sound, then saw a long shape falling toward them.

Cynthe twisted around, staring up at it. "What—"

"Cover your head!" Diello cried. He pushed her down, shielding her with his body. His staff smacked into him, stinging hard.

"Ow!" He juggled to get a firm grasp on it.

Cynthe straightened. "Good catch," she said.

The bottom of the shaft proved to be a second trapdoor. It opened beneath them and they fell again. This time there was nothing but thin air and the ground far, far below. Diello flipped over and flew to one side, tapping Cynthe as she hurtled past him. She flung out her arms, stopping herself, and rose until she was floating beside him.

Breathing hard, they looked at the closed trapdoor above them. As they watched, it faded from sight, leaving only a sheer cliff of rock in its place.

"A long fall to your death," Cynthe muttered. "If you couldn't fly."

"But Tescorsians can," Diello said. "What an odd trap to use."

The trapdoor reappeared. It opened, letting a stream of rotten meat, vegetable scraps, and broken crockery tumble down. Diello and Cynthe flew apart to avoid it.

She wrinkled her nose. "So we're no better than garbage to them?"

Diello flew up toward the trapdoor, but he couldn't catch it in time. Staying close, he waited until it opened to eject more trash, then he lunged and caught it. "Come on!"

"No," Cynthe said. "Not that way. Not now."

The magical door was shaking in Diello's hand. He

wedged his shoulder into the opening and looked back at her. "Don't argue. It's the last thing they'll expect."

"We can sneak back in when things have calmed down."

"We tried sneaking, and it didn't work. I'm getting that scabbard."

Squirming through the trapdoor, Diello braced his back against the stone shaft and held the door open with his foot while Cynthe wriggled after him. Then the door snapped closed, surrounding them in smelly darkness.

"It stinks worse in here than before," Cynthe grumbled.

"So we'll wash later. Hurry!"

Diello pushed off, rising swiftly up the shaft until he could see glimmers of light through the floorboards above him. Slowing down, he raised his left hand and touched the wood surface, feeling for the first trapdoor. He could hear squawks and trills along with a great deal of laughter.

His face flamed. *Are they laughing at us?*

Putting his eye to the crack, he tried to see what the Tescorsians were doing. Reeshwin's voice rang out, the words unintelligible but her tone defiant. He saw a foot and the hem of a robe but not much else.

Cynthe floated up beside him. Her bow was in her hand. She held an arrow ready.

Diello tightened his grip on his staff. He could feel the power thrumming inside the weapon. Its proximity to the scabbard was feeding the magic he'd created in it. The magic was building inside him, too, vibrating in his bones. *I've got to control it,* he warned himself. *This is probably our last chance.*

"Get ready," he told his twin. "When I open this door, you go through. Fly for the king if you can. One of us has to get the scabbard. If you reach it first, get out of here. Don't wait. Don't look back."

Cynthe drew in an audible breath. "The same goes for you," she insisted.

Diello frowned. She touched his cheek. "I mean it. This is for Amie."

He nodded because he had no choice.

"Let's get this done," Cynthe said. "Make yourself invisible."

"Not this time."

"Diello! Stop worrying about what's fair."

"I'm not. I don't think I can handle invisibility along with the rest of this magic," he admitted.

She squinted as though she didn't believe him, but she stopped arguing.

Carefully he rubbed his palm along the symbols he'd carved in his staff. The magic surged inside him. His bones ached from the force of it. He could feel the scabbard's awareness of him nearby. Eirian's voice murmured in the back of his mind, very faint and far away. He ignored that, wanting no distractions now.

He struck the trapdoor with the end of his staff, channeling his power through it.

The door exploded in a shower of sparks and splinters. Several pieces of wood caught fire as they sailed through the air. Diello soared through the smoke into a scene of confusion. Crying out, people were backing away or running.

His blast had taken out part of the steps to the king's dais. The whole structure was tilting at a crazy angle. Guards were shouting, and Uruoc was standing next to his canted throne. If the dais fell over, Uruoc would topple with it.

The king held one of his gold-clad hands upraised while his other fumbled along the seams of his heavy costume. Diello saw that some of the outfit's jeweled catches had sprung open, but the others remained fastened. Uruoc struggled to open them.

Attendants and guards were pushing at the dais in an effort to right it. They didn't seem to be succeeding. Uruoc continued to utter fierce commands, but Diello couldn't see that anyone was paying much attention to him.

Diello headed for the helpless king. From his left, a large shape knocked him sideways. It was one of the guards in eagle form. But the creature's wide wingspan was hampered inside the chamber, giving Diello the advantage.

Diello struck back with his staff. There was another explosion, and the guard vanished in a cloud of ash and smoke.

Half blinded, Diello heard Cynthe calling behind him, but he couldn't see her. Then the smoke ahead of him cleared, revealing Uruoc. The king had managed to free both arms from his costume. Now he was tugging at the ornate mask. Cynthe flew at the king, angling fast for the jeweled scabbard swinging at his waist.

Another guard attacked her. Diello struck him from behind, turning him to ashes, but Cynthe was pushed off course by the blast. She circled the room, but it had cost her time.

It's up to me, Diello thought. He saw the king toss his glittering mask aside, revealing a bald head, stooped shoulders, and a small mouth pursed in anger. Uruoc swung his sceptor at Diello. It was a diamond-crusted rod ending in gold talons clutching an enormous ruby. As Uruoc attacked, razor-sharp knives projected from the fake claws.

Diello dodged, but not quite fast enough. The weapon slashed his sleeve and the skin underneath.

One of Cynthe's arrows hit Uruoc's hand, and he dropped the sceptor. Diello lunged close and yanked the scabbard off the king's belt.

Uruoc shouted in desperation. He gripped the other end of the scabbard and pulled. Hanging on tightly with one hand, Diello struck the dais with his staff and shattered the main timber still supporting it. The structure toppled over, crashing onto the floor and taking Uruoc with it.

"Got it!" Diello shouted, waving the scabbard in triumph.

"Look out!" Cynthe called.

When he turned, he saw more eagle guards flying toward him. All the courtiers were now changing into eagles. Uruoc—apparently unhurt—transformed into a huge white bird. Stretching his wings, the king screeched a predator's cry.

Reeshwin transformed, too. Her drab, brown bird looked small next to the king's. As her guards joined the rush toward Diello, Reeshwin flew between them, blocking their attack before she soared out of one of the large windows.

The delay gave Diello his chance. He tucked the scabbard and his staff close to his chest and dropped down the open shaft. He didn't fly; he let himself fall, plunging as fast as possible. Just before his feet struck the second trapdoor, he aimed his staff and blasted the wooden panel to pieces. Out he went into the open air. He flew across the sky.

Below him, a cloud wreathed the mountain, covering the lower canyons in a layer of fog. The sinking sun crowned distant hills in gold.

Cold wind whistled in Diello's ears, and he heard a voice in his thoughts: *How may I serve you, Master of Eirian?*

Zephyr! he replied gladly. *May I ride with you again?*

The breeze surged beneath him, lifting him high as it circled. Diello rendered himself invisible, riding the wind with more confidence than before. But he would not let it take him away from here.

"Cynthe!" he called aloud, searching the skies. "Come on. Where are you?"

Finally he saw her, a small speck coming from the temple side of the mountain. She must have gone out a window while he was falling through the shaft. A brown eagle was flying with her. *Reeshwin,* Diello thought in relief.

But even as he spotted them, so did the others. The sky filled with eagles. Reeshwin flapped her wings, rising to meet them while Cynthe flew on alone.

Diello tried to make his twin invisible, but he wasn't able to do it from a distance the way Vassou could.

Vassou! he called. *Cynthe needs help!*

The wolf didn't answer. Diello forgot his promise to escape without Cynthe if necessary. He slipped off the zephyr's back and flew toward his twin.

Young master! The zephyr swept under him again, lifting him once more. *You cannot outfly the eagle warriors alone. Let me help you.*

Help Cynthe, Diello pleaded as the eagles caught up with his twin. *Please!*

Suddenly Cynthe was moving faster. She zoomed away from the eagles just as they were about to attack, and they couldn't overtake her.

Diello nearly whooped in joy before he remembered that he was invisible. *Thank you, Zephyr,* he said as an astonished Cynthe passed him. He went after her.

"I'm here!" he called to Cynthe as he caught up. He made himself visible.

"What kind of spell are you working now?" she yelled.

"We're riding the winds!"

And then it was impossible to talk, because they were dropping through layers of cloud. Lightning flickered and thunder boomed around them. Diello threw back his head, enjoying the danger. He didn't mind the pellets of sleet stinging his face or the numbness in his cheeks and hands. The wind currents bore them along even faster, breaking through the cloud into a world of shadows and dusky twilight. Boulders and scrawny, wind-twisted trees ringed the snowy clearing where Vassou and Scree were huddled beside a tiny fire.

There! Diello called to the zephyr. *I see our friends.*

Let me take you far from this land of eagles, the zephyr whispered in his mind. *You are not safe. They will hunt you.*

My friends cannot fly, Diello said, wishing he could accept the offer. *Thank you, but I won't abandon them.*

The zephyr said no more, bringing him down gently. When Diello's feet touched the ground, he stumbled, unable to find his balance.

Scree jumped up with a startled cry, but it was Vassou who reached Diello first.

The wolf leaped around him. "I didn't know if we would ever see you again."

Scree hung back a little, staring at the scabbard. The firelight made its jewels glitter brightly. "I am very glad to see you, Diello," Scree said. "But that is a dangerous thing."

"Yes, it is." Diello tucked it away in the battered rucksack.

"And you are different," Scree went on. "You are not the same Diello who is my friend."

"I'm no shape-shifter," Diello replied. "I'm still me."

Scree's face puckered. "Where is Cynthe?"

Diello pointed at the sky. "She's coming. See her?"

"You have found power beyond your Gifts," Vassou said, assessing Diello. The wolf stretched out his forelegs and bowed. "You have become a mage."

Just then Cynthe landed. Her eyes were glazed, and she

looked pale with exhaustion. Vassou ran to her, uttering little yips. She hugged him tight.

Scree greeted her, too, but he kept glancing over his shoulder at Diello.

Not knowing how to reassure the goblin-boy, Diello kicked out the fire. "We need a hiding place for the night," he said.

It was almost dark. Diello heard the eagles coming, their cries strident. Everyone ran for the giant rocks, crouching in the shadows as the birds circled once and flew on.

"What about Reeshwin?" Diello whispered.

"She gave me a chance to get away. That's all I know. Do you think they'll search all night?" Cynthe asked. "If they were real birds they'd stop to roost, but what will shape-shifters do?"

"I'm not sure," Diello said. "I'm too tired to keep going tonight, but this is a risky place to camp."

"Ahem," said a voice at their feet. "Perhaps I might be of assistance?"

Diello looked down and saw a round, gray rock by his ankle. Two eyes were staring up at him, and a patch of lichen beneath them almost seemed to form a face on the stone's side. "Qod!"

"May I be the first to offer you congratulations for your successful mission?" Qod said.

"We had a lot of help," Diello told the tomtir. "More than we expected."

"I know what is different," Scree said suddenly. "You smell of shape-shifter magic. Are you really Diello?"

Diello didn't want to explain now, but Scree looked so worried. "I'm really me. When I was in their temple, handing over the *stona*, I accepted a gift from a Tescorsian spirit. That's all."

"All?" Qod echoed, sounding impressed. "*All?* It's unheard of. Such a thing hasn't happened in these mountains for—for—" The tomtir broke off, as though finally at a loss for words.

"We'll tell you everything later," Cynthe said, yawning. "Let's get out of here."

"I saw some caves farther down the mountain," Vassou said. "If we can shelter there for the night, the eagles won't find us."

"Close by?" Diello asked as the tomtir shrank down to pebble size and bounced into his pocket. "We're very tired."

"Better to be weary than captured," Vassou replied. "Follow me."

They clambered over the rocks, stumbling along a steep trail that they could barely see.

"Why weren't you sheltering in these caves already?" Cynthe asked.

"We were waiting for you," Scree said.

"You needed a signal fire," Vassou added.

"You're right. We did," Cynthe said. She yawned again. "I could eat an entire haunch of venison all by myself."

"Flesh and grain," Qod's tiny voice grumbled inside Diello's pocket. "Always flesh and grain. You really should vary your diet. Perhaps you might develop a taste for gravel?"

"No," Diello said.

"Pity. If you could only bring yourself to sample crushed red limestone, I'm sure you'd come around."

"Hush," Vassou warned. "They're making another pass."

Everyone scrambled for cover, silent and tense as the eagles flew over again.

This time the birds landed, their wings whipping up dust. As they perched on ledges and outcroppings all around, Diello counted at least fifty.

How do they know we're here? How will we ever escape?

chapter seventeen

he air shimmered, and it was as though moonlight poured over each of the Tescorsians. They changed shape, becoming men and women. Diello saw Reeshwin among them. She was arguing with one of the men. He gave her a shove and stormed away, ordering the group to fan out and search.

Fifty against four, five if we count Qod, and six with Reeshwin. Still terrible odds, thought Diello.

Qod popped out of Diello's pocket and rolled away, then returned, bumping Diello's ankle. "The caves are ahead," it said quietly. "I'll show you."

Diello beckoned to Cynthe. She broke from her hiding place, scuttling low to join him. "Caves, nearby," Diello whispered. "Stick close to me. I'll turn us invisible again."

"I'd rather use Vassou's *cymunffyl.* Then we don't have to hold hands all the time."

Vassou appeared from the rocks and joined them. He nudged Cynthe's palm with his nose. "Diello's protection is safer for you," he said. "It's stronger."

"He's worn-out," Cynthe protested. "He's not used to working so much magic."

"Very well," Vassou said. "But in future remember that you and Diello have your own magic now. You have grown beyond the need of mine."

"Please," Cynthe said. "Let's hurry."

"Everyone, follow Qod," Diello whispered.

Cynthe disappeared as Vassou's magic surrounded her. Diello felt her touch his cheek before she was gone. Vassou trotted after her, a gray shadow that melted into the rocks.

Diello looked around impatiently. *Where's Scree?*

As though summoned by his thoughts, the goblin-boy touched Diello's arm.

"You go ahead," Scree whispered. "I have a pine bough. I will clear away our footprints."

The goblin-boy was invisible—thanks to Vassou. Diello saw one of Cynthe's tracks being rubbed out.

"I think they hunt by sighting their prey," Diello said. "They won't be tracking us."

"Oh," Scree mumbled. "I wanted to help."

"But go ahead," Diello said hastily. "Our tracks could give our position away."

"That is what I thought," Scree agreed.

Diello patted his shoulder in approval. While Scree bent to his work, Diello traced the symbols he'd carved in his staff. He closed his eyes as he drew on the magic inside. His skin prickled all over, and when he opened his eyes, he couldn't see any part of his body. His staff and the rucksack containing the scabbard were invisible, too.

Satisfied, Diello crawled forward. Now that he was invisible, he could have walked without attempting to hide, but he couldn't bring himself to do it. Scree followed close at his heels, now and then bumping into Diello as he scratched at the ground.

A whistle from one of the Tescorsians told Diello that the eagle-folk were closing in. The predators had scattered and were systematically clambering over the tops of boulders and inching their way sure-footedly along narrow ledges above the trail that Diello and Scree had taken. Their shapes were silhouetted against the moonlit sky.

Diello quickened his pace. He didn't want to risk bumping into the searchers.

But in his haste he kicked some pebbles that went bouncing and clattering down the trail. Diello froze, but Tescorsian shouts drove him forward. He glimpsed Vassou ahead, watching for him.

Vassou took cover, but Diello aimed for the spot where he'd seen the wolf. He zigzagged from boulder to boulder, leaving as few tracks as possible and above all trying to stay quiet. Scree was slower, still intent on obscuring their trail.

Diello stumbled once and lost his footing but caught himself before he fell. He would be safer flying, but the effort required to keep himself invisible was draining him fast.

A Tescorsian jumped at him from above, landing just inches away. Diello was certain the man's keen hearing would detect his breathing. The eagle-man's back was to him. The Tescorsian stepped even closer to the edge, keeping his balance fearlessly as he gazed down the hillside.

Diello itched to get out of there.

From behind him, he heard Scree approaching. The Tescorsian whirled around, and Diello struck with his staff. He knocked the man off his feet, sending him tumbling down the rocks.

"Come on!" Diello called to Scree.

Without waiting, Diello angled down the sharp slope away from the trail. He squeezed through an opening between two tilting boulders. Ahead and below he could hear the soft chuckle of running water. He headed for the stream.

More shouts cut through the air. Diello sprinted into the open, no longer caring if they heard him. Beyond the stream, a sheer cliff face rose toward the night sky. Qod's cave *had* to be there.

Vassou appeared on the stream's opposite bank, pale in the shadows.

Diello splashed his way across, shivering, and touched Vassou's back. The pup stood immobile, watching the pursuing men.

"Where's Scree?" Diello asked. "Is he coming?"

One of Vassou's ears swiveled in Diello's direction. He didn't answer, and Diello felt a shudder run through the wolf pup's body. A dark shape swept overhead, outstretched wings black against the largest of the twin moons.

Can the Tescorsians sense the scabbard's presence? Diello wondered. *Why doesn't Scree hurry?*

He heard splashing and saw the water kicked up by Scree's invisible feet. The stream was shallow, no more than knee-deep at the point where Diello had crossed. But the water ran fast, and the stones lining the streambed were slippery.

There was a big splash, accompanied by a muffled cry. More splashing showed Diello exactly where Scree was floundering to regain his footing.

The Tescorsians saw as well. They swarmed down the slope into the water.

Diello dropped the rucksack and his staff next to Vassou and ran for the stream. Scooping up a fist-sized stone, he resisted the temptation to bean the closest Tescorsian and threw the rock upstream. It hit deeper water with a loud *ker-plunk.*

The simple ruse worked. The shape-shifters turned, heading that way. Diello threw another stone, making sure it thudded on the bank. The Tescorsians converged on the spot.

Diello grinned, even though he knew his trick would work for only a few moments. Just as he stepped into the water, Scree bumped into him. Diello grabbed blindly, and his fingers found Scree's wet tunic. He turned, dragging the goblin-boy with him. Scree's teeth were chattering.

"I—I am sorry," Scree said. "I did not mean to fall. I have caused us much trouble."

"Quiet," Diello said, and shoved him along faster.

A shrill whistle warned him that the Tescorsians were coming back.

"Run!" Diello told Scree.

As they left the stream, Vassou emerged from cover and joined them long enough to put his paw on Diello's foot before loping away with the rucksack's strap in his jaws. As the wolf ran, he faded from sight within a *cymunffyl* of his own. Diello picked up his staff and hurried Scree along the bank.

Both boys were stumbling. The effort to stay invisible was too much for Diello. His legs seemed to be trapped in a vat of syrup. They wouldn't move fast enough. Even worse, Diello saw his hands and arms beginning to reappear. They looked transparent, then solidified. Now his legs were materializing. Halting, he tried to regain control of the spell and couldn't.

Vassou materialized again. He turned around and came bounding back to them.

"No," Diello said. "Go on. Take the scabbard to safety."

Without answering, Vassou ran behind them and used his head to bump Diello forward.

Diello was entirely visible now. He felt Vassou's magic slide around him and then melt away without working.

"I can see you!" Scree cried. "What are you doing? Are you trying to trick them by showing yourself? I think you are foolish. I think you should vanish again."

"Can't," Diello said through gritted teeth.

Diello concentrated on running. Vassou was streaking ahead of them, and he did his best to keep up. But he was so tired. Now it was Scree's turn to support him, Scree who pulled him along.

"Faster!" Scree urged him. "You must go faster!"

Excited shouts came from the Tescorsians. They were gaining.

The cliff wall rose ahead of Diello and Scree.

If we can't find Qod's cave, we'll be trapped, Diello thought.

But Vassou never faltered as he led the boys along the cliff's base and ducked beneath a low overhang. Diello looked back. Several of the eagle-folk were throwing spears. Just as Diello dropped to his knees, one of the weapons bounced off the jutting ledge of rock, missing him by a finger's breadth.

"This way!" Vassou called.

It was dark under the ledge, the ground cold and clammy with the smell of damp. Unable to see Vassou, Diello felt desperately along the cliff base, but his fingers found no opening.

"Where's the cave?" he muttered.

Scree elbowed past Diello. "I see it!"

A Tescorsian war cry filled the air. Strong fingers gripped Diello's clothing from behind. He twisted in the eagle-man's clutch and used his staff like a cudgel, striking hard. He was able to yank free. Another reached for him, and Diello kicked to fend him off.

"Scree!" he cried. "Vassou!"

"Here," Vassou replied. "Keep coming!"

"I'm...trying," Diello gasped. He thumped his opponent with his staff, only to find his arms clamped in a fierce grip.

Pinned, Diello kicked and writhed, but the Tescorsian outweighed him.

A loud rumble overhead made both of them pause in their struggle. The ground was shaking, and the deep, growling sound above them was one that Diello recognized all too well.

"Avalanche!" he yelled.

Dirt and snow rained down. The shelf of rock above them cracked. The Tescorsian looked up, his grip loosening as he whistled a series of notes.

Diello kicked violently, knocking the man off balance. Another loud noise came from the rock overhead. Part of the rock tipped dangerously low. The Tescorsian rolled away from Diello, flailing his arms as he tried to scramble clear.

Diello scuttled as far beneath the overhang as possible. The ground was still shaking. The roar of snow and dirt overwhelmed everything. The outer section of the overhang collapsed in front of Diello. Snow was piling on top of him, burying him alive.

Sharp teeth closed on his upper arm, pulling him forward. Diello realized Vassou was dragging him through the cave's mouth.

Diello flipped over on his stomach and pulled himself through an opening. His shoulders wedged in the tight space, but he squirmed, eeling his way through. The snow spilled into the tunnel behind him, covering his feet.

"Diello!" Scree's voice reached him through the din. Wiry fingers tugged at Diello's shoulders and arms.

"Pull harder!" Diello shouted. "Don't let me get stuck in here!"

"Become smaller," Scree said in ragged breaths. "Stretch yourself out."

The cave tunnel was pitch-black. Diello strained forward, but he couldn't get through.

"I'm stuck!"

More snow was pushing in around his legs, filling the small space and covering his back. *I'm going to die in here.*

He smothered his panic. "Where's Cynthe?" he called.

"I'm here," she said.

He felt his twin grip his hands. *At least she's with me.*

"Cynthe, I—"

"Quiet," she said. "Vassou told me that your magic is fighting the spell that protects Qod's domain."

The snow was pressing around Diello's shoulders. He could feel the icy touch of it on the back of his neck. "What?" he cried.

"Don't argue. Push your staff forward."

Diello didn't understand, but he pushed the stick ahead of him.

"Ow!" Cynthe cried. "Careful!"

The snow was sliding along his ears. "Don't let go of my hand," Diello pleaded.

"I won't. Take the staff, Scree."

Diello heard Scree yell.

"What's happening?" Diello asked just before snow pushed over his head and covered his face.

He sputtered, but there was no escaping it now. Ice coated his eyes and filled his mouth. He puffed out his breath, fighting to keep snow out of his nostrils. Frantically he cupped his free hand over his mouth and nose, creating a tiny air pocket.

"Diello! Stop fighting," Cynthe said urgently. "Remember when you really learned to fly? Relax and allow Qod's magic to help you."

I can't! Diello wanted to yell. *I can't!*

"Trust Qod," Cynthe said. "Trust *me*."

She brushed the snow from his face, letting him breathe. Something in her touch tingled through his flesh. He forced his tense muscles to loosen.

The tingling grew more intense—like hot sparks popping off a fire. It spread across his hands and into his wrists. He felt his body shrinking, as though his bones were being compacted. His clothing grew looser.

Then he realized that he was moving. Finally he was being drawn through the opening.

As soon as his feet cleared, magic surged around him, sealing off the opening. The thunder of the avalanche faded. Dazed, Diello noticed little glimmers of illumination here and there.

The darkness faded to shadow, and shadow became light. Rubbing his eyes, Diello sat up.

He found himself staring into one of his sister's green eyes, an eye as large as Diello's head. Her face—gigantic now—loomed over him. Her breath blew his hair back from his brow.

Diello closed his eyes tightly, then opened them. Cynthe remained huge.

"What's happened to me?" he cried.

"Oops," said Qod.

chapter eighteen

"What did Qod do?" Diello's voice sounded small and shrill.

Cynthe tried to touch Diello, but her finger looked like a tree branch. Diello dodged away. He bumped into a wooden wall, then recognized a carved symbol on it and figured out that this had to be his staff, lying on the ground.

Vassou's muzzle swooped over him, each sniff like a gust of wind. "Qod shrank you."

"It saved your life," Scree boomed.

Diello stared up at his friends. His twin's enormous hand came toward him again, knocking him down before he could get away.

Kicking furiously, he rolled upright and dusted himself off. "What are you doing?"

"Trying to pick you up," Cynthe said. "I don't want you to get hurt."

"Then stop pinching me like a woolly bug you're picking off the marrows," Diello told her.

"Sorry."

"How did the rest of you get through the tunnel?" Diello asked.

"The same as you," Cynthe told him. "Only, as soon as each of us came through, we were back to our full size."

"Where's Qod?" Diello demanded. "How come the spell didn't work on me?"

"Part of it worked," Scree reminded him. "The important part. I think you should remember that and be glad. I am glad for you."

"Thanks," Diello said, forcing himself to calm down. "But I can't stay like this."

Cynthe giggled. "I could carry you in my pocket, *little* brother."

He made a face at her, seeing nothing funny about his situation.

A boulder came rolling toward Diello and halted before him. Qod's dark eyes blinked rapidly.

"This doesn't seem to have gone as it should," the tomtir said.

"No, it didn't," Diello snapped. "Change me back!"

"There's no need to be so cross, Fae-boy."

"Look, Qod, I'm very grateful to you for saving my life. But this spell has to be corrected right away."

Qod hesitated. "Are you sure you wouldn't rather eat first? You look quite pale. I can tell you aren't yourself."

Cynthe laughed again.

"No, he is not himself," Scree burst out before Diello could speak. "He is too small. I like small things, but I do not like my friend this way. He should be himself."

"Qod," Diello said firmly, "I wish to be changed back to my normal size."

"Please!" Cynthe added.

Vassou growled loudly.

Qod looked at Cynthe. "If you will kindly move that mage-stick away from us both."

Cynthe picked up Diello's staff. Her foot came down too close. He was only as tall as her ankle.

"Watch out!" Diello shouted.

"Oh! Sorry."

"Give us plenty of room," Qod requested. "And, everyone, mind your feet."

While everyone else moved back, the tomtir began rotating around Diello, going faster and faster.

Tingles ran up and down his arms and legs. He felt icy cold, then very warm.

Dizzy, he closed his eyes. He could feel his arms and legs growing longer.

"Oh no!" Cynthe cried. "Diello!"

He opened his eyes and bumped his head on the cave ceiling. Cynthe, Scree, and Vassou looked like ants at his feet.

"Too big!" Diello said. His voice was a roar that echoed off the stone and sent trickles of dust raining down.

Cynthe and Scree clapped their hands over their ears.

"Stay calm," Qod's voice piped up. "It's all a matter of adjustment."

Suddenly Diello lost his balance and landed on his

bottom with a jolt. Stretching out his arms, he patted himself all over. He was back to his normal size.

Qod circled him. "As I said, simply a matter of adjustment. It isn't easy to size-shift crystal bones. Anything broken?"

Diello shook his head. "I don't think so."

"Thank you, Qod, for putting him back together," Cynthe said. She gave Diello a swift hug, then elbowed him.

"Uh, thank you, Qod," Diello said.

"It was my pleasure," the tomtir replied. "Welcome to my realm. You have no worries now. You're quite safe here. Please come this way."

As Qod rolled away, the companions exchanged glances, then followed the tomtir into a low tunnel leading from the cave.

Although reluctant to crawl into another narrow space, Diello had no other option.

The dim light faded. Clutching his staff to his chest, Diello groped his way cautiously. The place smelled of damp soil and tree roots. Scree gave him a nudge from behind, but Diello couldn't go faster. He tried to flick fire to light his way, but the magic sputtered and died on his fingertips.

"Neither your magic nor mine works here," Vassou said in the darkness.

"Please keep moving," Scree whispered. "I do not like this dark place. It reminds me of—"

"What?" Diello asked.

"Nothing. It is nothing. I have nothing to say. I wish to go."

"Did anyone see Reeshwin before we escaped?" Diello asked.

"She was after us like all the others," Cynthe replied.

"No, she was just pretending."

"I did not see her," Scree said.

Diello would've liked to have told her good-bye. He hoped she was safe. He crawled a little faster over gravel that dug into his palms and kneecaps. Then his outstretched hand touched nothing at all. He teetered on the edge of a drop, one he could sense but couldn't see. Scree pushed at him. As Diello struggled to keep his balance, a hand closed over his wrist and yanked him forward.

He tripped, swallowing his cry, and landed on top of someone.

"Get off." Cynthe gave him a push.

He hung on to her sleeve. "Are we in another hole?"

"I don't think so."

"Can't see."

"Vassou can."

"I can!" Scree joined in, jumping down beside Diello. "I can see very well in the dark. I will help you."

Vassou brushed past Diello's leg. "The tunnel stops here," the wolf said. "I don't understand."

"Has Qod vanished again?" Diello asked.

"It seems so," Vassou said. "I'll search for another passage." After a moment, the pup said, "Yes, here's one."

"The one we came through?" Cynthe asked.

"No. It's much bigger."

Diello wiped his face wearily. All he wanted to do was make camp. *Why does Qod have to play games with us?* As Vassou led them forward, Diello shuffled along in silence. At least he wasn't crawling.

He saw a glimmer of light ahead. It quickly grew stronger. The passage curved; and as Diello went around it, he saw a chamber filled with light. The warmth in the air welcomed him.

A fire blazed merrily, its smoke spiraling upward to escape through a fissure. Along the walls, chunks of quartz glowed. There was a circle of seats made from stacked stones. Jewels as vivid as those adorning Eirian's scabbard floated in the air. Sparkling, they bobbed and spun. When Diello tried to catch one, his fingers touched nothing but air.

"What are these?" Cynthe asked, jumping for another in vain.

"Illusions," Diello answered.

"This food is real," Scree declared.

Diello saw a feast spread along a ledge: thinly sliced beef surrounded by creamed taties and marrows, bowls of steaming sprouts, an array of cheeses, and a basket of fresh-baked bread. Inhaling their mingled fragrances, Diello found his mouth watering.

"Come on, Diello!" Cynthe called, picking up a wooden plate. She tossed it to him. As Diello caught it, he felt a surge of magic behind him. When he turned, he saw that the passage they'd entered from was gone.

He should have felt trapped, but the atmosphere of

serenity inside this chamber made him feel relieved instead. An unfamiliar sense of well-being spread through him. He hadn't felt this safe since the morning of his birthday when he'd last seen his parents alive.

Qod's magic at work, Diello told himself.

He was afraid to let himself trust it, yet he couldn't resist. Across the chamber, Cynthe was laughing with Vassou. Scree sidled closer to the food, his hand darting out to grab a bun.

The twinkling jewels swirled through the air, clustering together and then flying apart. An enormous diamond—the size of two fists clenched together—was revealed. Sinking to the ground, it glittered brilliantly in the firelight. Then two round, dark eyes opened in its side. They gazed up at Diello.

"Qod?" Diello asked uncertainly.

The diamond grew in size until it reached higher than Diello's knees. "Welcome, dear guests." Qod's voice was unmistakable. "May you enjoy my hospitality for as long as you please, and may you wish for as many gifts and pleasures as I'm able to grant. Come now and put down your belongings. There is warm water to wash with, food aplenty, and—when you are ready—soft blankets and beds for your comfort."

Cynthe came over and smiled down at the creature. "Thank you, Qod. This is lovely."

"It is my pleasure. In the eons to come, I shall be able to say that I served Queen Sheirae's granddaughter and grandson as my honored guests. As the last of the elder tomtirs, given the duty to watch over these mountains, I can only repeat that you are most welcome. Most welcome."

From the corner of his eye, Diello saw Scree sneak another handful of food. Diello frowned. "Scree! Wash first."

Scree froze with his grubby fingers in the taties. His guilty gaze moved from Diello to Cynthe before he hung his head. Still, he managed to scoop taties into his pocket.

"There's plenty for all," Cynthe said. "You don't need to steal."

"I am sorry," Scree said. "I am so hungry. It is hard to wait through speeches. I do not like speeches. Do you?"

"Well, no, but it's rude to say so," Cynthe told him. She pointed at the basin of water. "And it's good manners to clean your hands before you eat. You know our rules."

Scree slinked away to wash.

"May I offer you new dishes?" Qod asked.

Diello nodded gratefully. "Please."

"Then it is done."

A trail of light sparkled across the food. All the items that Scree had dug into vanished, and fresh delectables appeared in their place. Diello's stomach was growling.

"There's no need to wait," Qod announced. "Eat all that you can hold. Eat more. You are safe tonight, and for as long as you choose to stay with me."

Cynthe was already splashing water on her face and scrubbing her hands.

"Thank you, Qod," Diello said. "But I have some questions—"

"Mind your feet!"

Qod spun, faster and faster, and then it disappeared.

chapter nineteen

It had been a long time since any of them had felt so secure. Even their brief stay in Embarthi had been perilous. Diello slept without bad dreams, waking to eat another delicious meal before falling asleep again.

Sometime later, he awoke and drowsily munched on hot cakes oozing with sweet cream and sprinkled with nuts. This time only he and Scree were eating. Cynthe was lazing around on a pile of cushions. Vassou was curled up with his bushy tail over his muzzle, fast asleep.

The chunks of quartz illuminated the underground chamber. The fire crackled and hissed steadily. It never needed fresh logs to replenish its flames.

Qod had showered them with gifts. All of them—except for Vassou—had new clothes and footgear. A fine leather belt and pouch for Scree. A necklace of smooth agate disks for Cynthe. A flute of polished silver for Diello. Although the flute was pretty, Diello missed the wooden bird whistles that Pa had carved for each of his birthdays. All but one of the whistles—now safe in his pocket—had been burned when the goblins attacked their farm.

I'll play the flute after I have a nap, he thought, stifling a yawn.

Diello finished his last hot cake, licking his fingers. One remained on the platter. Diello saw Scree eyeing it and smiled.

"Go ahead, Scree. I've had enough."

"There is never enough," Scree said. Grinning, he crammed the cake into his mouth and chewed vigorously.

Diello noticed that the goblin-boy looked plump. *How can Scree be fat? He's always been scrawny.*

"How long have we been here?" Diello asked. He tried to think back, but his recollection was hazy. "Cynthe?"

Instead of answering, she rolled onto her side. He poked her arm, but she was asleep.

Diello yawned so wide he felt his jaws pop. His eyelids felt heavy. He was warm and full. No one could bother him here—not the Tescorsians, not Brezog, and certainly not Uncle Owain. Yet something teased at his mind, something he needed to remember.

Idly he picked up his flute and puffed a few solitary notes. Lowering the instrument, Diello pulled the jeweled scabbard from the rucksack and hung it on his belt. It seemed a waste to hide such beautiful workmanship. He found himself rubbing the colored stones while he hummed a little tune. He realized it was the song Mamee used to sing to his little sister at bedtime.

"Amalina," Diello blurted out. His mind cleared, and he fought off his lethargy. How could he laze about when she was still in danger?

Standing up, he kicked his twin's foot. "Cynthe, wake up. Wake up!"

She roused, grumbling as she swept her hair back from her face. "What?"

"How long have we been asleep?"

Her cheek was red and creased from her pillow. "What are you talking about?"

"Wake up! Look at Scree."

She snuggled deeper in her blankets. "Why should I? Go back to sleep."

"Look at Scree!" Diello insisted. "He's getting fat."

"You're dreaming," she mumbled.

"No. That's just it. Since we've been here, I've not dreamed once."

"Good. You need the rest."

He shook her shoulder. "I've had enough. More than enough."

"I haven't. Go away. Stop worrying. We're safe."

"We're *too* safe. You have to wake up!"

"Oh, all right." She sat up and flung her arms wide in a stretch. "I don't understand what you're worrying about. Scree and Vassou are both sleeping. It must be the middle of the night."

"But *which* night?"

"What?"

"Which night?" Diello repeated. "How many nights?"

"You're daft."

Diello took her hand and pulled her over to where Scree now lay snoring on the floor, cake crumbs smeared at the corners of his mouth. Diello patted Scree's cheek, but the goblin-boy didn't stir.

"See?" Diello said, tapping the pudginess under Scree's chin.

Cynthe was yawning. "So?"

He pressed her fingers to Scree's side. "Feel any ribs?"

"Of course not! Wait." The drowsiness cleared from her eyes. "You're right. He's always been skin and bone no matter how much we fed him. Now he's downright chubby."

"That didn't happen overnight," Diello said. "We've been here longer than we think."

Standing up, they stared at each other. For the first time in a long while their eyes were level.

Diello gasped. "I'm as tall as you!"

"You aren't as tall." Cynthe stretched her neck. "Not . . . quite."

"Closer than I used to be. I've *grown*."

"Or maybe Qod didn't adjust your size right after all. No . . . wait. My hair's longer," Cynthe said, fingering the ends. "What's Qod doing to us?"

Diello crouched beside Vassou. He blew in the wolf pup's ear, making it twitch. "Vassou, can you hear me?"

The pup opened one eye, rolling it in Diello's direction. "Of course."

"How long have we been here?"

"Twenty-eight days and nights." Vassou rubbed his muzzle with his paw.

"What! Why didn't you say something?" Cynthe demanded.

Vassou sat up. "I—I couldn't. The spell has held me enthralled, too."

"Are we Qod's prisoners?" Diello asked grimly.

"No."

"What then?" Cynthe asked. She smacked her cheeks and shook her head. "It's so hard to stay awake."

"Perhaps I am the best one to answer your questions," Qod said from behind them.

Diello spun around, but he didn't see the tomtir. "Please tell us why you're keeping us here."

"Is that your wish?"

"Yes!" Diello said. "I wish you to tell us the truth. I wish you to explain *everything*."

"And I wish you to stop making us sleepy," Cynthe added.

The quartz lights lifted off their wall niches and floated in the air. Their illumination grew brighter, revealing Qod glittering on the opposite side of the chamber.

"Qod's still a diamond," Cynthe whispered.

"I am not a diamond," Qod said. "I told you I was made from the scraps of magical ore when Eirian was forged."

"Eirian's made of glass," Cynthe argued.

"Not so. The ore is called *chthon*. It is found only within this mountain."

"It looks like glass," Cynthe said. "It's not steel. We can touch it."

"Not exactly," Diello mumbled.

Cynthe ignored him.

"Master of Eirian," Qod went on, "you have held the sword. You know its voice. Touch my surface and decide if I'm telling you the truth."

"Be careful," Cynthe said.

Diello didn't need her warning. Slowly he approached Qod and leaned over. Qod's dark eyes blinked up at him. Diello brushed his fingertips across the top of the tomtir.

"Press your hand to me," Qod ordered. "Do not be afraid. Have I ever harmed you?"

Diello heard no lie in the tomtir's tone, yet they'd been tricked into staying here for nearly a month. Qod could have stolen the scabbard while they were all asleep—if that's what the tomtir was after—but Diello wasn't ready to trust it.

He tried to look at Qod with Sight, but nothing happened.

"Well?" Qod said.

Diello placed his palm against the tomtir's surface. It didn't have the cold feel of stone. Instead, he felt a warmth—a vibrancy—beneath that gleaming surface. He closed his eyes, feeling a flow of power up his arm. It was exactly the same as the first time he'd held Eirian. Except this time, the sword's voice didn't murmur in his thoughts.

"Is it as I've said?" Qod asked. Diello's eyes snapped open. "Do you recognize the magic?"

"Yes," Diello said. He backed away, reluctant to break

contact. His hand still tingled. He could feel a stirring in his bones, and across the chamber the carved symbols on his staff glowed faintly to life. "It's the same."

"Then put aside your fears and mistrust. I shall obey your wishes and answer your questions."

"And you'll let us go," Cynthe said.

"I do not keep you here against your will," Qod told her. "What a pity your parents taught you such wariness. You cannot sort friends from foes, can you?"

"We do all right," Diello said curtly. "Have we really been here twenty-eight days?"

"By your reckoning, yes."

"Why? You know how important it is for us to find Eirian and save our sister."

Scree woke up and edged closer to Diello. "What is wrong?" he whispered, licking the crumbs from his mouth. "Why are you angry with Qod?"

Vassou put his paw on Scree's foot. "Be silent," the wolf pup growled.

Scree obeyed without protest. The twins exchanged a quick look. *It's like how they used to be,* Diello thought, *when Vassou criticized Scree all the time.*

Diello turned his attention back to Qod. "Why put a spell on us to make us so sleepy?"

"You needed the rest."

"Not this much!"

"Yes, you did," Qod countered. "You have been struggling on a most difficult journey since the summer."

"Look, Qod, you've been awfully kind to us. We

appreciate your help and all the delicious food. But we've a long way to go still."

"Which is why you needed this opportunity to recuperate," Qod said. "Consider all you've been through. The stress and turmoil, not to mention the dangers—"

"We know," Cynthe said. "But we must keep moving. It's a long journey across Antrasia to the Barrens."

"And back again," Diello murmured.

"We can't afford to grow soft or—or happy," Cynthe went on. "We have to stay tough."

Diello nodded.

"No one doubts your courage," Qod told them. "But Scree's leg needed to finish healing. Vassou has had a chance to grow bigger and stronger. And you, Diello, you do realize what Thugar has given you?"

"Wisdom."

Cynthe snorted before she clapped her hand over her mouth. "Sorry."

"I asked to always know the right thing to do," Diello said as though Cynthe hadn't interrupted. "And it was supposed to be granted to me."

"Very sensible," Qod said. "You've needed to adjust to Thugar's gift."

"I have?" Diello asked. "I don't understand."

"Why don't you use your newest ability now? Consider. Are you really going to trudge all the way to the Barrens, exposing yourselves to many terrible risks during the journey, when there are alternate means of travel available to you?"

Diello stared at Qod thoughtfully.

"And furthermore, how do you intend to take Eirian away from the goblin leader?"

"We'll think of something," Cynthe said. "We got the scabbard back, didn't we?"

"Through a great deal of luck and Tescorsian ineptitude."

"That's not—"

"Cynthe," Diello cut in, "we both know Qod's right. King Uruoc was nothing compared to Brezog."

Cynthe shrugged. "I suppose."

"Don't be so stubborn. We can't afford to forget how dangerous Brezog is, especially since Queen Sheirae's curse will kill him if he loses possession of the sword."

"Owain's worse," Cynthe said.

Diello silently agreed with her, but they had to deal with one thing at a time. He turned to Qod. "Can you get us to the Barrens magically?"

"Precisely! What a clever Fae-boy you are. You have only to wish."

Diello wanted to believe Qod, but part of him remained doubtful.

"You'll help us," Cynthe said, "in exchange for what?"

"Oh dear. Such ingrained mistrust. Lwyneth should not have put her fears inside you."

"Mamee wasn't afraid," Cynthe snapped.

Diello jumped in. "If we can't trust you, it's because we've been tricked and manipulated by almost everyone we've sought help from. The baron we thought a friend to our father stole our farmstead. Even our own grand-mother banished us."

"She didn't appreciate what we tried to do for her," Cynthe added.

"Our uncle tried to kill Cynthe and is holding our little sister hostage," Diello continued. "So, you see, Qod, we *want* to trust you. But tricking us this way—however well-intentioned—makes us suspicious."

"Then there is something I will show you," Qod said. Part of the stone wall slid away, revealing a poorly lit pas-sageway. "Please follow me."

No one took a step except Vassou. He positioned him-self between Qod and the twins, blocking their path.

"It isn't far, I assure you," Qod said, rolling forward. "Come along. Don't dawdle."

"All of us?" Cynthe asked.

"Yes, yes, all of you. Mind you, keep to the path. No wandering off to explore. What looks like a puddle may in fact be a bottomless lake."

Cynthe began filling the rucksack.

"No need for that," Qod said. "Your belongings are quite safe. Come along!"

chapter twenty

they didn't walk far before the passageway opened into a cavern so vast it could have held all of Wodesley, the village near their farm. The cave's ceiling stretched high, lost in the shadows. Long panels of stone hung in drapery-like formations. Soft light glowed from behind stacks of stone or from within the stalactites themselves. Glowing chunks of quartz seemed to be everywhere. And Qod glowed, too, giving off a radiance that shone ahead of them.

"I never imagined there could be anything like this underground," Cynthe marveled.

"Is that a lake?" Diello asked, pointing at an area of glistening black.

"The water is so cold it would freeze you solid, and the fish that swim in it are blind," Qod replied.

"Blind!" Cynthe said.

"Fish!" Diello chimed in. "How can they live here? Why don't they freeze? What do they eat?"

"Qod feeds them," Cynthe guessed.

"I am the caretaker of this mountain," Qod said. "This was the task set for me."

"By whom?" Cynthe asked. "Uruoc?"

"No. Try again."

"The Guardian?" Vassou guessed.

"No, no. You can do better than that."

"Eirian's maker?" Diello said.

"Quite right! You truly are a clever creature, Fae-boy, when you put your mind to it. Now behold this."

The shadowy vista began to change. The smooth ground grew hilly, even mountainous. The black lake widened, changing to a silvery blue so clear that Diello could see rocks and ledges far below the surface. Trees and grass sprang up. A pale sunlight shone down from above. It was like looking at the world in miniature. The slopes were lush. Deer grazed under the alert eyes of the herd sentry. Birds fluttered in the tree canopies, and small game foraged in the undergrowth. Along the mountain slopes, jewels littered the ground; and gold glinted from rock crevices, reflecting the light.

"This is Tescorsa as it once was," Qod said.

"There is more gold on the ground than in six trog hoards," Scree breathed, staring.

"More than *all* the trog hoards," Diello said.

Scree nodded. "May I walk there? May I have the gold that I see?"

"Stay where you are, all of you," Qod said sharply. "Don't leave the path."

Scree moved forward as though he hadn't heard. Diello gripped his sleeve and held him back.

"You can't have it," Diello said. "None of us can. It isn't really there."

Scree lifted disappointed eyes. "Nothing is real? But why show us such a sight? I do not like to look at things that are false. I do not understand."

"Qod's going to explain."

Scree shook his head and turned away.

"It's beautiful anyway," Cynthe murmured. "I used to dream Embarthi would be like this."

Diello shot her a look, wondering if Qod had drawn from her imagination.

Qod bumped against Cynthe's foot. "The realm of the Fae is far lovelier than this vista."

"I don't think so," Cynthe said. "This is better than any part of Embarthi that I've seen."

"Is that why you brought us here?" Diello asked Qod. "To look at scenery?"

"Long ago," Qod replied, "these mountains were so full of wealth that it lay everywhere, as common as pebbles. The people of this land did not value their prosperity. They had no need for gold. They did not understand why others came to take the pretty stones, so they didn't fight to protect what was theirs."

"Who conquered them?" Vassou asked.

"The ancient gods fashioned armor and weapons from the special ore that could only be found here," Qod continued. "When the Age of Mortals began, a greedy race from far beyond the Land Now Lost came to plunder and squander. Then the Fae opened mines, burrowing deep into the mountains. Later, the first Antrasin barons ventured from the lowlands to fill their treasuries. To this day, every knight in the Order of Carnethie wears a star stamped from Tescorsian gold."

Diello drew in a breath. Their father had been a Carnethie Knight once, a member of the elite fighting force in Antrasia. Wide-eyed, Cynthe pulled out Pa's star, which she wore on a leather thong around her neck.

"But the wealth here was not infinite," Qod said. "As the mines closed one by one, the Tescorsians were no longer needed for labor. They were turned out of the shelters built for them. As they suffered, their chieftain climbed to the highest peak—where the eyrie is now. He prayed for help. The gods were silent, but a roaming spirit answered."

"You?" Cynthe asked.

Diello elbowed her. "Thugar."

"That's correct," Qod said. "Thugar gave the Tescorsians the *stonas* that turned them into shape-shifters. Their chief became a king. He fashioned the last of the gold and jewels into a garment to remind his people of what they had lost."

"What about the magic ore?" Diello asked. "The *chthon*?"

"It was used up long before men plundered the rest of Tescorsa. No more swords such as Eirian could be made."

Diello heard a voice in his mind—very faintly: *Come to me quickly.*

Diello put his hand to his temple.

"Of course, many continued to seek *chthon*," Qod went on. "Mages summoned small spirits called naesirs and sent them forth to find veins of *chthon* for mining."

Come, the voice murmured to Diello.

He felt hot and dizzy. *Why did I think the voices couldn't reach me through Qod's protection? I'll never be free of them. Is it Eirian or Brezog that calls me now?*

"Do you know of the naesirs?" Qod asked.

Cynthe and Vassou shook their heads.

"Creatures of bog and wood," Scree answered dreamily. "They steal into villages in the dead of night and take away the unwanted babies. Just as I was taken."

"Scree!" Cynthe said, shocked. "Is that true?"

"You cannot see a naesir," Scree continued. "You never see the hands that reach into the cradle and lift you. You want to cry. But there's a spell on you, like a cowl drifting over your face, and you do not whimper. Then you're outside, and the dew falls cold on your skin. You're pressed tight against clothing made of moss, so tight you cannot breathe. You're afraid, but you never cry. And then . . ." Scree shuddered. "And then you're left. In the marsh, by a rotting log, or on a creek bank. You're alone and little, so very little. The night is dark. The woods are dark. The spell ends, and the naesir is gone. You are alone; and although you cry and cry, there's no one to hear you."

Scree's voice faded. No one spoke for a moment.

Diello gave the goblin-boy a light shake, but Scree went on staring at nothing.

"I'm not sure if he was telling us his own memory," Diello said. "He doesn't usually talk this way." Diello's gaze swept the concerned faces of Cynthe and Vassou before he turned to Qod. "Was it *your* memory?"

"What a peculiar question. Was I ever an infant?"

"*Were* you?" Diello persisted.

"I am made of *chthon*, as you can see and feel," Qod said. "I have never been human."

"Then it's Scree's memory," Cynthe said. "How awful."

"There are too many versions of Scree's past," Vassou grumbled. "Which is truth and which are lies?"

"You stand in a place of truth," Qod said. "Consider that."

Diello wasn't satisfied with Qod's slippery answer. "But we're staring at an illusion right now."

"The scene before you is a record of the past. Surely you can discern the difference."

"I'm not sure I can," Diello admitted. "All this time, I thought you were a stone. But now you look like a huge diamond."

"Absurd. Diamonds cannot compare to *chthon*."

"Why change your appearance?" Cynthe asked. "Why look like a muddy old rock?"

"Outside my domain, it's more prudent to blend in with my surroundings."

"So you really are a shape-shifter," Cynthe said.

"No," Qod replied. "I've told you, I am a size-shifter. I have no *stona*. I don't serve Thugar or Uruoc. I owe no allegiance to the eyrie."

"My sister wasn't trying to offend you," Diello said. "We want to understand. That's all. Now, please take us back to where we left our belongings."

"There is no hurry," Qod said. "Time has no meaning

here. Years are as weeks. Weeks are as years. Days, we do not count at all."

"You may ignore time, but we cannot," Diello said. "Our little sister needs us. Unless you can bring her here."

"Why didn't I think of that?" Cynthe cried. "Qod, I wish you to bring Amalina here to us!"

"I cannot."

"Do you know where our uncle is keeping her?"

"I do not."

"Can you take Eirian away from Brezog so we don't have to confront him?"

"No." Qod's shining surface grew dull. "You have found the limits of what I can grant."

"What about getting us to the Barrens faster?" Cynthe asked, exasperated. "You *did* promise that."

"But you can't possibly leave just yet," Qod said. "Not when I have the loveliest surprise planned for you."

"What sort of surprise?" Vassou asked.

"I like surprises," Scree said. "Surprises can be very pleasant. Of course, sometimes they are bad; but when they are not bad, they are very fun."

"The surprise is only for Diello and Cynthe," Qod said. The tomtir bounced forward on the uneven path. "Please watch."

"Watch what?" Diello asked. "Are we supposed to follow you?"

But the tomtir had vanished again.

"What's Qod doing now?" Diello sighed. "All this talking, for what?"

"Diello," Cynthe said in a peculiar voice. She sounded breathless, like the time she fell out of the tallest tree in their orchard. She pointed behind him. "Look!"

But Diello had already seen: Mamee and Pa were coming their way, walking hand in hand.

chapter twenty-one

Mamee wore long robes of silvery white. Her hair hung unbound down her back, sparkles glinting among its strands. Her pale skin glowed with the full glamour of Fae magic. Beside her, Pa walked proudly—a warrior in a hauberk and spurred boots. The insignia of the Carnethie Knights was embroidered on the front of his cloak. A sword hung at his hip, and his arm and hand were no longer withered from the injury he'd received when he stole Eirian from the Fae.

That's when Diello knew for certain that this was only a dream—a vision. He averted his gaze from his parents' faces.

When he lifted his head again, the couple had vanished.

"Where did they go?" Cynthe cried. "Did you see them? Where are they?"

She ran forward, but Diello caught her.

"You can't go after them," he said. "Are you listening? Cynthe!"

His twin lifted her coppery-green eyes to his. They were brimming with tears. "I know," she whispered, and wiped her face.

"You're right, Scree," Diello said, clenching his fists. "We shouldn't have to see things that aren't real."

"They looked real," Scree said softly. "They looked very real."

"If all of you saw them, then it wasn't a vision. Not the kind I usually have." Diello rubbed his eyes. "Let's go back. I'm tired of this place."

Diello started back the way they'd come. The path had dimmed since their arrival. He stumbled a few times.

Cynthe steadied him from behind. "Slow down! What if you fall into one of those bottomless puddles and are frozen solid? I think we should wait for Qod to come back."

"No, Diello is right," Vassou said, padding at Scree's heels. "We shouldn't stay here, staring at things that don't exist."

Cynthe looked back over her shoulder. "I miss them so much," she whispered.

"I do, too," Diello said. "But we must keep going."

She stopped. "If we could just talk to them for a moment!"

"No." Diello gave her a small push. "They're gone."

The light from the quartz cubes was fading fast. He could barely see where to place his feet. The path seemed to twist more than he remembered. Behind them, the vista of Tescorsa had vanished.

"Wait!" Diello shouted. His voice echoed all around the cavern. "This isn't right. We've taken the wrong path."

"There's only one trail," Cynthe said, "and we're on it. Besides, we've walked only a few steps. We aren't lost."

"We are." Diello reached out and patted the stone wall beside him. "This wasn't here before."

"But—" Cynthe broke off. "You're right. We were in an open space."

"A large cavern," Diello said. "Now we have this wall crowding us. And—*Great Guardian!*"

Another wall had appeared on his left. They were now hemmed in a narrow passageway.

Cynthe smacked her palms on the walls. "Everything feels solid. If it's an illusion, it's a good one."

"It is not good, Cynthe," Scree said. "It is a scary illusion."

Diello looked behind him, but the darkness had closed in. Extending his hand in front of him, he edged a step forward, only to bump into yet another wall.

"We're boxed in on all sides," he said, trying to keep his voice steady.

"This way lies open," Scree said, gesturing behind them.

"I don't want to go there," Diello protested. "It's deeper into the cavern."

"Well, it's go that way or stand here forever," Cynthe said. She tugged at his sleeve. "Come on."

Following her, Diello ducked through a low opening into a small, circular room lit with an eerie blue light. The light came from what looked like smears of liquid dabbed on the walls. Diello dipped his fingers into the liquid and sniffed, but he detected nothing other than a mild tingle of magic on his fingertips.

The air grew moist and warm, filled with steam rising off a pool of bubbling mud ahead of them.

"A bog?" Diello said. "How odd."

"The passage behind us has vanished," Scree announced.

"What?" Cynthe cried.

"No retreat," Diello murmured. He hefted his staff in both hands, wondering if he dared blast through these barriers and risk causing a cave-in.

"There is still an exit," Vassou said.

"Past the mud." Cynthe shook her head. "I wish we could fly."

"Not if it means abandoning Scree and Vassou," Diello said.

"I don't intend to leave them." Cynthe studied the mud. "I could jump it if I had a running start."

"No, you couldn't," Diello said. "It's growing. It stretches across the entire passageway now. We have to walk through it if we're going anywhere."

"What if it's bottomless, too?" she asked.

"I'll try it," Diello said.

"No." Scree pushed him aside. "I will do it."

"We'll tie a rope around you first," Cynthe suggested. "That way, we can pull you out if needed."

But they didn't have any rope.

"Hold my hand," Diello told Scree. "Cynthe will hang on to me. Vassou, stand in front of me so I can brace myself against your weight."

As soon as the wolf was in position, Diello spread his feet and locked fingers with Scree. But when the goblin-boy reached the edge of the mud, he dropped Diello's hand and went bounding across before Diello could stop him. Whooping, Scree danced along the opposite side, slinging mud off his feet as he went.

"It is safe," he said. "It is warm. It has leaked inside my shoes."

"You're daft!" Cynthe yelled. "You could have vanished forever."

Diello touched her arm. "It's no good scolding him now. Who's next?"

"I'll go." Vassou sniffed the mud before trotting through it. On the other side, he shook splatters of mud from his coat. "It's very shallow."

"Now you, Cynthe," Diello said.

She tiptoed into the rippling, belching mud. Her face was scrunched with distaste. Halfway along, she halted. "Oh!"

"What is it?" Diello shouted. "What's wrong?"

"It just seeped inside my moccasin," Cynthe said. "I've got mud squishing between my toes."

"Is that all? Go on!"

She picked up a blob of mud and threw it at him before skipping the rest of the way.

"Scree's right," she called. "It's warm. Come on, Diello! Don't dawdle." She sounded like Qod.

Halfway over, Diello heard something. He paused, cocking his head.

"Now who's got a leaking shoe?" Cynthe said. "Hurry up!"

Raising his hand for silence, Diello listened harder. The noise sounded like singing. Deep voices, tiny voices, coming from all around him, yet so very faint he wondered if he was imagining it. *Is it the mud? How could it be?*

"Diello!" Cynthe called, her voice reverberating around the chamber.

He squelched forward and jumped lightly onto dry ground, only to have Cynthe push him against the wall.

"What were you doing?" she asked. "Do you realize how long you stood out there? If you were making fun of me—"

"I heard singing," Diello said. "How can mud sing?"

"Oh, but it does," Qod said, rolling up against Cynthe's ankle. She jumped with a shriek. "Most of the old ones still have voices. A few of the ancient ones have fallen silent, of course."

"What old ones?" Cynthe asked.

"This is a sanctuary for them," Qod said. "And you should consider yourself honored to have heard them."

"I don't know what I heard," Diello said.

"Maybe you should sit down for a while," Cynthe told him. "You're as pale as a bowl of porridge."

He shook off her concern. "I'm all right."

"Certainly he is!" Qod said. "There's nothing to fret over. I must say that I didn't expect the young Master of Eirian to be so timid about new experiences."

Diello stiffened his shoulders. "I'm not—"

"What is this place?" Vassou asked.

"I told you. A sanctuary," Qod replied. "When tomtirs achieve extreme age, they fade from existence. All that's left of the oldest ones remains here. I do grow lonely. I come here to visit them, but their voices are very faint."

"You made this bog for them," Diello said.

"As long as they're bubbling and singing, they're still alive. In a way."

"Did we hurt them, walking on them?" Cynthe asked.

"Not at all."

Cynthe whispered to Diello, "Do you think Qod knows I threw one?"

"I hope not."

An opening appeared in the wall, and Qod spun around. "There's something else for you to see."

The next cave they entered was cold and gloomy. The same eerie blue light glowed on the walls. Precise rows of stones were lined up on the ground like knights in formation, but no two appeared alike. Diello saw chunks of granite, porous limestone riddled with holes, and sharp-edged flint. He counted thirty of them altogether.

"Little tomtirs?" Diello guessed. "Your children?"

"Once this was the place of *giami*—the beginning. Now no spirits fill the stones."

"You said that the rock that fell on Scree was your child," Cynthe noted. "Is it the only one that's alive?"

"You begin to understand," Qod answered. "Sometimes, about every five or six hundred years, a fleck of *chthon* is found inside a stone. I bring it here. If the faintest spark of life occurs, then I place the young stone on the outside of the mountain. And I wait. A pity your crystal bones cannot amplify my powers." Qod turned to Diello.

"Our magic is simply incompatible, except in the most basic way."

Diello tried to imagine himself kneeling in the snow next to a small boulder, trying to coax it to speak or move; but the whole concept was too strange truly to grasp. He was relieved to know there wasn't anything he could do.

"Alas," Qod said, "I know my task is futile. The bits of *chthon* are too small. The mountains are dead hulks. There is only one way to spark *giami* now. Through Eirian."

Diello stiffened. *This is what Qod's been after the whole time!*

"No," Diello said.

"We can't give you Eirian," Cynthe added. "We don't have it anyway."

"You will," Qod said. "I shall get you to the Barrens as I promised. And in exchange—"

"Our little sister comes first," Diello said.

"Would you really put flesh before spirit?" Qod asked.

Diello struggled to hold back his anger.

"It's sad what has happened to Tescorsa," Cynthe said, "but Eirian doesn't belong here."

"Eirian *belongs* in Antrasia," Qod replied. "Antrasia has no other source of magic. After the sword was forged, the Guardian decreed that the sword should be in human hands to keep the balance of power equal among all creatures."

"That's what our parents tried to do," Cynthe said.

"Your parents had the courage of the ancients and the will of true heroes," Qod said.

"Thank you," Diello said, surprised. "No one else has praised them."

"But Stephel and Lwyneth were naive to think they could change the way of the world so easily."

It wasn't easy. Pa was crippled, and Mamee had to surrender her magic. They didn't even finish their task, and now the sword is in the wrong hands. . . .

"At least they tried," Cynthe said.

"Nonsense!" Qod retorted. "What does *try* matter when there is no good *result*? You're both very young, but don't console yourself with such a feeble excuse. Even an ancient edict cannot—indeed, should not—always be followed."

"Why not?" Diello asked.

"Antrasia is overrun by goblins and is easy prey for anyone possessing serious magic," Qod said. "Even a Faelin child could break its defenses. As for Embarthi, it has no stability at all. Its line of succession is threatened, the queen is in danger of being overthrown, and the whole realm teeters on the brink of civil war."

Diello looked away.

"We know all this," Cynthe said.

"Do you know that fate can be altered?" Qod asked. "When Eirian was placed by the Twelve Watchers of Afon Heyrn within the Wheels of Silver on the Isle of Woe, the sword became bound to Embarthi and its people. The Fae prospered. As good neighbors, the Fae permitted a little of their prosperity to leak into Tescorsa. Enough for the shapeshifters to live happily within their own borders. Now, the

Tescorsians are desperate and starving. They are driven to foolish actions."

"Like stealing the scabbard?" Diello asked.

"Precisely. Uruoc has no idea how to control such magic."

"So you want to do it for him."

"I want only to keep the scabbard safe while you confront Brezog. If you take the scabbard into the Barrens and fail, Brezog will be invincible."

I can't trust the tomtir that much, Diello thought. *To leave the scabbard behind when Amalina's life depends on our bringing the entire sword back to Embarthi . . . it's too risky.*

"Diello," Cynthe whispered, looking scared. "What are you thinking? You mustn't do it."

"Brezog has crept into your mind before, young Master of Eirian," Qod said. "He knows that you have the potential to destroy him, yet he's capable of controlling you, especially now while you are young. I must say that Clevn has been very slack about your training."

"We can't give you Eirian," Diello said.

"I seek only to help you," Qod replied. "I have no ambition of my own—"

"Untrue!" Vassou declared. "You want to revive the *giami*. You want more tomtirs to inhabit these mountains."

"And why not?" Qod said. "Clevn could not do it when I sought his help years ago. But with the scabbard here to bring these young ones to life, there is a real chance of success."

"The destiny of Cynthe and Diello lies elsewhere," Vassou said. "You must not interfere."

Qod moved closer to Diello. "Think for yourself, Faeboy. Do not repeat your parents' mistake. What a terrible error they made!"

"They were doing what they thought was right," Cynthe said.

Diello rubbed his hand over the symbols carved in his staff.

"Who has treated you better, the Fae or me?" Qod asked. "Who has been cruel to you? And who has been kind?"

"You have been kind," Diello said slowly, "but we don't owe you Eirian."

The tomtir sighed. "I didn't want to do this. I felt it unscrupulous. But now, I see that I must."

Scree and Vassou looked at Diello. Diello turned to look at Cynthe. Then they all stared at Qod.

chapter twenty-two

iello steeled himself for an attack. Instead, the small cave containing the rows of stones vanished. Diello and his friends found themselves back in the vast cavern. This time, it held a scene of Wodesley Castle, the familiar turrets rising tall above the village roofs. Diello could even see smoke curling from the house chimneys.

"Watch closely," Qod said. "Study the road winding up from the village."

"People are moving," Scree said. He leaned forward past Diello, pointing. "See there?"

"Yes." Diello could make out a couple walking along the road.

"It's Mamee and Pa again!" Cynthe cried.

"Don't believe what you see," Diello warned her, but his eyes were stinging with tears. "They'll fade in a moment."

Their parents were less than ten steps away. Stephel and Lwyneth smiled calmly.

"You're hurting me," Cynthe said.

Diello realized he'd been gripping her wrist. "Sorry." He released her.

Vassou moved in front of the twins and bowed. "Hail, Lady Lwyneth."

Mamee inclined her head regally. A halo of light shone around her, glinting off the elegant points of her ears and sparkling in her long hair. "Thank you, Vassou." The sound of her voice sent shivers through Diello. "I've had no chance to express my gratitude to your mother, Shalla, for her loyalty and service. Your clan has paid a heavy price, and yet you have still served me well by helping my children."

Diello forced his gaze up. To hear her speak, to see her smiling at Vassou . . . He wanted to run to her, but he wouldn't let himself move.

"Mamee!" Cynthe rushed forward, avoiding Diello's swipe at her sleeve, and hugged first her mother, then her father. "Oh, Pa!"

With a laugh, Pa swung Cynthe around.

Then he met Diello's gaze. "Son?"

The knot in Diello's throat kept him silent. He watched Cynthe laughing as she moved from Pa to Mamee and back again, chattering away as she tried to tell them everything that had happened. Mamee was fingering Cynthe's hair and stroking her face. Pa listened, nodding his head.

It isn't real, Diello thought. *It can't be real. Once Cynthe realizes it, she'll grieve even more.*

"Why are you doing this?" Diello asked Qod. "Why torment us this way?"

"What you see is no illusion," Qod replied. "Within

my domain, there are no barriers that spirits cannot cross. They have been apart, your parents, but here they can be together . . . for a short time."

"How have you conjured their ghosts? How did you bring them here?"

"There are no ghosts here," Qod answered. "They *are* your parents. Believe it."

"I believe," Scree said, gazing wistfully. "I wish I could know such gladness."

Diello squeezed his friend's shoulder. Until the twins had befriended the goblin-boy, Scree had seldom experienced kindness. He'd scrounged for survival on his own. Diello's happy home had been a blessing, one he'd taken for granted until the day it was taken away.

"It's wonderful, Scree," Diello said, "but it's not really happening. I was with Pa—holding his hand—when he died. I heard his final breath." Diello's breath caught a little. He made himself keep talking. "I put the shroud across my mother's face. I saw her buried."

Cynthe's laugh rang out across the cavern.

Scree's eyes were shiny. "Will you not speak to them? How can you turn away? Cynthe has let herself be happy. I wish you to be happy also, Diello. I wish it very much."

Vassou nudged Diello's hand. "Don't fear this gift. Accept it."

"I c-can't."

Stephel stepped away from his wife and daughter, beckoning to Diello. "Come here, boy."

That voice, deep and slightly gruff, held a tone of

command that Diello had obeyed all his life. He found himself walking toward his father.

Then he was running until he crashed against Pa's chest and felt those burly arms tighten around him.

"Pa," Diello whispered. "Pa!"

"You've grown," Pa said. "You're taller, stronger."

Diello choked, unable to talk.

"Diello," Pa said softly. "Come, let's walk a bit."

Pa led him across an expanse of meadow grass. In this magical place, there was no snow. The trees were budding and green. A creek ran full and clear, as though recently fed by spring rains. But there was no scent in the air, no fragrance of growing things.

Don't believe it, Diello told himself. *Be careful.*

Pa said nothing, just strolled along with his hand on Diello's shoulder. *We're nearly the same height,* Diello noticed with surprise. He glanced sideways at his father. Pa looked calm and assured. *He's younger here,* Diello realized. *Those lines carved in his face are gone. He must have worried a lot, back on the farmstead.*

"Now," Pa said. "Tell me how things fare. You have the deed seal safe?"

Diello thought about lying but couldn't do it. "Well, sir," he said. "It's with Amalina right now."

Just before Pa died, he'd given Diello the seal, a shiny silver disk engraved with a land description which proved their ownership of the farm. Later, Diello had discovered how to use it to unlock Mamee's spell guarding Eirian's hiding place.

"No seal," Pa said flatly. "And the farm? Have you prepared the seed for planting? Is the plow sharpened, ready to break ground as soon as there's spring thaw? You've remembered to plant New Field first? The old one will flood when the creek overflows its banks."

"We lost the farm," Diello said, his face burning with shame. "Lord Malques took ownership. He said that Faelin couldn't inherit property."

Pa didn't speak.

"I made a mess of everything, Pa. Cynthe and I traveled all the way to Embarthi, but the queen wouldn't help us; and Uncle Owain—he hates Mamee for what she did. He hates all of us."

"Where's Amalina?" Pa asked. "Why isn't she with you?"

"Uncle Owain has her."

"You left Amie with him?"

"He—he kidnapped her from Wodesley Castle after he set the goblins on you and Mamee. He wants us to give him Eirian for Amie's return." Diello dropped his gaze. "I'm sorry."

He ached for his father to offer forgiveness and understanding, but that wasn't Pa's way.

"You should have left the sword hidden," Pa said. "The goblins couldn't get at it. No one could. And it was in Antrasia, where it belonged."

Diello stared at a point over his father's shoulder. There was nothing Pa was saying that he hadn't already told himself.

"Why did you hide Eirian on the farm?" Diello asked.

"Why didn't you give it to the Antrasin king?"

"He has no way to use it and can't protect it. I'd intended to put the sword in the Carnethie stronghold; but Clevn's accusations were believed, and I was expelled from the Order. That's when Lwyneth and I decided to hide the sword. Eirian's magic would seep into Antrasia slowly. The people would prosper, and no one would be corrupted by its power. That was our plan."

"Why didn't you and Mamee tell us? If we'd known more, we wouldn't have made so many mistakes."

"You're right," Pa said, startling Diello. "We thought you were too young to know. And we believed that the more you knew, the worse you'd feel about being Faelin and not having magic ways."

"But we *do* have magic," Diello said. "We can fly, just like full-blooded Fae. I can ride the wind now. And when Uncle Owain tried to kill me with mage fire, I fought back. Cynthe can break things with her voice. She's—"

"We planned to tell you and Cynthe everything when you turned fifteen," Pa interrupted.

He still doesn't want to talk about our magic Gifts, Diello thought with frustration.

"I've got Eirian's scabbard now," Diello said. "So how do we infiltrate Brezog's stronghold? Sheirae hit him in the heart with an arrow, but he can't die as long as he holds Eirian. He's bound to be weakened from his wound, but you've always told me a wounded animal is twice as dangerous. Can you tell me how to fight goblins?"

Pa didn't answer.

"Even if we can get the sword back, how do I trade Eirian for Amie? I don't want to put its power in Owain's hands." Diello tugged on his father's sleeve. "Did you hear me? I said—"

"Keeping a vow always means paying a price," Pa said. "You promised me you'd protect your sisters."

"I'm *trying*."

"Trying's not enough, son. You've got to do it."

"I'm not the only one who failed. You broke your vows as a knight. You stole the sword and killed a Watcher."

"I killed no one!" Pa snapped. "Owain killed the Watcher and blamed me. I took the sword—aye, because your mother asked it of me. She wanted to break the line of succession because she knew what Owain was. Knew that when the time came for the two of them to rule as queen and mage, she wouldn't be able to control him. Owain was already going mad. He planned to take Eirian for himself. When Lwyneth found out, she tried to tell Clevn, but he wouldn't believe her. The queen wouldn't listen either. So Lwyneth turned to me. I was just a visiting knight at the Liedhe Court then, but I would have done anything for her. I agreed to help her flee. It was the only way to stop him."

"Mamee said that if something ever happened to her or you, we were to find Owain and he would help us. That's how we got into so much trouble. We *trusted* him!"

"Lwyneth didn't want to lie to you." Pa looked sad. "Secrets became twisted into lies; and once that begins, where does it stop? Your mother knew the Fae would never stop hunting her. And if Owain learned about you and Cynthe, he might destroy you. That's why she discouraged your budding magic and wouldn't train you."

"But why lie to us about Owain?"

"To keep you safe."

"I don't understand. We walked right into his trap."

"Lwyneth couldn't break the bond between her and Owain. I'm not sure she truly wanted to. You know how you and Cynthe are always aware of each other? When Cynthe got lost in the forest in that rainstorm, you led me right to her."

Diello nodded. They'd been eight or nine. Cynthe's tracks had been washed away, but Pa had listened every time Diello "felt" they should take a certain turn. *I'd forgotten that.*

"Aren't you aware of Cynthe's feelings, if they're strong enough? You know when she's using magic?"

"Usually."

"It was the same with Lwyneth and Owain as twins. She didn't want him to suspect the true reason she'd fled Embarthi. He thought it was because we were in love and I wanted to steal Eirian for the glory of it." Pa snorted.

Diello's head ached with confusion. He tried to comprehend that his mother could have treated him and Cynthe this way. "We've been used as pawns. This wasn't about protecting us at all, was it?"

"She couldn't send you directly to Clevn. He'd never believe you."

Diello nodded again. He could understand *that.*

"But you and Cynthe continue to worry Clevn. Pressure Owain enough, and he'll betray himself at some point. Then Clevn and Sheirae will have to face the truth."

"This is too complicated."

"Did you think that being royalty was simple?" Pa replied.

"Aren't you angry?" Diello asked. "Didn't you care about losing your knighthood because of Mamee?"

"It had to be done. I love her," Pa said. "I always have."

"But—"

"Your mother was born to be a queen. She was never meant to live on a farm among humans, forced to walk instead of fly. She deliberately destroyed her future to save her people and keep Sheirae's throne as secure as possible. She hid her suffering from you children, but exile was agony for her."

"We knew, Pa," Diello said quietly. He swallowed the rest of his questions about the past. "How do I get Eirian away from Brezog and save Amie from Owain?"

"You want me to give you permission to hand Eirian back to Owain, to undo everything your mother and I accomplished—but I cannot."

"What other choice is there?"

"Owain is afraid of you," Pa said. "Use that as your weapon."

"I want to do the right thing," Diello whispered. "I can't afford to fail."

Pa tilted his head as though listening to something Diello couldn't hear. "I must go."

Diello gripped Pa's arm. It didn't feel quite solid. "You can't leave yet. I need help."

"I would sacrifice my sword arm a second time to stay with you," Pa said, "but I can't. I'm glad to have seen you once more, son. Now it's time to say good-bye."

"You have to stay!" Diello cried.

Pa seemed to have walked away without Diello seeing it. He was fading from sight. Raising his hand in farewell, he vanished, leaving Diello standing alone.

chapter twenty-three

When Diello turned around, he found Cynthe right behind him.

"How did you get here?"

"Where's Pa?" she asked. "I thought you were together."

"He left. . . . Where's Mamee? I wanted to talk to her."

"And I wanted to talk to Pa."

"Did she leave, too?"

Cynthe nodded, blinking back tears. "I was telling her about meeting the queen when Mamee kissed me and left. I thought perhaps I'd made her too sad."

"Something seemed to be calling Pa away. I think I should tell you what he said."

When Diello finished talking, his twin looked angry instead of sad.

"Couldn't he have told you *something* to use against Brezog?"

"Maybe he doesn't really know how to fight the goblins."

"Of course he does!" Cynthe said. "He was a knight."

"But they killed him," Diello reminded her gently.

Cynthe kicked at the ground without speaking.

Diello sighed. "As for what he said about Mamee lying to us—"

"I don't want to talk about that."

"We'll have to discuss it before we face Owain."

Cynthe shook her head. "Not right now. Let's deal with Brezog first."

"I wish we didn't have to." Diello paused. "I'm scared."

"Me, too," Cynthe said. "We'd be daft not to fear the goblins."

Diello smiled in gratitude. "Well, I've been thinking about a way to reach Brezog. It's risky."

"Risky is okay."

"I'll walk in there with Scree," Diello continued. "I'll pretend to be dazed, like Scree's taken over my mind."

"*Scree?* Are you joking? Brezog will kill you," Cynthe said. "No. We have to come up with something else."

"So what's your plan?" Diello asked.

"I think we should slip inside under a *cymunffyl* and sneak the sword out."

"Brezog's holding it, remember? Are you going to pull his fingers off the hilt, one by one?"

"Here are the problems with your plan." Cynthe held up her index finger. "One, it's a bad idea to just walk into a goblin lair." She held up another finger. "Two, you'll have to rely on Scree, and we've seen how Brezog can control him."

"Scree won't let that happen again."

"Are you sure enough to stake your life on it?"

"He's the only one who can get us close to Brezog."

Diello expected Cynthe to keep arguing. Instead, her mouth trembled, and she pressed her hands to her eyes.

He hated seeing her cry. *She's more scared than I thought.*

"Cynthe, we *have* to do this."

She rubbed away her tears and nodded. "At least let's stay together."

"If we're apart, we have two chances. Together, we have only one."

"I hate this plan! It's the worst thing you've ever thought up."

"I know."

"But if you think we can do this, then we're going to do it. Together. I'll be invisible," she added before Diello could protest. "I'm not waiting outside, twiddling my thumbs while they tear you open."

Diello swallowed hard. "Agreed. As soon as Scree and I distract Brezog, I'll grab the sword and hand it off to you. Promise me that you'll run with it and won't look back. And really mean it."

"Diello!"

"You broke your promise at the eyrie."

"So did you. I won't leave you behind. And don't ask me to."

"We have to get the sword out of there." Diello spit on his palm before holding out his hand. "Sworn promise!"

"No. I won't abandon you. No matter what, we stick together as we always have."

"But to save Amie—"

"I won't, not even for her." Cynthe spit on her hand. "We do this as a team, from start to finish. Will you give your promise to that?"

Diello hesitated, but clasped hands. "I promise. Let's talk to Qod about getting to the Barrens."

As they walked back to where Vassou and Scree were waiting on the path, Wodesley Castle and the village faded from sight. Vassou and Scree greeted them eagerly.

"What did you find out?" Vassou asked. "Were your parents helpful?"

"No," Diello answered.

"We have a plan that we'll explain later," Cynthe added. "Are you ready to leave these caves?"

Scree shook his head. "I do not wish to leave. The food is good here. I do not want to go to the Barrens. I want to stay here and eat, not leave and be eaten."

Qod rolled over Scree's foot, making the goblin-boy yelp. "May I be of assistance?"

"We're going," Cynthe said. "We'd like our things, please."

"Mind your feet," Qod said loudly. The tomtir spun around. Their packs and bundles appeared on the ground.

Diello and Cynthe gathered them up, distributing the load among themselves and Scree while Vassou paced, impatient to depart.

"I am hungry," Scree said to Diello. "I think we should wait another day."

"We've waited long enough," Diello said. "Tie these flaps, please."

After Scree tied his pack shut in a sloppy knot, Diello hefted the rucksack. It was filled with food that smelled delicious.

It's good to know we won't starve for a while, Diello thought.

"So hasty," Qod complained. "All this rush and bustle. I should much prefer you stay longer."

Diello knelt in front of the tomtir, placing his hand on the creature's smooth surface. Magic tingled against Diello's palm. "We couldn't have made it this far without your help. We're deeply grateful."

"I haven't delayed you. And if you stayed longer, you still would not be delayed."

"Perhaps," Diello said, not entirely understanding what Qod meant. "But our little sister needs us. We have to go."

"I hoped you would enjoy talking with your parents' spirits. Instead, they've unsettled you. Shall I summon them again? Another conversation might achieve a different effect."

It was tempting, but Diello shook his head.

Qod sighed. "It has delighted me to have you here. Good-bye, my young friends. If you will all please stand in this spot and remain very still. . . ."

"Wait," Diello said. He untied his belt and slipped off the scabbard.

"What are you doing?" Cynthe said. "Are you *sure*?"

Diello laid Eirian's jeweled scabbard in front of the tomtir.

"I'm leaving this in your guardianship for safekeeping," Diello said. "If we return—"

"When," Cynthe said.

"*When* we return," Diello continued, "we'll need it back."

The creature rolled against the scabbard and turned a rainbow of hues, reflecting every color of jewel adorning it.

"Trust," the tomtir murmured. "Given freely. Your heart has won over your head. Young Master of Eirian, you have indeed honored me."

Diello wasn't sure if he was doing the right thing, but he couldn't risk Brezog taking the scabbard.

"We're counting on you, Qod," he said. "I hope we see you soon."

"When you are ready to return to me, repeat the following: *Spiritus chthon, redeimi giami est.* Now, make your wish," Qod told him.

Holding Cynthe's hand and beckoning for Vassou and Scree to stand very close, Diello said, "I wish you to send us to Brezog's stronghold."

Twinkling jewels rained down from the cavern ceiling, spilling over Diello's hair and shoulders. Cynthe laughed in delight, and Scree cupped his hands to catch as many as he could.

"Look!" Vassou said.

The cavern had disappeared. A dark opening yawned before them.

"This is it," Diello said, and stepped forward.

chapter twenty-four

there was a moment of darkness. Then Diello was surrounded by swamp and jungle. The stifling, moist heat wrapped around him. Already he was sweating. Dropping his staff, Diello shrugged the rucksack strap from his shoulder and peeled off his winter clothing.

He was down to his undertunic when Cynthe stepped into sight. She'd shed her heavy clothing, too, rolling them into a bundle that she'd corded neatly. With her came Vassou, panting, trapped in his thick fur.

"Where's Scree?" Diello asked.

"I thought he came through with you," Cynthe said.

"Look, everyone!" Scree called, running up in excitement. He opened his cupped hands to reveal a mass of squirming worms. A multilegged insect with long feelers slithered up Scree's wrist, disappearing under his sleeve. "I have found good things to eat already."

Diello drew back. "Uh, that's good, Scree. You go ahead and enjoy your snack. I'm flying up to get my bearings."

Diello rose into the dense, damp air, ducking tree

branches. Emerging above the canopy, he floated on his stomach, staying just above the treetops. Before him, the jungle stretched all the way to the horizon.

Why call this place the Barrens? he wondered. *It looks lush to me.*

Behind him, he saw a gray edifice rising up from the mud, less than a half league away. Whether it was made of stone or mud, he couldn't tell. But it was as tall as a turret of Wodesley Castle.

"Brezog's Rock," Diello murmured.

He descended at once, brushing aside twigs and branches as he dropped. Cynthe and the others had stashed their bundles in the low fork of a wide-spreading tree. Diello landed on a patch of mud nearby.

He tried to lift his foot, but it was stuck. Before he knew it, he'd sunk as deep as his ankles, then his knees.

"Hey!" he called in alarm.

Now he was in as far as his thighs. . . .

"Cynthe! Scree! Help me!"

They all came running. Vassou reached him first, then whirled around with a snarl, keeping Cynthe and Scree back.

"No closer," Vassou said. "It's quicksand."

Cynthe turned to Scree. "Fetch some vine from over there!"

Now the quicksand was up to Diello's waist. He held out his arms, more scared than he wanted to admit. "Bring my staff. I can hold on to it and lever myself out."

Cynthe hurried to fetch it but dropped the staff as soon

as she picked it up. "I can't hold it! It's glowing. Are you using magic?"

"Not on purpose," Diello gasped. "I wish I knew a spell to get out of this."

"If the quicksand reaches past his shoulders, we'll never get him out," Vassou said.

"Hurry, Scree!" Cynthe yelled. She ran to help the goblin-boy, yanking the lengths of vine from his hands.

The mud was sliding around Diello's ribs, making it difficult for him to breathe. Cynthe threw a vine at him, and it smacked him in the face.

"Get hold!" Cynthe said. "Put it under your arms!"

Diello hooked his elbows over the vine and held on firmly with both hands despite the prickly stickers growing on the underside. "Ready!"

The others had lined up: Scree first, next Cynthe, then Vassou at the rear with the vine in his teeth.

"One, two, three . . . pull!" Cynthe ordered.

Diello felt himself rising slightly. "Good! Keep going!" he cried.

Scree slipped in the mud. Cynthe grabbed him.

The awful, sucking quicksand drew Diello down. It was up to his chest now, slopping greedily over his right arm as he struggled to hang on to the vine. He wanted to scream but fought back his fear.

"I'm all right," he made himself say. "Try again. Don't worry, Scree. It wasn't your fault. One . . . two . . . three . . ."

"Pull!" Cynthe yelled.

Diello barely moved. *I'm in too deep now,* he thought. He tried kicking, but he couldn't shift his legs.

"Don't struggle," Cynthe said breathlessly. "Everyone, pull!"

He slid upward an inch.

"Pull!"

He was only hip-deep now, and he could breathe again. They dragged him forward onto his stomach. Diello focused on keeping his face clear and resisted the urge to kick and flail. His legs were still caught, but he felt them moving. Only his feet and ankles remained trapped. He wanted to say something encouraging to the others, but he couldn't seem to find his voice.

There was a loud, gurgling noise, and at last he was free.

They dragged him to higher ground and collapsed around him, whooping for breath. Diello lay there, more relieved than he could say, not minding that he was covered in quicksand and smelled vile. He wondered how many hapless creatures had fallen into that trap and died there, their bones rotting in the muck.

Then Cynthe was kneeling over him, pulling away the vine gingerly. She grinned down at him. "Never do that again," she said, her voice shaky.

"I won't. Help me up."

Diello found that his knees didn't want to hold him. He was trembling all over and had to sit.

"Sorry to be so stupid," he mumbled.

Cynthe patted his shoulder.

Scree crouched next to him. "Do you know you have

lost your moccasins? And your bronze knife. That is a shame."

Diello slapped his belt. Sure enough, his knife hilt was empty. "I've had that since I was ten years old," he said. He started emptying his belt pouch. At least his other treasures—his bird whistle that Pa had carved, his tinderbox from Pa for his thirteenth birthday, and a bit of amber from Mamee's broken keepsake box—remained secure. *I might have lost Eirian's scabbard if I'd been wearing it. . . .*

"Should I find you some food?" Scree asked. "I would be happy to dig grubs for you, but I know you don't like them. Are you thirsty? The water tastes bad here. I think it will hurt your stomach. There is Qod's food. We do not have to save it for later when we camp."

"No, thanks," Diello said. "I don't feel very hungry."

"You stink like a pig wallow," Cynthe noted. "As soon as you think you can walk, let's wash you off."

Diello stood again. Cynthe and Scree supported him as he crept down the bank to the water's edge. Stagnant, with scum on top, the water almost smelled worse than he did.

Diello hesitated. He also didn't like the way the trees grew in the water, their roots protruding like knees. Very little sunlight filtered through the thick branches overhead. *Anything could be lurking in this water.*

"Get on with it," Cynthe said, poking him.

He stumbled into the green water. It was only knee-deep, until he stepped off a ledge and went under with a yelp. He fought his way back to the surface, sputtering, and slung his dripping hair from his eyes as he paddled.

Giggling, Cynthe leaned over to offer him a hand. Then her gaze locked on something behind him. "Get out of the water now," she said.

Diello floundered, trying to climb out. Cynthe grabbed his arm and yanked, hurrying him away from the edge just as teeth snapped behind him in the water.

At the top of the bank, Diello looked back. He saw only a big, dark shadow. It slid beneath the surface and vanished, leaving bubbles in its wake.

"What was that?" Diello gasped.

Cynthe's fingers were digging into his arm. "It had orange eyes," she whispered. "I saw them glowing just on the surface. It was coming right for you. I—Scree, do you know what it was?"

Scree was even farther away from the water, clinging to a tree trunk. "Swamp wraith. Very bad."

"We just got here," Cynthe said, "and we've already had two close calls."

Vassou paced, his head moving from side to side. "What other dangers are in the water, Scree?"

"Crocs," Scree said. "Biting monga fish. Leeches. All bad."

Diello looked around. The jungle seemed eerily quiet and still, yet he had the feeling of being watched. "And on land?"

"Why do you ask me so many questions?" Scree burst out. "I do not come here. I do not know goblin ways. I am scared. I do not like it here."

Drums started beating. Diello and Cynthe raced for

their weapons, then stood back-to-back. Cynthe drew her bow. Diello gripped his staff. Vassou circled, snarling.

The noise was faint, as though coming from a distance. It didn't seem to get louder; but it was a steady, throbbing sound that wore on Diello's nerves.

He wiped his face, trying to breathe normally. "Brezog's Rock is that way." He pointed. "I think the drums are there."

"Can we reach it by land?" Cynthe asked. "I'm not swimming there."

Diello glanced at Scree for guidance, but the goblin-boy was crouching on the ground with his hands clapped to his ears. "I don't think so. We'll have to build a raft," Diello answered. "If only we had an ax to fell some saplings."

"The water is not safe, not even in a boat," Vassou said.

Cynthe was studying the jungle. "Look at how the branches grow. These massive trees spread wide; and they connect, most of them, if you go high enough. Vassou, let's put on your harness. You can walk along the widest branches, and we'll fly, carrying you from tree to tree. Scree can climb."

Vassou trotted to the pack containing his harness. He brought it back and laid it at Cynthe's feet. "If I were older, I could fly with you," he growled.

"Maybe that's why Qod wanted us to wait," Diello said.

"And how do you suppose Uncle Owain's been treating Amie in the meanwhile?" Cynthe asked.

Diello felt sick just thinking about it. He gathered their gear, tying his straps snugly before tapping Scree's shoulder.

"Come on, Scree. There's no need to panic," he said. "We aren't under attack."

Scree kept his eyes squeezed shut, even after Diello forced his hands down from his ears. "Death drums," he moaned. "It will be dark soon."

"Scree, calm down," Diello said, shaking him. Scree's eyes popped open. "We need to rely on you."

"I am no help here," Scree said. "I cannot be brave as you are. I do not want to be captured. I do not want to serve Brezog."

"That's not going to happen. I've seen your courage, and I know you can do this. Now, listen. We're going to the stronghold. In the morning, you and I will go inside."

Scree clutched Diello's wrist. "No, no, no! This I cannot do."

"We'll pretend that I'm your prisoner," Diello went on. "You'll carry a knife, and we'll have my hands bound loosely. You'll be 'giving' me to Brezog."

Scree stared at him in horror.

"The gorlord will be pleased with you; and since he'll probably think I have the scabbard, he'll let me get close to him. That's when we attack. Cynthe will be with us, but invisible. As soon as I grab Eirian, we'll turn invisible, too. I'll give Eirian to Cynthe, and you and I will keep the goblins at bay until she's out. Then, in the confusion, we'll escape. See? Simple."

"No," Scree whispered. "You do not understand. Brezog will *know*."

"He's dying," Diello said, ignoring his own doubts.

Repeating the plan again and again didn't make it stronger. "The gorlord will be weak."

"He is strong. He cannot be tricked. When he sees me, he will know."

"Lie to him," Diello said. "Think of how cruel he's been to you. He let Eirian burn you because he was too cowardly to touch the sword himself. He forced you to betray us, and then he abandoned you to the Fae. You have to strike back at him. This is your chance."

"I cannot take revenge on him," Scree whimpered. "I cannot do it."

"Aren't we your friends? Haven't we taken you in and treated you better than anyone else?"

Scree lowered his head and wouldn't look at Diello. *I shouldn't be doing this to him,* Diello thought. *But this is the only way to save Amie.*

Cynthe came over. "Scree," she said, "we need your help. Without you our plan can't succeed. We're all scared, but we have to do this."

"I want to help you. I want to do as you ask, but I will fail you."

"No, you won't," Diello said.

"I will! I will fail. Brezog will eat you. He will torment me and let his horde torment me until I scream for death, and then he will . . ." Scree shuddered.

Diello curbed his frustration. "All right then," he said, standing up. "I can't force you. Let's go. We'll think of something else when we get there."

"Diello," Vassou said, "why do you intend to give Eirian

to Cynthe? Why not claim it for your own and fight with it? The goblins cannot beat you then."

Diello couldn't meet the wolf's gaze. *Because I'm scared of its power,* he wanted to say. *Because I don't know what it might do to me or how it might change me.*

"We'll stop halfway there and camp in the trees," Cynthe said, breaking the silence. "I want to be in a position to spy on the stronghold at daybreak."

As they moved away, Scree came scrambling after them. "Are you leaving me? I do not wish to stay behind. I am afraid to be in the swamp by myself."

"We aren't leaving you," Diello said. "Grab your things and hurry."

Scree stared up at Diello with huge, miserable eyes. "Even when I defy you, you are kind to me. I will never understand you, Diello. You know I will let you down. I can gather food and firewood. I can wash cups. But real help—the kind that matters—that I cannot give you. Yet you keep me. You are not angry. You do not shout at me. Why?"

"You're my friend," Diello said quietly. Then he walked over to join Cynthe in checking Vassou's harness.

chapter twenty-five

In the morning, Diello awoke bruised and sore from his encounter with the quicksand. Sleeping propped up in a tree fork hadn't helped. He yawned, wincing at his aches. The sun was only a fiery band on the horizon, but already he was sweating in the moist heat.

Brezog's Rock rose on a jut of land sticking out from the swamp. To the east, the jungle thinned and opened up to reveal a broad, sluggish river. Weed-choked marsh lay on the opposite bank.

A stinger-fly buzzed in Diello's ear. He slapped at it, smearing blood. He was covered in itchy bites. He and Cynthe had coated their skin with mud last night, but he'd sweated off most of his protection.

Thunder rumbled close by. The skies were overcast with dark, swollen clouds. Diello inhaled deeply. The air smelled like rain. When the thunder boomed again, he felt it resonate through him. He wanted to climb higher, to fly into the clouds and catch lightning. A bolt flashed nearby, sizzling the swamp water, and Diello saw tiny flames ignite on his fingertips. He picked up his staff, drawing the storm's power through it. His crystal bones were thrumming.

Cynthe's foot on his shoulder distracted him. She gripped his hair to steady herself as she climbed down from a higher limb and dropped beside him. "What are you doing?"

"Trying to channel the lightning."

"Well, stop it. If you set this tree on fire, the goblins will know we're here."

The flames on Diello's fingers snuffed out. Once more, the storm was just clouds in the sky, and he was a boy separate from it.

Fat drops of rain spattered them. Cynthe picked a handful of leathery leaves.

"Let's make cups and catch rainwater," she said. "I'm thirsty, aren't you?"

Diello got busy helping her. Leaf cups were simple to make, requiring only a large, heavy leaf and a quick flicking of fire to seal together its pinched edges. Too much fire charred them. Too little allowed water to leak out. He'd made four, his fingers moving deftly, when Scree clapped a hand over his.

"No more magic," the goblin-boy whispered. "Too dangerous."

A torrent of rain burst over them. Diello and Cynthe held up a cup in each hand. The drumming downpour filled the cups almost immediately.

Diello placed one where Vassou could lap it. He handed another to Scree before taking a cup from Cynthe to drink from himself.

The water tasted sweet and clean.

Cynthe had climbed back up to a higher perch. With her legs wrapped around the branch, she filled more cups and poured their contents into the waterskin. It was a tedious job, but she stuck with it patiently. As soon as everyone's thirst had been quenched, Diello collected the cups and filled them again, adding their contents to the waterskin. They'd almost finished their task when the rain stopped. The gloom lightened, allowing a few rays of watery sunlight into the jungle.

A toneless horn sounded, giving a signal. Goblins poured from the stronghold, shoving and arguing. More peered down from the many openings carved in the structure's walls. The place looked like a rudimentary keep tower. Crudely made of logs and mud, it rose for several stories and was larger than it had looked yesterday. Ramps made of packed dirt zigzagged up the sides. There seemed to be no doors, just holes for access and exit. At its base, a crude wooden jetty stretched out into the river. Several boats and skiffs were tied to it. Around the stronghold, the ground was trampled to a muddy bog.

The tall gor-goblin sentries carried weapons and were quick to push or kick any of the lesser breeds that jostled too close. The majority of the horde carried only pointed sticks and sacks.

Scree inched closer to Diello. "They're coming for us."

"No," Diello said. "Look. They're on food patrol."

The goblins spread out, most of them heading toward a cluster of trees by the river. Their pointed sticks were used to stab fruit. A deft twist, and the fruit was brought down and dropped into the sack. Others climbed into skiffs and rowed out into the slow-moving water. They speared fish: long, oily-scaled creatures that flopped in a growing pile. By the time they returned, a large crowd of goblins of all colors and sizes had gathered, including females and children.

The yelling and jostling grew fierce as guards tossed food to the crowd. The fish was fought over most violently, with the stronger goblins robbing portions from the weaker. A few of them tucked fish under their arms and scuttled back into the stronghold, but most ate it raw where they stood. The fruit was ignored until all the fish was gone. Diello saw mothers gobbling fish, even chewing the bones, while ignoring their children's cries. Adults did not help the little ones. The young did not make way for the old.

The smallest, hungriest children were the first to eat the fruit. Grubby, many of them naked, they crouched in the mud and smacked and gnawed, letting the juice run down their arms. As soon as the adults started eating the fruit, all the noise and squabbling stopped. They grew drowsy and slow. They crept about or sat down, staring slackly at nothing.

"What is going on?" Diello asked Scree.

"Why do you ask me? I do not know."

"I have heard my pack elders talk of this fruit," Vassou said. "It's called *potok*. The gor-goblins like to make a fermented drink from it called throat-fire."

"It sounds nasty," Cynthe said.

"Eat a little of it raw, and you're lazy. Eat too much of it, and you're poisoned."

"Why eat it at all?" Diello asked. He nudged some leaves aside to continue watching the goblins.

Scree teetered uneasily on his branch and grabbed the massive trunk to steady himself. "Less trouble?"

"I'm sure you're right," Diello agreed. "It keeps them docile, doesn't it? Once they eat the fruit, they don't care if the gatherers fail to catch enough fish."

"There was enough fish for everyone, if they'd shared," Cynthe said.

Diello nodded. The children were as bony and thin as Scree had been before Qod had fattened him up. Many of the adults looked gaunt. All were ragged.

"You do not understand goblin ways," Scree said. "You want goblins to be fair like you. They are not."

"They could be," Diello said.

"They are not."

It was obvious that the gor-goblins ruled the others. They kept most of the fish and ignored the fruit. They swaggered around, picking their teeth with fishbones, and ganged up on the other breeds to steal from them.

Although the goblins were impoverished and cruel to one another, they were somewhat cleaner than the Tescorsians. As soon as all the food had been eaten, any peelings or offal was gathered up and thrown into the river to float away.

Someone screamed. Diello saw a short hobgoblin

running on stumpy legs, dodging among the others. The creature was clutching a folded piece of cloth to his chest. Three gor-goblins chased him, swearing and shouting. The hobgoblin reached a vast cauldron hanging over a cold heap of ashes. His pursuers caught up with him. One smashed a mace into the hobgoblin's back, knocking him down.

The others pounced, pummeling him before dragging him upright. They tipped the cauldron over, rolling it out of the way, then tied the hobgoblin's hands and hung him from the cauldron's hook.

"I can't watch," Cynthe said, looking away.

Diello stared with sick fascination, unable to stop himself. It reminded him of when Brezog had beaten Scree. He put his arm across Scree's shoulders, feeling the goblin-boy flinch each time a blow fell.

"Barbarians," Vassou muttered behind Diello.

"What did the wretch steal?" Cynthe asked, peeking. "A blanket?"

A gor-goblin was holding up the square of cloth, revealing a hole and a tattered edge. He shouted at the hobgoblin, hissing as he slashed through the creature's bonds. The hobgoblin fell to the ground, mumbling something that Diello couldn't understand. The tormentors kicked their victim one last time and strode off, waving the blanket like a trophy.

"All that," Diello asked, "for a useless—"

"It is not useless. It is good cloth. Very good still," Scree whispered. "It is hardly worn."

Diello wondered what their own possessions must have looked like to Scree when he first joined them. *We have almost nothing, and we're rich compared to these creatures.*

"I didn't know goblins were so poor," Diello said gently. "They're always raiding Antrasia. Where's their gold and plunder?"

"In Brezog's treasury," Vassou answered.

"They don't have to live like this," Cynthe said.

"I know the eagle-folk can't farm in the mountains," Diello added. "Poor soil, short growing season. But the goblins could clear some of these trees to make small fields. They could dry and salt fish so there's always a good supply."

"Goblins don't farm," Vassou said.

"Why do they put up with it?" Cynthe asked. "Why don't they leave?"

"Goblins cannot live alone," Scree explained. "Even I, who am only half-blood, feel the loneliness of not belonging to a clan."

"You belong with us," Cynthe said.

"Yes, I am lucky to have good friends. But them? Where would they go? What would they have?"

"They don't have much right now," Diello said.

"They must be with the gorlord. Where he is, they are."

"But if he doesn't take care of them, why are they loyal?"

"There's no time to worry about this," Vassou grumbled. "Remember what's most important."

Diello nodded. "You're right. Let's get some of that *potok*."

"Why?" Vassou asked. "Goblin stomachs are tough. It might make you sick or even kill you."

"I don't intend to eat it. But if I smear some on my face and hands, then I can pretend to be drugged."

"That's too flimsy a disguise," Vassou insisted. "You'll never fool Brezog."

"I don't have to. I just have to get past the guards. And to them, I'll look more convincing as Scree's prisoner."

"But I will not follow your plan," Scree said in alarm. "I told you this. I cannot do it."

"Scree, you must. Otherwise, Cynthe and I have to go in there alone."

"You were clever with the Tescorsians. You can be clever again."

"Staying invisible means using magic. The goblins are more sensitive to that than the eagle-folk. They'll know we're in there. We'll never reach Brezog if we aren't more devious."

Cynthe touched Scree's sleeve. He jumped and almost fell off the branch. "If you don't help us, our little sister will be given to Brezog. She'll have to live here."

"I am sorry," Scree said, "but you cannot make me."

Cynthe's mouth compressed in a thin line. "You owe us," she said. "Now you'll do what we tell you to do."

Scree stared at her as though she'd whipped him. His eyes looked dull. "I thought you were my friends. If I must serve, I will serve. As long as I can."

"What does that mean?" Cynthe asked.

"You will not betray them, goblin," Vassou said. "If you fail, it will be my teeth that you'll feel."

"Stop it, both of you," Diello said to Cynthe and Vassou. "Don't threaten him. He's just scared."

"We're doing this for Amie," Cynthe said.

"It's no good," Diello said. "If we force him against his will, then we're no better than those gor-goblins."

Cynthe's face reddened.

Diello turned to Scree. "You aren't—and never will be—our slave. We can't force you. I've asked you because we need your help and I trust you."

Scree lifted his head. "Despite what I did to you?"

"Brezog forced you. It wasn't your fault. I've told you that before."

"You said it," Scree whispered, "but I could not believe you meant it."

"I believe in you, Scree. I'm scared, too. If it wasn't for my little sister, I wouldn't come within a hundred leagues of this place."

"But you *are* here."

Diello nodded. "You can wait for us out of sight. I won't blame you; and if Cynthe and I come out alive, we'll still be your friends."

Vassou nudged Scree. "It is hard for me to trust goblins, but Diello is right. You have a good heart."

Scree's mouth fell open. He stared at the wolf.

"I'm sorry," Cynthe mumbled.

Scree grinned at each of them, too overwhelmed to speak.

"All right, then." Diello picked up his staff. "We will follow our alternate plan. Let's stay under cover and get as close as we can before we turn invisible. Vassou, are you ready to put a *cymunffyl* around Cynthe?"

Vassou nodded.

Diello looked at Scree. "We'll leave our packs with you."

"No." Scree stood up, clinging to the trunk. "I will not stay behind. I will not be a coward. I do not think I can disobey Brezog's orders once he puts his spell on me, but I will do all I can." His small chin jerked up. "If I should turn against you, please know that it is not by my will. I am weak, too weak. You understand that?"

Diello clasped Scree's shoulder. "You won't let us down."

Tears ran down Scree's grubby face.

Cynthe took his hand. "We're all orphans. We've all survived horrible things. The four of us are family now. That matters more than anything."

"To say such things to me," Scree murmured. "To say such things and mean them."

The foursome looked at one another.

"Time to get that fruit," Diello said, breaking the moment. "Come on, before I lose my nerve."

chapter twenty-six

the fruit smelled sickly sweet. Just putting it on his skin made Diello dizzy. Shaking off the effect, he removed his belt pouch and emptied his pockets into the rucksack. If he didn't, he knew the goblins would rob him. Tearing their thinnest blanket into strips, he wrapped his staff in cloth to disguise its carved symbols. The carvings were casting a faint glow. As his hands moved across them, he could feel Eirian's power. Diello resisted the temptation to reach out to the sword. It would warn Brezog of their arrival.

While Diello worked, Cynthe and Vassou kept watch and Scree wrung his hands nervously. They'd taken cover in a thicket, but just hearing goblin voices nearby made Diello look over his shoulder often.

"I'm ready," he whispered.

Cynthe tied her bow and quiver to Vassou's harness before studying Diello's disguise. He was barefooted, his clothing torn and smeared with mud. He'd tied a cloth around his head and across one eye. The *potok* juice had dried on his chin and hands. Hoping to make his twin smile, he let his mouth sag open and crossed his eyes.

Cynthe grimaced.

Diello straightened with a frown. "Well?"

"It's better than I expected."

He grinned. "Good. So let's get started."

"Diello, I—" Cynthe bit her lip.

"We're doing this for Amie," he told her.

She nodded. "For Amie."

Vassou worked a *cymunffyl* and slid it around Cynthe. She disappeared from sight.

Diello drew in a long breath. Despite the sticky heat, he felt cold. He nodded at Scree. "Let's go."

The moment Diello and Scree stepped out into the open, shrill goblin howls rose in the air. The goblins came running and surrounded them.

Diello kept his expression vacant, reacting slowly even when one of the sentries poked him with the butt end of a spear. Scree looked gray with fright.

Diello worried that the goblin-boy had forgotten what he was supposed to do, but suddenly Scree found his voice.

"I have brought Lord Brezog this gift," he announced. "Take me to the gorlord at once!"

"No," a sentry replied in Antrasin, spitting near Diello's foot. The venom hissed, burning the trampled grass. "No one sees Brezog. Khuno will accept this prisoner. Khuno is in charge."

Diello saw a gor-goblin standing apart with an entourage of his own. Khuno's eyes blazed with disdain. Silver bracelets covered his wrists. His long fingers were playing with a stout rod that had a skull mounted on one end.

Diello's courage sank. The skull-mace was Brezog's weapon. Had the gorlord died?

"I—I have brought this prisoner," Scree cried.

The sentries laughed at him, and one of them jabbed Diello in the leg, drawing blood. It was all Diello could do not to yelp.

"The prisoner is for Lord Brezog," Scree said.

Diello swallowed a groan. *Say something else!*

Khuno swaggered forward and pushed Scree to the ground. "We will eat the prisoner tonight, and you will feed the swamp wraiths."

All the goblins roared and thumped one another with merriment. They shoved Diello back and forth, tearing his tattered clothing even more.

Diello tried to look drugged, but his thoughts were racing. *Do I confront Khuno? Do I reveal who I am? If Brezog is dead, it won't help us. But if I don't do something now, Cynthe's going to—*

"Fool!" Scree shouted.

Khuno bared his teeth. "What did you call me?"

"You are not gorlord here," Scree said. "The prisoner is for Brezog, not for you."

"Give me no orders, you piece of dung."

Scree didn't flinch.

One of the gor-goblins murmured something in Khuno's ear. "You are Brezog's half-blood whelp?" he said.

"I am Scree. S-son of Brezog." Scree's voice quavered, but he continued to stare up at Khuno defiantly. "Who else would bring Brezog such a fine gift? Not you. Not any of you!"

"Have you come to challenge me?" Khuno asked.

The roar of laughter drowned out Scree's reply.

Diello stared at the ground. *Keep going, Scree!*

"Let us pass," Scree said when the noise died down.

A green hobgoblin pushed through the throng. "The gorlord says you are to come to him."

Khuno turned on the messenger, swiping with his skull-mace, but the hobgoblin dodged the blow.

"Bring the prisoner *now*," the hobgoblin said.

Scree stood and started forward. Diello was given a shove from behind that almost knocked him over. Staggering, he shambled along, trying to look docile. He leaned heavily on his staff as though his bleeding leg hurt. Through the wrapping, he could feel the power pulsing inside the wood.

We're in!

A sliver of pain lanced through his temple, and something slid through his thoughts.

You've come to me at last, Faelin morsel.

Diello masked his excitement. Brezog thought he'd sprung a trap around Diello and Scree. Now he had to keep the gorlord from guessing the truth.

Eirian has brought you to me, Brezog whispered in his mind. *Hurry. Hurry!*

Diello drew on his staff's power to close his mind to the gorlord.

Inside the stronghold, torches of burning pitch filled the air with oily smoke. Diello coughed as he climbed the winding ramp of dirt and stone leading up inside the tower. Scree crowded Diello's heels, his fingers clamped on the back of Diello's belt. The green hobgoblin led the way, and gor-goblins—grumbling and muttering—brought up the rear.

At each level, the ramp branched into a passageway riddled with holes. Goblin faces peered out from these holes, staring at the procession. *Is that where they live?* Diello wondered. He felt the stirrings of pity. Maybe this was why they were so angry and mean.

A young goblin tottered toward Diello. He tried to fend off the child with his staff—pushing gently. The mother came scuttling from a hole and dragged the infant back. She snarled at Diello, spitting out words he didn't understand.

He recoiled slightly and bumped into something he couldn't see. *Cynthe!* Careful not to give away his twin's presence, Diello continued up the ramp.

"Quickly!" the hobgoblin called.

At the very top of the stronghold, the floor was open and spacious. Windows on all sides let in light and air. Diello sighed in relief.

Treasure lay heaped in every corner. Bags of gold pieces spilled across the floor. Silver goblets, jeweled necklaces, and fancy rings were piled with silks and velvets. Weapons were stacked haphazardly without any kind of order. Crocks and jugs, odd fragments of furniture, and even an assortment of village banners lined the walls.

At the center of the room was a large square stone. A

cushion and a necklace of hammered gold lay on top of it. Diello supposed this was Brezog's throne. But today, the gorlord reclined on the floor, propped up by a number of cushions and covered—despite the sweltering heat—by several blankets. Eirian lay across the gorlord's lap. Brezog's right arm rested on a stack of cushions, and Diello saw that a strip of dirty cloth bound the goblin leader's hand to the sword's hilt.

Brezog's eyes were shut. He seemed to be asleep, his breathing heavy and laborious. He looked gaunt. A tray of uneaten food set nearby, crawling with flies. Queen Shei-rae's silver arrow still projected from Brezog's bare chest, and the flesh around the wound was black.

Eirian's translucent blade had turned dull. The magnificent hilt jewel was scratched, as though someone had tried to pry it loose.

Around the room, goblins perched silently on fat bags of money. They watched Diello with hostile eyes. Next to one of the windows, a stooped hag with gray hair hanging in her face stirred a cauldron of bubbling liquid. She stopped stirring and began snipping the heads off small, writhing lizards and dropping the carcasses into her brew. She was no goblin. Diello thought of the stories he'd heard about the Barrens and the creatures that lived here. *A myst-witch?* He sensed a miasma of magical power hanging over the crone. Whatever spell she was working made Diello's bones itch unpleasantly.

There was a cloying, sweet smell to Brezog. *He's rotting away, like his food,* Diello thought.

The gorlord opened his eyes. They were as fiercely red as Diello remembered.

Scree whimpered in the back of his throat.

"So," Brezog hissed, speaking Antrasin weakly, "the Faelin morsel has come to take Eirian from me."

Diello scrubbed the sticky fruit from his face. He didn't need his flimsy disguise now.

"Where is the scabbard?" Brezog shouted.

Then the gorlord lay back, resting on his cushions with his eyes half-closed. One of his attendants crept up to him and wiped the sweat from his face. Brezog growled, and the goblin scurried away.

"Where is the scabbard?" Brezog repeated. He raised a taloned finger, and a guard pushed Diello to his knees. No one had taken the cloth-wrapped staff from him yet. He laid it on the floor beside him. Ignored, Scree crept over among an assortment of crockery and hunkered there.

"The scabbard is in Tescorsa," Diello answered.

A murmur of displeasure circled the room, but Brezog's lips curled in amusement.

"You are not afraid of me," he rasped. "You think you are stronger than me."

"Did you know that Khuno is carrying your skull-mace?" Diello countered.

"Khuno is my son. He will be gorlord after me. But not yet. You will not find a goblin rebellion to help you take Eirian."

"Don't be so sure about that," Diello said. "Khuno is

feeding *potok* to everyone but the gor-goblins. That won't fill empty bellies."

"You lie," Brezog said. "They eat croc meat and fish. By my order."

Diello glimpsed the myst-witch's sharp look at the gor-lord. *She knows.* His gaze traveled the room. *They all know. Khuno is taking over, but Brezog isn't aware of it yet.*

"You have come here with foolish confidence," Brezog continued. "Did the Fae send you? Sheirae would never venture here. Her mage-brother will not sully his hands fighting me. So they let a Faelin child and a goblin mongrel come in their stead. Where is the girl?"

"In the jungle," Diello lied. "Ready to pick off your sentries if we don't come out soon. She's as good with a bow as Sheirae."

Several goblins jumped to their feet, shouting. The guards smacked Diello, making the corner of his mouth bleed. He sucked at his split lip, his head ringing.

"I've taught you this lesson before," Brezog said when the furor quieted, "but it seems you must be taught again. Bring Scree to me."

chapter twenty-seven

Scree tried to run but was caught easily. The guards brought him forward, kicking and panting with fear.

"Pick on me, not him," Diello said, jumping to his feet only to be shoved down again. "He's not a part of this."

"Isn't he? Who do you serve?" Brezog called out to Scree. "Me? Or this Faelin boy? Answer!"

"I—I—I serve you, my lord." Scree wouldn't look at Diello.

Diello hoped with all his heart that Scree was lying as he curled his hand around his staff.

Brezog suddenly sat up. "What is this magic? What are you doing? Who failed to take the boy's weapon?"

The guards made a grab for the staff, but Diello rolled out of reach. When he shook off the wrappings, the wooden rod was glowing white. Its carved symbols pulsed with power. Several goblins cringed back, shielding their eyes.

"Fae magic," the myst-witch acknowledged. She dipped a cup into her cauldron and stepped forward. "The boy is a mage. Beware of him, gorlord. He wears layers of lies and deceit."

Hissing, the guards brandished their spears and surrounded Diello. He held his staff ready, watching them. Outside, thunder rattled the skies. A part of Diello called silently to the storm, willing it closer. Vassou remained hidden outside the stronghold. His magic was working perfectly. *Have patience, Cynthe,* Diello thought. *Wait for my signal.*

Brezog cried out. As everyone turned to him, Diello saw that Eirian had begun to glow as well. The sword did not shine as brightly as it once did, but it was still coming alive. The runes on the blade threw off sparks, and Diello's bones hummed with the power he was summoning.

Brezog writhed on his cushions. His fingers shifted beneath the binding around Eirian's hilt as though trying to release it.

"Hold him!" the myst-witch ordered.

A pair of gor-goblins lifted their leader to his feet. Brezog whimpered and sagged, but they kept him upright. The crone lifted her cup to Brezog's lips. He drank greedily, slopping the liquid onto the floor.

"There, there," the crone said soothingly. "You can bear the sword's magic now. You are strong again. You are fearless."

Brezog stepped away from her and his attendants. The brew glistened on his lips and chin. His free hand curled around the arrow projecting from his chest. Diello thought he was going to pull it free, but the gorlord dropped his hand and walked toward Diello.

"A puny Faelin mage cannot make me drop this sword," Brezog said.

By now, Cynthe should be in position, Diello thought.

Brezog nodded to the guards surrounding Diello. Tensing, Diello lifted his staff like a club. At the same time he shouted at Cynthe. "N—"

A band of magic encircled his throat, choking him. Diello clawed at his neck. He staggered, growing dizzy. His staff was struck from his hand. A second blow drove him to the floor.

Diello tried to get up, but he was struck again. The world went black for a moment.

Diello opened his eyes. He could breathe once more. The guards pulled him to his feet. Brezog held Eirian's tip to Diello's chest, right above his heart.

"My heart for yours," Brezog said. "That's why I allowed you to come here. Eirian drew you exactly as I intended. Your sister is here, isn't she? Roving the room, wrapped in her samal spell. Did you think I couldn't sense her? Perhaps she is behind me now."

He gestured, and guards formed a semicircle at his back.

Diello said nothing. Scree was moaning.

"Have I told you how much I hate the Fae?" Brezog smiled, letting his fangs show. "Yet I am willing to accept a heart that's half Fae, willing to bear the discomfort, willing to drink witch-brew for the rest of my days to keep your heart beating for me. A Faelin heart in exchange for a Fae curse." He rasped out a laugh, wheezing slightly. "What will Sheirae say when I send your corpse back to her? The curse she put on me with this arrow will have destroyed you. And I will still have Eirian for my own."

There was nothing Diello could say. He had known Brezog would try something like this.

"Make the girl visible," Brezog ordered.

Diello shook his head.

Since Brezog would die the moment Eirian left his hand, everything hinged on whether Diello could pull the weapon free before his chest was torn open by the goblins. Diello shivered.

"That's better," Brezog hissed. "Drop your pride. Let me savor your terror. I'll deal with the girl later." He tapped Diello's chest with the sword.

Come to me! Eirian spoke to Diello's mind.

He closed his eyes, wanting to grab Eirian so badly it hurt. He forced himself to wait.

"Open your eyes and gaze into mine," Brezog said, his command charged with magic. "I will govern your mind so that you feel no pain when you die. I will be that merciful to you."

Diello's eyes opened. He saw Brezog drawing back his arm, but then something unseen bumped the gorlord. The bindings on the hilt began to tear away.

Brezog turned, shoving Cynthe. Diello heard a thud as she hit the floor.

"A child's trick!" Brezog snarled. He turned back to Diello and rammed the sword at him.

"Diello!" Cynthe screamed.

Pinned between the guards, Diello tried to make himself invisible but failed. Brezog's magic was too strong.

Scree jumped in front of Diello, and Eirian's blade plunged into the goblin-boy instead.

"No!" Diello shouted.

Slowly—looking stunned—Brezog withdrew the sword.

Wrenching free from the guards, Diello caught his friend's body as it crumpled. "Scree!"

The goblin-boy's eyes found his. Scree struggled to speak. "My friend," he whispered.

Scree's eyes fell shut. His breath stilled.

Easing the body to the ground, Diello hardly noticed as the guards pulled him upright.

"That was your son!" he shouted at Brezog.

Brezog beckoned to the myst-witch.

She crouched beside Scree's body, mumbling to herself as her hands touched his face. "There is nothing to be done."

Brezog didn't bother to wipe Scree's blood off the blade. Meeting Diello's gaze, the gorlord shrugged.

Diello jumped at Brezog.

"Hold him still, you fools!" Brezog yelled.

But they couldn't contain him. Diello lashed out and kicked Brezog in the stomach.

The gorlord doubled over. His attendants rushed to him, but he waved them off, coughing.

From the corner of his eye, Diello saw his staff vanishing from sight as it was lifted. *Cynthe!*

One of Brezog's attendants bent over with a grunt and toppled to the floor. As confused shouting broke out, the unseen staff walloped one of Diello's guards. Diello guessed at Cynthe's position and grabbed the staff from her.

As the staff became visible again, he let its full power flow through him. The wood blazed blinding white while lightning flashed in the window.

The storm had arrived.

Diello swung the staff, and a bolt of lightning jagged through a window. It connected with the staff, and Diello caught its strength as he'd been yearning to do.

The lightning vibrated through Diello's bones, making his teeth chatter. He held on to his staff with both hands, nearly shaken off his feet.

When he turned to face Brezog, the gorlord stumbled back, holding up Eirian for protection.

Then Brezog was jerked sideways, and he fell hard. Cynthe's invisible knife slashed through the bindings around the hilt.

Brezog screamed, but the other goblins—clearly afraid—didn't rush forward.

"Stop her!" Brezog ordered, his voice weak.

When the guards charged uncertainly in his direction, Diello aimed his staff.

A goblin was thrown through the air, charred to ashes. Diello burned another, and the rest of the guards retreated. Diello resisted the urge to destroy them, too. The power he was holding was so dangerous it frightened him.

He heard more goblins coming up the ramp.

"Diello, what are you waiting for?" Cynthe called. "Take the sword!"

"You will be destroyed if you take it from me by force," Brezog gasped.

Cynthe tried to wrench Eirian from him anyway, but Brezog clung to it with desperate strength. They grappled until the gorlord bit her. Cynthe cried out, and he struggled away from her, slapping at the air.

Diello held up his staff. "Drop Eirian now!"

"Sword against staff—which will win?" Brezog taunted. "Eirian is supreme. You can never take it from me."

Diello aimed the staff at the gorlord. Fire struck Brezog, knocking him back; but he didn't burn up like the others.

Brezog laughed, still holding Eirian. The sword twisted in his hand, and Cynthe cried out in pain.

She became visible, as though touching Eirian had destroyed the *cymunffyl*. She was kneeling, cradling her hand. Brezog moved toward Cynthe, but she rose in the air.

Khuno and a group of armed goblins burst into the room. They halted, looking uncertain.

"Capture the Faelin!" Brezog ordered.

But no one obeyed.

Disbelief flickered across Brezog's face. "So the boy spoke the truth," he said. "You're against me."

Khuno didn't answer.

Brezog looked down at Scree's body. "The mongrel would have served me better."

Diello flew straight at Brezog. He twisted the blade from the gorlord's grasp.

"No!" Brezog cried.

"For my mother and father," Diello pronounced, flying away from Brezog's reach. Diello curled his fingers around the hilt. The sword's magic surged through his body. White tendrils of power entwined around Diello's wrist and up his forearm. "For Scree."

"You cannot avenge Scree," Brezog growled. "You tricked him into betraying me. His death lies upon you, not me. Now, why do you not die? You take the sword by force, yet you do not burn?"

"I am Eirian's master," Diello replied. His bones were thrumming with Eirian's power inside him. "It speaks to me."

Brezog flung goblin fire at Diello, but Diello deflected it easily with the sword.

Then Brezog began to shake, gripping the arrow in his chest. Grimacing, he sank to his knees and gazed up at Diello. "You—you . . ."

Brezog shook again and collapsed.

No one moved or spoke until Khuno strode to the gorlord and knelt beside him. Swiftly, Khuno pulled off Brezog's gold bracelets and slid them on his own arms. Then he drew out the silver arrow and tossed it aside before facing the others. He held the skull-mace high.

"Brezog is dead. Khuno is gorlord!" he shouted.

The goblins knelt, pressing their foreheads to the floor. "Khuno! Lord Khuno!"

Cynthe landed next to Scree and bent over him.

"Come," Diello called to her while the goblins went on chanting Khuno's name.

Smoothing Scree's hair, Cynthe kissed his forehead and folded his arms across his body. Then she picked up the silver arrow and flew out the window. Diello, holding both Eirian and his staff, followed her.

Jubilant yells poured from the stronghold, Brezog's Rock no longer.

chapter twenty-eight

Cynthe was crying as they landed in the jungle. "We shouldn't have left him behind."

"We had to," Diello said.

"But we could've done something for him. With Eirian's power—"

"It doesn't work that way."

"Maybe Qod could have saved him!"

Diello shook his head sadly.

"Scree doesn't belong there," Cynthe insisted. "They'll throw him out like garbage."

In the distance, the drums started up again, faster, rapping out a beat that sounded like a celebration. A column of smoke rose above the treetops.

"Brezog's funeral pyre," Diello guessed. *Is Scree burning there with his father?* Diello couldn't bear to think about it. "It's my fault."

"Forget what Brezog said."

"If I hadn't given Scree the idea that he could be brave, he'd still be a coward. He'd still be . . . alive."

Vassou came running up to them, panting. "You have

Eirian! Well done." Then he flattened his ears. "What's happened? Did Scree—"

Cynthe put her hands over her mouth, and Diello gathered her in his arms, hugging her close while she sobbed.

"He saved my life," Diello told Vassou. "He was so scared that he'd betray us, but he died a hero."

"And we left him behind," Cynthe wailed. "I'm so ashamed. He never asked for much from us. He didn't deserve to be abandoned, with no rites, no—"

"Cynthe," Vassou said, "we will give him rites. We will bid him farewell, but not here, not now."

"Vassou's right," Diello said. "Soon Khuno will stop celebrating and want Eirian back. We have to go."

Cynthe swiped at her eyes, gathering their packs and slinging them into a pile at their feet. Diello wanted to clean the sword but didn't dare venture near the dirty water. He could see pairs of baleful orange eyes gathering out in the swamp and moving closer to land as though drawn by the shining sword.

Let us fight, Eirian said to him.

"*Spiritus chthon,*" Diello murmured, "*redeimi giami est.*"

Eirian trembled in his hand, growing so heavy that Diello struggled to hold it up. His staff shone like a beam at the brooding clouds. Lightning crackled above the trees, and Diello cried out. Thunder shook the ground, and rain poured down.

In the next moment, they were sucked from the Barrens into a gray void. Then the mist parted, and they were back inside the caves.

Jewels and floating bits of light sprinkled down on them before a shining, round stone came rolling their way.

"Welcome back!" Qod cried, spinning around them. "Master of Eirian, you return triumphant! A feast is ready to delight you. I shall offer you all your favorite foods plus new delicacies to tempt your palate."

"No thanks," Diello said wearily. The exhilaration of the storm had gone. Magic no longer pulsed through his bones. His head was aching, and his hand felt numb from gripping the sword. He crouched down, holding out Eirian's stained blade for Qod to see. "I have to clean this."

"Of course. You may do anything you like, only please follow me. Mind you, keep to the path where the quartz lights are shining."

"Qod, you don't understand," Diello said. "Scree is dead. I have to clean the sword *now*."

The joyous glow faded from Qod. The tomtir said, "I shall ask you no questions. I shall provide all that you require. Come this way."

A passageway appeared in front of them, and they trudged through it. Qod led them to a dark pool of water that reflected pinpoints of light on its surface.

"The water is pure and clean," Qod said. "It is shallow enough for you to bathe in."

"Isn't it cold?" Vassou asked.

"Not here. Diello and Cynthe will find it most comfortable."

A fire appeared inside a ring of rocks. Beside it, a screen

materialized to shield the bather, and on the other side were benches.

"Let's see," Qod murmured, "you will want clean clothing and towels. Anything else?"

"The scabbard, please," Diello said.

"At once," Qod said. The tomtir rolled away.

"What about your hand?" Diello asked Cynthe, trying to look at it.

She pulled away. "It'll be all right."

"Cynthe, you should bathe first," Vassou said. "Throw your clothing in the fire and wash away the filth of the Barrens."

"Maybe later," she said dully.

"Now." Vassou was firm. "It is part of the rites that we will give Scree."

Without further argument, she stepped behind the screen. Vassou herded Diello over to a bench.

Dark smoke billowed up. Diello smelled Cynthe's clothes burning and heard muted splashing. Eventually she emerged, her wet hair sleek and pale in the firelight. She wore a new green tunic that matched her eyes and the necklace Qod had given her. At Vassou's insistence, she dabbed some of their healing salve on her burned palm.

We will fight, Eirian whispered to Diello. *We will conquer the world.*

"Diello," Vassou said, "go and wash. Eirian first and then yourself."

It was an effort to move. Diello's limbs felt leaden. His

head still ached. He found the jeweled scabbard lying next to the pool's edge. He knelt and washed the blade, scrubbing away the last of Scree. As he worked, he cried silently for his friend, wishing he'd been kinder and more patient, wishing he'd left Scree behind with Vassou, where he would have been safe.

I used him. I didn't listen when he said he was scared. Why couldn't I let him be?

Diello dried the sword carefully and slid it into the scabbard. Eirian's voice faded from his thoughts, and his headache went away. The magic tendrils had disappeared from his arm, but they left red marks that he couldn't rub off his skin. Sighing, he removed his dirty clothing and burned it, then stepped into the pool with a shiver.

The water was warm. Diello wondered why Qod hadn't provided soap until he realized the water alone washed every streak of mud off his body. He sank beneath the surface, feeling bubbles along his scalp. When he stood up, slinging his wet hair from his face, he had never felt so clean.

Diello climbed out, drying himself and putting on the clothing that Qod had provided. When he picked up his belt, he found that his possessions had been placed back inside his belt pouch. He wanted nothing that he'd owned before. Reeshwin's feather floated to the ground. For a long while Diello weighed the wooden whistle and tinderbox on his palm. As gifts from Pa, he'd treasured them. Now they looked silly, and he didn't know why he should keep them. They were a child's things.

Diello tossed them. The tinderbox sailed into the fire, but the whistle bounced off one of the stones. He shrugged. *Is this what it means to grow up?*

"Diello?" Cynthe asked, peeking around the screen. "What are you doing?"

She used her knife tip to knock the tinderbox out of the fire. Its sides were charred, and one corner of the lid had burned away; but the rest remained intact. Picking it up along with the whistle, she turned to Diello.

"Destroying the past isn't the way," she said. "You're angry, but later you'll regret losing what Pa gave you."

She lifted the Carnethie star from around her neck and put it in Diello's hand. His fingers curled around it.

"We're not children anymore. I don't need my old toys or this," he said, holding out the star to her. "Go on and keep this. I don't want it."

"Stop sulking," she said. "It doesn't help."

"What about you?"

"I'm sad. There's a difference. You're not thinking about Scree. You're thinking about yourself. You want to blame Pa and Mamee, but that's no good."

"We've had no peace. We've been used and manipulated. What's the good of it, Cynthe? What's it for?"

"Amalina," Cynthe replied.

Diello shook his head. "It's more than that. Mamee shouldn't have lied to us."

"Maybe," Cynthe said. "Don't you think living as she and Pa did, out in the woods away from everyone, living without her magic—don't you think that affected her?"

"That doesn't excuse—"

"She missed Embarthi so much. She always talked about it as though it were perfect."

"To deceive us."

"To cherish her memories of the home she loved."

"What about Owain? She told us that he was kind, that he'd help us."

"I've thought about that a lot," Cynthe said. "And Mamee always talked about him in the past. She'd say, 'Your uncle *was* the kindest person. He *had* so much good in him.' And then she'd change the subject and talk about the gardens or the parties."

"I . . . I don't remember," Diello said.

"We invented the story we wanted to believe until we forgot that it might not be true."

"She still misled us," Diello said.

"Whether she did or not, we still have to plan for what comes next."

"Why?" Diello said. "We're going to give Eirian to Owain and make him invincible. It's that simple."

"But—"

"No, I'm done talking. We swap Eirian for Amie, and then we leave Embarthi forever. Owain can do whatever he wants. I don't care."

"You do care!" Cynthe cried. "You have to!"

"Well, I don't." Diello pushed past her to rejoin Vassou.

Ignoring the food that Qod conjured for them, they opened Scree's pack and took out his meager belongings. Odd-shaped pebbles, a crimson leaf, six coins of goblin gold, a spare tunic, and his blanket. *When we first met him, he didn't own even this much,* Diello thought.

Tracing the edge of the leaf, Diello began to sing an old ballad that Scree had liked:

> *Hush-a-bye, cries the maiden.*
> *My Tohnny's coming home.*
> *Hush-a-bye, my heart's cravin'*
> *All the fine things we'll own.*
> *Hush-a-bye, cries the maiden.*
> *Wedding my Tohnny I'll never rue.*
> *Hush-a-bye, cries the maiden.*
> *My heart, my heart will always stay true.*

"He was silly to like that one so much," Cynthe said. "He was always silly."

"Not always," Diello said. "He liked the simple songs about love and family, didn't he? I guess that's what he wanted most."

"He belonged with us," Cynthe said. "We gave him that much."

"I wish it had been more."

Sighing, Cynthe hummed a little and then sang another song, one they'd learned from Mamee:

> *Sweet grows the wild rose, the wild rose, so true.*
> *I miss you, my darling. I'm longing for you*

To meet me by the old wall and smile as before.

To greet me with soft posy and a heart that holds more.

There were several verses to the song; but Cynthe's voice broke, and she couldn't continue. In the silence, Vassou moved away from the crackling fire. He tipped back his head and howled a medley of cries so mournful that Diello wanted to cry out, too.

Cynthe leaned against Diello. He put his arm around her and let his tears come.

chapter twenty-nine

W hen they woke in the morning, the fire had died to
ashes. Fresh food had replaced what they couldn't
eat the night before. Cynthe held out Diello's whistle and
tinderbox. He took them and stowed them away in his belt
pouch.

He could remember Scree saying, *It is good to have gifts.*
I would like to give you something, Diello. I found this pebble
on the ground today. It looks like a newt, and that is why I
carry it. Do you like it? I will give it to you gladly.

Diello had replied indifferently, accepted the pebble,
and later when Scree wasn't with him, he'd dropped it on
the ground. *The way I used to throw away the flowers Ama-*
lina brought me.

This morning, with a clearer head, Diello understood
that the sacrifice had been Scree's choice. Whether Diello
felt guilty about it didn't matter. *Scree's life was the most*
valuable gift of all. I will never throw it away.

Diello searched until he found the feather Reeshwin
had given him in friendship. He put it back in his pouch.
Then he attached Eirian's scabbard to his belt, getting used

to the weight of the sword at his hip. Eirian was finely balanced—wearing it was no hardship. *Not that I'll have it for very long.*

"Good day, my young friends!" Qod's voice sang out. "I hope you are in better spirits. Saying good-bye is hard, but we go on, don't we? Now, young Master of Eirian, I have a surprise for you. Come and see it."

Another visit from Mamee and Pa?

Diello followed the tomtir reluctantly. Cynthe and Vassou trailed behind.

Qod took them to the surface. It was a shock to leave the dim underground and stand on a snowy hillside, blinking against the sunshine. The mountain slope towered above them, with fresh snowfall softening its angles. Diello saw stones, roughly knee-high, positioned everywhere.

"The little tomtirs?" Diello asked. "The ones you showed me before? Have they—"

"Isn't it thrilling? The *giami* has worked. Just the proximity of Eirian's scabbard has been enough to give them a spark. Now, blessed by sunlight, they may—just may—come fully to life in a few hundred years. I have great hopes. I cannot thank you enough for the trust you awarded me."

"Let's do better than that." Setting aside his staff, Diello drew Eirian and walked among the scattered stones, touching each of them lightly with the blade. He did this to a half dozen before he felt something stir.

A fleck of *chthon* glinted, as though reflecting the sunlight. A bit of life unfolded inside a lopsided piece of limestone. The entity was as tender and new as one of Pa's seedlings sprouting in New Field. Diello closed his eyes, letting his crystal bones enhance the power flowing from Eirian. "*Chthon* to *chthon*," he murmured, not knowing where the words came from. "Live. . . ."

He moved to the next stone and found no response. But the next, a rugged chunk of granite, burst to life so violently that the rock rolled from side to side.

Qod bumped into Diello's ankle. "Did you see that?" the tomtir cried. "It moved. It's—"

"Are you always so loud?" a shrill voice piped up. A pair of eyes popped open in the granite, glaring at them both. "Who's blocking the light?"

Diello hastily moved to one side.

"My child!" Qod said. "My dear child."

"Who are you?" the granite tomtir demanded. "Why are you bigger? How fast will I grow? How long do I have to stay here? Can I have a hole of my own? What is this cold substance around me? Do you have any dust to eat?"

Qod spun around, unable to keep up with the barrage of questions.

Grinning, Diello finished tapping Eirian against the stones. More than half of them responded, but none were as vocal as the piece of granite.

"I am not alone!" Qod said, rolling around in joy. "I have so much to do. The underground passages must be widened. I need more shale. Dust simply won't provide the sustenance that young tomtirs require."

"I don't like shale!" the granite tomtir shouted. "I want onyx dust, with flint chips mixed in."

"Congratulations, Qod," Diello said.

"Oh, forgive me. I'm so excited I nearly forgot it's time to bid you farewell."

"We'll never forget you," Diello said.

"I owe you a bigger debt of gratitude," Qod replied. "You will all be forever welcome here. But now . . ."

Diello looked at Cynthe and Vassou. They both nodded. "I wish for the three of us to save Amalina from Uncle Owain," he said.

"I wish for us to defeat Uncle Owain," Cynthe added.

"Good-bye again, my young friends," Qod said.

Diello slid Eirian back in its scabbard and picked up his staff. "Good-bye, Qod. Enjoy your new family."

"Mind your feet!"

The tomtir spun in a blur around them. Then they were rising in the air.

Greetings, my friend, murmured a voice in Diello's mind.

"Zephyr!" he cried.

"Who are you talking to?" Cynthe asked. "How are we going to fly Vassou all the way to Embarthi?"

Vassou—his legs dangling—was staring at the ground as it grew smaller beneath them.

"We're not flying," Diello answered. "We're going to ride the wind."

He felt the strong breeze lift beneath him. Cynthe, her hair whipping around her face, whooped in delight. Vassou was crouching awkwardly on the wind. His ears were flat to his skull. Diello held on to the wolf's harness on one side. On the other side, Cynthe did the same.

The zephyr swooped them straight up, then looped them upside down before shooting forward. Diello had one dizzying glimpse of eagles flying in the distance. He wondered if one of them was Reeshwin and wished he could have thanked her properly. Then they were racing along too fast to see the world below.

Good-bye, Reeshwin!

Everything became a blend of color and shape. The air was icy cold, but just when Diello grew so frozen he thought his numb fingers would drop his staff, Vassou shielded them with a *cloigwylie*.

"That's better," Cynthe said, sitting straighter. "This is faster than we could ever fly. How do you like it, Vassou?"

"When I am grown into my full powers, I'll fly like this every day," Vassou replied. "Well, perhaps not as fast."

Both Diello and Cynthe laughed.

The sun was sinking in the late-afternoon sky when Diello saw the gigantic *cloigwylie* that guarded the Embarthi border. Shimmering with colors, it looked—from a distance—like sunlight dancing on a river. But as they drew closer, the protective spell rose tall and thick—an infinite wall reaching for the sky. Diello had tried to fly over it once but had never reached the top.

Zephyr, be careful, he said. *We're coming to the border.*

I know no boundaries, the wind replied. *I go where I please.*

If the Fae spell resists our entry, we could be injured, Diello said.

"Why are we slowing down?" Cynthe asked.

Diello pointed, and she stood up, holding out her arms to keep her balance as she teetered.

"I see the *cloigwylie!*" she shouted. "I couldn't see it the last time we were here, but I can now. It's beautiful!"

Diello sensed the barrier's magic and felt the criss-crossed strands of the woven spell. *I understand how it's made,* he thought in amazement. *I could make one like it if I wanted!*

Cynthe dropped to a crouch beside him and took hold of Vassou's harness again. "We're still slowing. Why?"

"You've seen a sparrow fly into a windowpane," Diello replied.

"But we can go through it."

"I couldn't before, and it's closed to me now. I sense it."

"That's daft. You're just worrying as usual. Vassou will get us through."

"Not this time," Vassou said. "The border *cloigwylie* will enforce the queen's order to banish us."

"We have to think of an alternate way to get in," Diello said.

The zephyr rose. Vassou scrambled a bit, and Diello tugged on the wolf's harness.

Zephyr, Diello called, *why are you taking us higher? Can we go over the top?*

Yes, the wind replied, *so high the sky ends, and there is only night and stars.*

Zephyr, turn back! It's too high for us.

The wind shifted and raced downward.

Swallowing his nausea, Diello said, "Vassou, can I pierce the barrier with Eirian?"

"I don't know," Vassou growled, his head low. His protective *cloigwylie* faded away. "The sword is not meant for that."

Let us fight the spell, Eirian said to Diello. *Let us try!*

"Will mage fire cut through?" Diello asked the pup.

"Probably, but you'll warn Owain and Clevn of our return."

"Owain made a fool of me last time," Diello said. "Everything we tried, he turned against us."

"You can't play tricks on him," Cynthe said. "Not with Amie's life at stake."

"And you can't give him the sword," Vassou added.

"But that's the only plan I have," Diello said. "We get Amie back, and the Fae have to deal with Owain."

Vassou snarled.

"What do you expect me to do?" Diello asked. "Fight him?"

Yes! Fight. Let us fight.

"Why not?" Cynthe replied.

"Owain is probably watching us right now."

"I don't care," Cynthe said. "You have to come up with something. You've got *all* of Eirian, remember? He can't be stronger than you now. Why are you afraid to use the sword and all your magic?"

Diello thought of when Clevn had taken him inside the Cave of Mysteries and warned him about the dangers of Eirian's power. *Eirian's no ordinary sword. If I can't handle it properly, all kinds of destruction could happen. And what if Owain hurts Amie because I try to be a big hero?*

"What if she dies like Scree? I can't live with that," he said.

"Just try," Cynthe said.

The wind bore them along the side of the border *cloigwylie*, sliding past it so closely that Diello could feel sharp prickles of magic trying to repel him.

"I don't like it!" Cynthe cried, rubbing her arms. "It hurts like iron."

Diello stood up, seeking his balance as the zephyr dipped and climbed. He lifted his staff, pointing it at a few white puffs of cloud. The clouds moved together, growing in mass. They darkened, and thunder muttered faintly.

"Diello!" Cynthe gasped. "Are you going to pull lightning to us like you did at Brezog's Rock? You could kill us."

"Not if I catch it," Diello answered.

He aimed toward the storm clouds. They grew taller, their tops spreading out wide and flat. More thunder rumbled. He could see the lightning flickering here and there.

"But, Diello!"

"Quiet, Cynthe," Vassou said. "Let him focus."

She opened her mouth to argue, and just like that, the world froze. The wind stopped. Sounds stopped. The storm Diello was trying to capture grew silent.

A column of light appeared in front of Diello. He saw a cold, pallid face inside it. Merciless eyes glared at him.

"Clevn," Diello said. He couldn't hide his disappointment. He'd hoped it would be Owain.

"So you and your twin have returned in defiance of the queen's order," Clevn said. "The mark of Eirian is on your arm. You've used it in battle, then. Knowing that to spill blood was forbidden by the Afon Heyrn since the sword was first placed under the guardianship of the Watchers, you've dared defy—"

"I've killed no one with it," Diello declared.

"Eirian is awake. Even while contained in its scabbard, it speaks. I heard it leagues away. Every mage and Watcher in Embarthi will be listening to it now. Do you not realize the danger? Did I not explain to you that the sword must not be stirred to full awareness? Now that you've killed—"

"I told you: the life it took wasn't by my hand."

"You wear the mark. The responsibility is yours."

Do not accept rebuke, Eirian murmured. *Make him serve you.*

"Does the queen want the sword or not?" Diello asked, trying to ignore the voice in his head.

"The queen has no part in this."

"You don't seem very grateful. Do you really hate us so much?"

"This isn't about hate. It's about power. Which you don't know how to use. Give Eirian to me. I'll see that it's sent to the Watchers."

"Amalina's safe return comes first," Diello said.

"She's unimportant compared to the—"

"She's *not* unimportant."

"You're wasting time. Owain will come soon from his villa, and then you'll—"

"Owain is here now," said a familiar voice. "Hello, Uncle Clevn."

Blue light flashed across Clevn's face. He grimaced in pain. Then the column of light vanished, and Clevn was gone.

The world began moving again. Diello looked around, watching the sky for any sign of Owain, but he saw nothing except the brewing storm.

"If you're going to try catching lightning, do it fast," Cynthe said.

Diello blinked. She seemed unaware of what had just happened.

Mages step between time, he realized. *That's what Qod was doing, shifting time so we could talk to Mamee and Pa. That's how Mamee spoke to me at the cistern the day I found the pieces of Eirian. And that must be where Owain is hiding Amie . . . between time.*

"Cynthe," Diello said, "you and Vassou get ready."

"Has Owain come?" Cynthe asked. "I don't see him."

Zephyr, please circle in this spot as slowly as you can, Diello requested.

The wind grew so gentle and smooth, it was almost like standing still. Diello watched the storm, feeling the air growing dense and charged. As they circled, he waited for just the right bit of lightning.

A forked bolt crackled through the sky, coming directly at them. Diello shouted, swinging his staff high to meet it. The lightning connected, jolting its way through the wood. This strike was much stronger than what he'd caught in the Barrens. His bones felt as if they were ablaze. Flames danced off his fingertips.

Then Diello concentrated, pulling the raw energy under his control. He managed to channel it toward the border *cloigwylie*. As the spell shattered, the barrier screeched like a live creature. Cords of magic whiplashed back and forth. Diello ducked and watched in awe as the barrier collapsed. Colors intensified and ran together, changing to garish shades that hurt his eyes. The noise was deafening. Cynthe clapped her hands over her ears, and Vassou howled in agony.

Diello felt as though his eardrums were bursting. He couldn't use his hands to protect his ears because he was still hanging on to his staff. Lightning danced off one end of it, and mage fire was shooting from the other. Eirian's power surrounded him, glowing white. He didn't need to draw the sword. Both the storm and the sword united their magic in him.

"You've done it!" Cynthe shouted. She pounded on his shoulder. "You've broken through. Stop it now! Shut it off!"

But he couldn't. Diello was becoming the lightning. He was a part of the storm. He had no body, no shape. He was destruction and fire. Eirian's voice filled his mind. . . . *Destroy!*

"Diello!"

Cynthe's fist connected with his jaw. The pain snapped him out of his daze. He realized the staff was splitting along its wood grain. He threw the staff as far as he could just before it exploded. Pieces flew everywhere. He dodged them, throwing his arms across his face, but a splinter gouged deep into his hand.

The breeze had stopped circling and was moving forward again. Something seemed wrong with Diello's vision and his balance. He swayed and sat down, guided by Cynthe, who was clinging to him.

"Your hand," she said, her voice distorted by the ringing in his ears. "You're bleeding."

He wanted to speak to Cynthe. There was something very important to tell her, but Diello couldn't pull his wits together. While Cynthe dabbed at his hand, he looked up over her head and saw Owain's eyes staring down at him from the clouds.

Once he'd seen his uncle's eyes gazing at him the same way . . . just before a lethal attack had almost knocked the royal barge from the sky.

"Stop trying to speak," Cynthe said. "Just sit quietly and you'll feel better."

"N-N-No," he mumbled. "Vassou."

The wolf was staring in the wrong direction. "We're in Embarthi," Vassou said. "We're violating the queen's order. Any guard can take our heads for bounty."

"Worse thing to worry 'bout. Look . . . *look!*"

"Where?" Cynthe asked. "I still don't see anything."

"Watch out!" Diello yelled.

A torrent of hail fell from the clouds. The icy pellets hurt. Cynthe and Vassou huddled together. Diello struggled up, drawing the sword. The magical tendrils wrapped around his wrist tightly.

Fight, Eirian urged him.

How? Diello looked in all directions. Owain's eyes had vanished. The hail pelted Diello harder. He cringed, holding his free arm above his head. Inside, his determination was growing. *Zephyr,* he called. *Get us away from this.*

I'm sorry. As fast as I fly, the hail meets us.

Can another wind help us?

The breeze dipped beneath them. Vassou growled.

"What can we do?" Cynthe cried.

An unexpected gust whipped Diello's hair back from his face. A strong easterly wind swept the hail away.

Cynthe rose to her feet. "That's better!"

A huge boulder covered in flames hurtled near them. Flinching, Diello nearly lost his balance.

Cynthe grabbed his sleeve to steady him but released him quickly.

"Is that Eirian's magic I felt?" she asked. "Can't you use it?"

"I haven't figured out how," Diello replied. Another fiery boulder fell, closer than the first one. "I can't bat these things away with a sword."

"Let me try." Cynthe looked up and pointed at another boulder coming their way. *"Break!"* she shouted, using Voice.

The boulder crumbled into dust and particles.

Cynthe whooped and shook her fists at the sky. "Is that all you can do, Uncle Owain?"

"Don't taunt him—" Diello cried, too late.

A whirlwind came spinning toward them, throwing up

dust from the ground as it grew larger. Although the zephyr tried to evade it, the tornado changed directions and closed in. Then they were spinning as the tornado caught both the zephyr and the east wind and twirled them together. Diello could hear the zephyr's voice calling out to him before it faded.

The air was completely still. There was nothing to hold them up.

Vassou was the first to fall, plummeting fast.

"I've got him!" Cynthe called, flying after him.

Diello searched the sky, turning this way and that. "Your tricks don't work!" he shouted at Owain.

A shadowy net dropped from the clouds, catching Cynthe and Vassou. Diello flew to their aid; but before he could cut them free, a second net appeared, covering him.

Cynthe pushed against the magical, smoke-like strands. "What is this?" she cried. "What's happening?"

"He's playing with us." Diello slashed at the net with Eirian before squirming through the hole he'd made. "I'll have you out in a moment."

A spike of pain jabbed through his head, and Owain was suddenly in his mind.

Do you really think this is a game? Owain asked.

Get out of my head! Diello fought to push away his uncle. Owain had controlled him before, and Diello wasn't going to let him do it again.

The pain intensified, worse than any headache. It felt as if his skull was being crushed. He tried to draw strength from Eirian's power.

The pressure on his head lessened, and Diello grinned.

Then he was hit harder than ever. He felt Owain tearing at his thoughts, attempting to take command of his will. Although Diello resisted, something was wrong. The world was turning gray, as though all the color was being bled from it. He felt oddly weak. He couldn't sense Eirian's presence anymore. Had he dropped the sword? He wasn't sure. Everything started spinning, then the grayness became black.

chapter thirty

He was floating along like a leaf in the breeze.

Shifting his head, Diello wanted to keep floating, but now there were faces crowding around him. Mamee's pale beauty, her hair glinting silver. Pa, frowning with concern as he laid his callused hand on Diello's brow. Queen Sheirae speaking sharply, but her words made no sense. Amalina, blowing bubbles through her fingers, laughing as she dipped her hands in a dish of soapy water.

"Diello. Wake up, Diello."

It was Mamee's voice, low and urgent.

He stirred. She touched his face, and the prickle of magic in her fingertips jolted him to full consciousness. Dreams and illusions faded away—except for Mamee.

Diello blinked, staring at her. When he tried to sit up, she pressed him down.

It was dark. He couldn't see where he was. It didn't feel like a dream or a vision, but it had to be. Now and then, he had the sensation of swirling in midair, but that confused him more.

"Where—"

"Hush. Listen to me. There's little time."

Diello squeezed his mother's fingers. They seemed solid, tangible. "I don't understand. Another dream?"

"No dream, my darling. Neither of us is real here. That's how I can talk to you."

He looked around. The air appeared opaque, with a sheen that reminded him of a *cloigwylie*. "But where are we?" he asked.

"We're between time, floating in one of Amalina's soap bubbles. She's playing make-believe, and we are in the nowhere that lies between your world, hers, and mine."

Diello gaped. "I *must* be dreaming."

"Stop thinking as a human," Mamee said sharply. "There is much to explain. You need to pay attention."

Diello drew out the long splinter embedded in the edge of his palm and sucked at the blood. It tasted real enough. "Where's Cynthe? Uncle Owain attacked us. We have to find her. He'll kill her!"

"He won't dare now. Clevn has seen you. He knows you two brought back the sword."

"Clevn's never helped us before."

"Oh, Diello," his mother said, sighing. "He is not your enemy."

"He *is*," Diello said. "He stopped your Death Wind from carrying your dust back to Embarthi."

"Is that all?" Mamee asked.

"All! Isn't that bad enough?"

"When I left Embarthi years ago, I accepted the terms

of my exile," Mamee said. "I have no regrets. Why should you?"

Diello hesitated, surprised that she wanted no sympathy. "Mamee, why didn't you tell us the truth about Uncle Owain? Now he's got Eirian, and I can't stop him."

"He doesn't have Eirian yet," Mamee said. "There is little time," she repeated, "such a tiny amount of time. You are between one heartbeat and the next, my son. I lied to you when you were children to protect you. Owain has watched me all my life, listened to my thoughts, spied on me. I didn't understand until we were grown that it was wrong of him to be so watchful, so jealous. He refused to share me with anyone else. He thwarted every suitor of mine until I found your father. Owain couldn't separate us, not even when he murdered a Watcher and blamed Stephel for his crime. After we escaped and hid in Antrasia, I severed every tie save the one that binds twins together. You know what I mean."

"Yes," Diello whispered.

"To keep you safe, I made you love Owain. If he ever found me, I hoped he would spare you because you admired him so." Mamee pressed her hand to her mouth. "It has worked for Amalina. Her innocence has protected her. Her fondness for him is sincere, and he hasn't harmed her."

"Yet," Diello said. "But why don't the queen and Clevn realize what he's like? Wasn't he a monster when you were both little?"

"We were as close as you and Cynthe are now. It wasn't until Owain began to grow up that he understood what it meant for him not to have crystal bones, not to have all the powers a true mage should wield. When our Gifts manifested, he changed. He grew so bitter and insecure." Mamee sighed. "And when I left, he became much worse."

Diello fell silent. He remembered the night before the goblin attack, when he'd heard a voice in the rainstorm calling his mother's name. *Was that Owain sending a warning to her? Surely not. Who then?*

"The night before our birthday," Diello said, "there was a voice in the wind. . . . Was it Clevn's?"

"No. That was my brother. Year after year, Owain called to me in my dreams and sent his voice along the winds. He hoped to trick me into answering. I never did, but eventually he found me anyway."

"Did you know what was going to happen . . . that day at the farm?" Diello asked.

"As soon as you had the vision of the Death Flock flying over the cottage, I knew the omen meant terrible danger. I sent you and Cynthe away and hid Amie. It was all I had time for."

"But why didn't we *all* run away and hide together?"

Mamee shook her head. "I couldn't risk it. You children would have died with us."

"But—"

"There are places along your life's road where you can change your future, just as there are places where you cannot. Before we left Embarthi, Stephel urged me to let him kill Owain, but I was too weakhearted. How I regret that decision! We thwarted Owain, but we did not *stop* him. Now it's up to you. Do you understand?"

"But I've already failed," Diello said. "As soon as I'm no longer inside this—this bubble—Owain will finish me and take the sword. How do I stop him?"

"Show the queen what he truly is. He's deceived her long enough."

"But why hasn't Clevn protected her? He's supposed to be a stronger mage than Owain."

"In some ways. But Owain has a cunning that Clevn lacks. And my mother will not accept the truth. When you love someone, you create excuses and blind yourself. Make them *see*, Diello."

"How?" Diello cried.

"You're as strong a mage as Owain already."

"But you always said—"

She caressed his face. "Forgive me. I have been as prejudiced as my people, as slow to accept change as they are. Faelin or not, you should have been trained from birth. Instead, I held you and Cynthe back, suppressing your Gifts and telling Stephel it was for your protection. But you have done it all by yourselves. You will be a great mage-chancellor someday, a worthy successor to Clevn. And Cynthe will someday be queen."

"No, we aren't going to rule Embarthi," Diello said. "Vassou took us to the Knower to have our destinies foretold, and it said—"

"Hush," Mamee whispered. "Sight will guide you later. Now, you must defeat Owain."

"But if Owain can fool Clevn, what chance do I have? Clevn hates me."

"Clevn doesn't hate you," Mamee said. "Give him proof as only a mage can."

"There must be something I can use against Owain," Diello said. "Something besides Eirian."

Suddenly Mamee faded away, and Diello could see Amalina. The child was sitting on a thick carpet in a room that Diello didn't recognize. Amalina babbled nonsense to herself as she played, splashing her hands in the soap and blowing more bubbles. He watched one floating toward him. *When it touches me, my bubble will shatter,* he worried. *Owain will know where I am.*

Diello saw the deed seal hanging around Amalina's neck by a blue ribbon. A faint aura of magic glowed around the silver disk, a remnant of the disguising spell that had kept Eirian hidden for years. That was probably why Owain hadn't realized that Amie wore it.

What can the deed seal do for us now? Diello wondered. *Mamee persuaded me to give the deed seal to Amie for protection—how might I use it?*

"Amie," Diello said, "give me the seal, please."

Amalina was dribbling patterns of soap across her dress. Ribbons tied back her golden ringlets from her face. She looked rosy and content. Yet Uncle Owain had threatened to sell her to the goblins. He'd also threatened to make Amalina forget Diello and Cynthe.

Can she hear me? Will she even know me?

The fat, glossy bubble was still floating toward Diello.

"Amie," Diello said urgently, "if you can hear me, give me the seal."

The child didn't look up, but he saw the seal lift from around her neck and float toward him. He reached for it eagerly. His fingers touched a barrier—the slick side of his bubble.

At that moment, the other bubble touched his. Both burst. Diello fell, only to be caught by Amalina's chubby hand.

She balanced him on her palm, peering at him. Her face looked enormous. It was like being size-shifted by Qod all over again.

"Hello, Del," Amalina said, showing no surprise at seeing him or his tiny size. "I've missed you lots and lots."

"I've missed you, too."

The seal floated above him, much bigger than he was. Amalina gazed up at it. Giggling, she caught it just before it soared out of reach.

"Isn't this pretty?" she asked. "When I wear it, no one can see it but me."

"It's very pretty," Diello said. "May I have it?"

She handed it over. As soon as Diello touched the warm metal, it shrank so that he could fit it around his neck. He tucked it beneath his clothing.

"You're fading away, Del," Amalina said sadly, poking him with her finger. "I wish you'd stay and play with me. I'm lonely. I want to go home."

"I'll come for you very soon," he promised, but in a blink she was gone and he was falling. . . .

A slap to his face brought the world back into focus. "He's breathing," said Uncle Owain.

Before Diello could do anything, he was struck again. He sat up with flailing fists but was held down by a Fae in servant's livery.

Owain stood over Diello. He wore a dark-red tunic patterned with gold threads and a chain of rubies. More rubies dangled from his pointed ears, and he had a jeweled ring on every finger. Sparkles glinted through his hair and close-cut beard. His boot was resting on Diello's shoulder. Smiling, Owain stepped back, releasing Diello.

Diello scrambled to his feet. Someone had untied his belt. When he stood up, he left Eirian lying on the floor. There was a titter of laughter.

Owain waved, bowing slightly to the crowd. Diello looked around. He saw polished marble floors and a gilded ceiling soaring high overhead. An empty throne stood at the far end of the room. *It's the Liedhe—the Fae court. Why did Owain bring me here?* Dressed in splendid silk gowns or ornate tunics, their glamour shining in their hair and on their skin, the Fae courtiers laughed harder, pointing at Diello.

Hot humiliation flooded him. He saw Owain's daughter, Penrith, standing in the crowd. His cousin was as pretty as ever—slender and elegant in a green velvet gown, her brown hair a silky curtain down her back. A delicate bow hung from her waist. She wasn't laughing openly like the others, but her smirk made Diello grit his teeth.

Diello bent to pick up the sword; but Owain was quicker, planting his foot on Eirian's scabbard.

"You've no right even to touch it," Owain said.

"Where's Cynthe?" Diello asked. "And Vassou?"

"Unnecessary distractions," Owain replied. He picked up Eirian, taking care to handle it only by the scabbard. When he turned to the courtiers and held it up, they cheered.

"I told you I would save Embarthi!" he cried.

They cheered even louder. Penrith held up her hands, conjuring two wreaths of white roses. She placed one wreath around her father's neck and the other on his brow as a crown of victory. Kissing his hand, she curtsied gracefully before him.

"My lord," she said.

His eyes shining bright, Owain beckoned to the courtiers.

The room quieted. It seemed at first that no one would approach, but then a courtier stepped before Owain and bowed to him. The next bowed with a greater flourish. Owain's smile grew. He stood there, holding Eirian across his arm as though it were a scepter and he were their king.

"Stop this," Diello said loudly.

The next courtier in line turned to Diello haughtily. "Will you not dismiss this Faelin servant, Lord Owain?"

"Where's the queen?" Diello demanded. "Where's Clevn?"

Owain spoke to the crowd: "The mage-chancellor is indisposed. Her Majesty is not holding audience today."

"So you *did* injure Clevn when you attacked," Diello said, pitching his voice to carry across the chamber.

A murmur of curiosity ran through the crowd.

"Does the court know that you need my crystal bones because you have none?" Diello taunted Owain.

Owain gripped Diello's shoulder. "That's enough. Or the next time you appear in this chamber, you'll have no tongue. Look here." He tapped the chain of rubies stretching across his chest. "Look very closely, and you'll see how strong I am."

Diello wanted to refuse, but he felt Owain's magic compelling him. He peered at the jewels. They were smooth ovals, lacking any facets to make them sparkle. He thought he saw a face in one of them. He looked closer. It was Cynthe—trapped inside. Vassou was frozen in another ruby. Inside a third, Diello saw Amalina.

Diello forced himself not to react.

"If I choose, I can throw these stones on the floor and crush them to dust," Owain said. "Is that what you want?"

Diello shook his head.

"Now, stand over there." Owain pointed at a nearby column. "And be quiet."

Diello obeyed him, looking at no one. Owain's spell on him released, but Diello remained where he was.

"Let us resume," Owain said to the courtiers.

They stopped murmuring and formed a new line to bow to him. Owain beamed, his hand stroking Eirian's scabbard proudly.

chapter thirty-one

a stir at the far end of the gallery stopped the pro-
ceedings. The double doors were flung open, and a
page trotted through. "Make way for the queen!"

The courtiers gathered along one side of the long room.
Owain was left standing in the center, with Eirian in his
arms. The wreaths he wore faded out of existence.

A black samal wolf entered the room, wearing a gold col-
lar that gleamed against his dark fur. This was Chorl, who'd
once bowed to Cynthe and Diello in front of the queen's
army, the first of Sheirae's subjects to publicly acknowledge
them. Behind the samal came Queen Sheirae. She walked
slowly to match Clevn's pace at her side. Her twin brother
was hunched and leaning heavily on his staff. His thin face
was drawn with pain. The queen's gaze swept the room.

Her silver hair was coiled atop her head. She wore a
gown of white, encrusted with silver beads and diamonds
that glittered as she moved. Her jeweled bow hung at her
waist, and diamond-dust earrings in the shape of miniature
arrows dangled from her ears.

Clevn straightened with visible effort. Unlike Sheirae,

he didn't hide his outrage as he stared at the guilty courtiers. His gaze flickered over Diello without acknowledgment. The queen had not yet looked in Diello's direction.

"Who called this assembly?" Clevn demanded. "The queen gives no audience today."

"I summoned the court," Owain replied, giving his mother and uncle a slight bow. "I have good news. I have returned Eirian to Embarthi."

"How have you done this?" Sheirae asked.

She believes him, Diello thought. *She won't even look at me.*

Diello ran to his uncle, shoving aside the servant who tried to step between them. As Owain turned, lifting the sheathed sword out of reach, Diello grabbed the ruby necklace instead. *How can I free them?*

Before he could flee, the guards caught him. They snapped shackles of glowing blue magic around Diello's wrists. One of them tried to take the necklace, but Diello hung on. In the struggle, one ruby popped free of its setting and went spinning away.

The broken necklace was returned to Owain.

"Forgive this disturbance, Your Majesty," Owain said. "As you see, the boy is nothing but a ruffian."

"Stop lying!" Diello shouted.

The queen still ignored him.

Please! Diello sent his thoughts to Clevn. *You saw Cynthe and me at the border. We brought Eirian back, not Owain. You know the truth. Don't let him trick you.*

Clevn didn't answer. Instead, he shut his eyes.

A man in a crimson-and-black uniform swaggered forward. General Rhodri was commander of the queen's army and one of Lwyneth's suitors before her exile. He wore a lion skin over one shoulder, a jeweled dagger at his belt, and a cuirass polished to a bright sheen. The fighting rowels of his spurs jingled with every step. Black tassels swung from his ears' pointed tips. The last time Diello and Cynthe had been in Embarthi, Rhodri had helped them secretly.

"Lord Owain!" he roared. "Identify this boy for the court!"

"No!" Sheirae commanded.

Owain smirked.

The queen gestured to her guards. "Remove the boy from this chamber."

Diello struggled. The guards levitated him and began towing him toward the door.

A woman picked up the stray ruby. She gave it to Penrith with a curtsy.

Tucking the sword under his arm, Owain beckoned to his daughter.

Don't! Diello tried to command her.

He had no idea if his cousin could receive his thoughts. The last time he'd seen Penrith, he'd wanted to like her. But she'd been stuck-up and unwilling to be friends. She was to replace Cynthe in the line of succession. He couldn't expect her to help him now. Still he had to try.

"Penrith," Owain said.

She started in her father's direction, but General Rhodri

intercepted the girl and took the ruby from her hand.

"Wait!" Rhodri called out. He lifted the ruby to the light and peered at it. "Before the boy is removed, perhaps the queen should see this jewel. It's most uncommon."

"The jewel is mine!" Owain snapped.

Clevn swayed, leaning on his staff.

"This is surely a happy day for all of us," Sheirae said. "There will be a festival to celebrate Eirian's return and my son's heroism in recovering it. But for now, you all have my leave to withdraw. Except for you, Owain. Guards, take that boy away as I requested."

The guards towed Diello along. *General,* Diello thought desperately, *if you truly loved my mother, help us now!*

"Bring that ruby to me," Owain commanded.

Rhodri's face went slack. He walked toward Owain.

Diello felt his bones itching. Owain was using him, drawing power through him to compel Rhodri.

Not this time, Diello vowed. *Eirian!* he called.

The sword, still in Owain's possession, began shining inside its scabbard. Using Sight, Diello could see the webs of magic reaching from Owain to Rhodri. He cut them. Then he severed his own magical shackles.

Rhodri blinked. He walked over to the queen and held out the jewel on the palm of his hand. "Will Your Majesty look at this?"

The queen shook her head, turning away.

"Please!" Diello said.

Owain stepped between her and the general. "You have

been ordered to withdraw," he said to Rhodri. "And I'll take that." He reached for the ruby, but Rhodri fumbled and dropped it.

"I beg your pardon, Lord Owain," Rhodri said contritely, while gripping Owain's arm to stop him from picking it up.

Owain shook him off. Courtiers swirled around in an effort to pick up the jewel.

"I'll get it!"

"No, I have it!"

"Here it is!" One woman held it aloft, laughing.

While the guards were distracted, Diello hurried toward her. As she reached to give it to Owain, Diello grabbed her hand and closed his fingers over the stone. Owain was muttering a spell, but Diello swiftly wrapped a *cloigwylie* around himself. Owain's spell bounced off.

Cynthe stared up at Diello from within the ruby. He still didn't know how to free her.

I am whole, Eirian whispered to him. *Use my strength. Let us fight.*

Pain spiked through Diello's head as his *cloigwylie* broke. Crying out, he dropped to one knee. An invisible noose tightened around his throat.

Diello gasped and strained. He could hear Rhodri shouting: "Will you let Lwyneth's son be murdered in front of you?"

Release the jewel now, Owain said in Diello's mind. Owain was choking him as he had once choked Cynthe.

Diello clutched the ruby. His lungs were aching, and Owain was drawing on his crystal bones again. Through Sight, Diello saw the twisted web surrounding Cynthe. With his strength draining away, he couldn't break it.

I can't pass out now. Eirian, give me more of your power.

The sword obeyed. One by one, Diello began to unwind the magic strands.

Eirian will soon obey me, not you, Owain said. *Then I won't need your magic.*

Diello clutched at his throat. He fought to remain conscious. *I can resist the spell choking me, but I can't release Cynthe at the same time.*

Diello! he heard Cynthe calling.

Just one more twist.

And she was released.

With a puff of crimson smoke, Cynthe appeared in the middle of the chamber. Diello reached for the spell binding Vassou. Another ruby in the necklace vanished into smoke, revealing the young wolf. Vassou bounded over beside Cynthe, snarling. The courtiers scattered away. Diello collapsed.

"Help him!" Cynthe cried.

Diello felt as though he were drowning. He needed to tell Cynthe that Amalina was still trapped in one of Owain's rubies.

Too late, he thought.

Cynthe faced Owain, and he smiled. Looking up at the enormous crystal chandelier overhead, Cynthe cried, *"Break!"*

It shattered, raining down slivers. The startled courtiers rose in the air to escape. Owain flew with them.

The spell choking Diello vanished. He sucked in a breath, coughing violently. As he got to his feet, he noticed that Penrith was among the few who hadn't flown away.

The girl held her cheek, blood dripping onto her silk gown. Her eyes were glazed with shock.

"Move aside," Cynthe said to her.

Penrith straightened. "I won't. You don't belong here. You never will."

"I won't tell you again."

"I'm the queen's heir. You can't give me orders."

Cynthe started to push her, but Diello said, "Don't, Cynthe. She's not our enemy."

"Oh, yes, I am!" Penrith cried. "I won't let a half-breed take my place."

Cynthe grabbed her wrists. Sparks shot off Penrith's skin.

"Ow!" Cynthe yelled, jumping back.

More sparks shot from Penrith's fingertips. Diello saw his twin raise her fists.

"No," he said. "You'll hurt her."

"I hope I do," Cynthe said.

"Listen to me! She's being directed by Uncle Owain. She's a distraction. Forget her."

The anger in Cynthe's face died to a simmer. She nodded, lowering her hands. Diello headed toward the dais where Sheirae and Clevn stood; but as Cynthe fell into step beside him, Penrith said softly, "Coward."

Cynthe spun around, flicking fire. Small flames ignited the hem of Penrith's gown. She screamed.

"*Out!*" Cynthe said, and the blaze was snuffed.

Penrith stared at Cynthe. "You . . . how can *you*, a Faelin, command such magic?"

Cynthe tossed back her hair without answering and walked forward with Diello. *The queen's seen and heard everything,* Diello thought. *She has to believe us now.*

The courtiers began to land along the edge of the chamber.

Owain came down in front of the twins, blocking them from approaching Sheirae. "These Faelin barbarians have defied Your Majesty's order of exile," he said. "They should be—"

"Uncle Owain!" Diello called out. "Why don't you tell Her Majesty exactly how you took Eirian away from Brezog?"

"The queen has no interest in your lies," Owain said.

Sheirae's gaze shifted to her son. "Tell me," she commanded.

He flushed. "I—well, the goblin is dead, of course. After that, it was simply a matter of—"

"*We* took Eirian from the gorlord," Diello said. He held up his hand and stripped back his sleeve, revealing the mark of Eirian. "My twin and I. We got the scabbard back from Tescorsa, too."

"A tattoo means nothing," Owain said.

Cynthe had lost her bow, but her quiver remained

strapped across her shoulder. She drew out the queen's silver arrow that had killed Brezog. Kneeling before Sheirae, Cynthe held out the arrow.

"Your Majesty."

Sheirae reached out, then hesitated. "Clevn?"

The mage-chancellor gestured for a servant to take the arrow. The servant then gave it to Clevn, who looked at it closely.

"Well?" Sheirae asked.

"My dear lady mother," Owain interrupted, "these Faelin creatures are trained by the one this court calls the Betrayer. Your daughter, Lwyneth."

"That's enough!" Clevn said. "You know better than to say that name here."

Sheirae's face revealed no emotion, but Diello saw her hand clenched at her side.

Owain continued, "This pair has come to bring chaos, nothing more. They speak nothing but lies. I beg Your Majesty to remove them from your presence."

Sheirae studied her son's face.

She still believes Owain, Diello thought in dismay. *It is no spell. No matter what she sees him do, she still believes him because she wants to. Why couldn't she have believed Mamee when she had the chance?*

"Your Majesty." Clevn held out the arrow. "This is yours."

When the queen didn't respond, Clevn touched her arm. Sheirae flinched.

"This is your arrow," Clevn said. "The girl speaks the truth."

Sheirae took it, running her hands across the fletching. She nodded. "I put this arrow in that vile creature's heart." She looked up at Diello and Cynthe. "You say Brezog is dead, then?"

They both nodded.

"There's a new gorlord called Khuno in his place," Diello added. "Our friend Scree died there, helping us regain Eirian."

"And you brought the sword back. Despite your banishment, you returned Eirian to us?"

Diello and Cynthe grinned at each other.

"Your Majesty," Owain said, "I directed these young Faelin. They followed my orders well. I am pleased that you approve."

"That's not true!" Cynthe shouted.

She turned to Diello, but his gaze was on Vassou. Unnoticed, the pup had edged closer to Owain. Vassou's eyes were focused on the broken necklace dangling from Owain's hand. *This could be our chance,* Diello thought.

Vassou leaped forward, nipping Owain's leg. Diello jumped at his uncle, who lifted Eirian out of reach. But it was the necklace Diello wanted. He grabbed it and backed away.

Swearing, Owain kicked Vassou, but the pup dodged him and hurried to Cynthe's side.

The guards surrounded the twins.

"Remove them!" Owain said. "And take back my necklace at once!"

chapter thirty-two

Cynthe and Vassou stood in front of Diello, trying to protect him from the guards.

"Hurry," Cynthe urged him.

Diello was busy peering at each of the jewels in turn. He found the one containing Amalina. He gave its locking spell a swift twist, and crimson smoke hit him in the face. When it cleared, Amalina was standing there. She knuckled her eyes, looking bewildered, then hugged his legs.

"Del! Oh, Del! Cynnie!"

They knelt, kissing her cheeks and stroking her curls.

"I'm hungry," Amalina announced as Diello picked her up. "I haven't eaten in a long time. Not since Ninka went away."

Diello remembered that Ninka was the nursemaid who'd been caring for Amalina. "How long?" he asked.

Amalina spread her arms wide. "This long!"

Owain trembled with rage. "Can these chattering children be removed and decorum restored?"

Amalina was busy pulling the deed seal out from beneath Diello's tunic. "Here it is!" she cried.

Clevn leaned forward. "What is that?"

"Our father's deed seal," Cynthe replied.

"Your father," Clevn said with scorn.

"An Antrasin peasant and a thief," Owain added.

Diello met Clevn's eyes. "You know better. Stephel was a Carnethie Knight. *And* a landowner."

"But human," said Clevn.

"Yes," Diello said proudly. He held up the deed seal. "It also holds an *amddif* spell—the one that kept Eirian safe for fifteen years. Look at it, Clevn. Can you recognize our mother's magic in it?"

"Proof of Lwyneth's treachery," Owain declared.

"Proof of her careful guardianship," Diello retorted. "She kept Eirian out of *your* hands."

Owain's eyes narrowed, but before he could say anything, the queen interrupted.

"Who is this child?" Sheirae asked, looking at Amalina.

Diello shifted Amalina in his arms to face Sheirae. "This, Your Majesty, is my younger sister, Amalina. Say hello to the queen, Amie."

The little girl waved at the queen and smiled. "Majesty," she said.

Sheirae's expression softened. "She looks exactly like her mother at that age. Three children," the queen murmured. "A lucky number."

"Your Majesty!" Owain shouted. "Are you forgetting your daughter's treason?"

"He's right," Clevn said, and glanced at a servant. "Send

for the Watchers. It is time Eirian returned to its rightful place."

"Eirian's rightful place is with me," Owain said.

"You have the least right to it of all," Clevn replied.

"These twins are the true heirs!" bellowed General Rhodri from across the room. "They have proven their loyalty and courage."

"You speak treason!" Owain shouted. "Guards, arrest Rhodri!"

But the guards did not obey. Instead, they looked at the queen. She gave them no order.

A tide of red crept up Owain's face.

"Owain," Clevn said, "put down the sword and step away."

Owain stiffened. "Eirian is *mine*."

There was a sudden flurry of movement in the crowd. Diello saw Penrith running for the doors. More guards barred her exit.

"I've done nothing but obey his orders," the girl cried. "The treason is his! I had no choice."

"Shut up!" Owain shouted. "Your Majesty, pay no heed to what she says."

"We shall question the girl later," Clevn said. "What's important now is Eirian."

Behind the queen's dais, a door opened and the twelve Watchers of Afon Heyrn filed into the chamber. They wore tan hooded robes. It was impossible to see their faces. Their magic shivered through Diello's bones. He remembered the last time he'd seen the Watchers. Clevn had tried to give them Eirian's blade, and they wouldn't take it. They'd claimed that an incomplete sword would cause disruption and disharmony. *If they'd helped us then*, Diello thought, *Owain wouldn't be holding all this power now.*

Keep me from their prison, Eirian said to him. *I am whole. Use me to fight.*

Diello tried to ignore the sword's plea.

"Eirian is not yours," Clevn said to Owain. "It can belong to no mortal hand save by its choice."

One of the Watchers stepped forward, bowing to the queen before addressing the mage-chancellor: "Eirian is awake. It wishes to wage combat. Great care must be taken with it now."

Clevn glanced uneasily at Owain, who was cradling the sheathed weapon in his arms and muttering under his breath.

"Rituals must be performed," the Watcher continued, "to control and quiet it."

"No one will silence Eirian!" Owain shouted. "I am now ruler of Embarthi. You have bowed to me—all of you! You have pledged yourselves to *me*."

The courtiers exchanged looks of alarm. Some shook their heads.

"Eirian wants war, and we shall wage war," Owain went on. "We shall take Antrasia for our own."

The Watcher turned toward Diello. "Lord Owain must be parted from the sword without delay or its effect on him cannot be stopped."

"I think the sword has driven him mad," Sheirae murmured.

Diello met Cynthe's gaze and guessed what she was thinking: *Owain's always been mad.*

Diello watched his uncle warily. He was reminded of the time a neighbor asked Pa to help him kill a rabid dog. Diello would never forget how the wretched creature would snarl and bark viciously one moment, then shiver and whine in bewilderment the next.

"Stand ready," Diello warned his twin.

Vassou growled in agreement.

Diello set Amalina on her feet and held her hand. Nervously, she sucked on her thumb.

"Owain, no one's going to start a war today," Clevn commanded. *"Put down the sword."*

The blue sheen of a *cloigwylie* appeared around Owain. He laughed. "You can't use Voice on me, Uncle. You're too old. And you're ill."

"I'll heal," Clevn said.

Diello was aware of the Watchers murmuring with their heads together. He didn't like the way they kept glancing from him to Owain.

"You cannot carry Eirian into battle, Owain, if you haven't mastered it," Clevn said. "Let's see if you have any right to it. Put it down. We'll let the Faelin boy try to draw it from its scabbard. Then we'll give you the same chance. The sword will tell us what it wants."

"That old trick!" Owain scoffed. "You want the Watchers to hide Eirian in the Cave of Mysteries, where no one can ever get at it. You want it to stay quiet, to be useless. Why, Uncle? Because you fear Eirian's power."

The Watchers stretched out their hands in unison and cried out, *"Release!"* The word reverberated through the chamber.

Eirian fell from Owain's arms and lay on the floor. Its hilt blazed with magic. The scabbard's jewels shifted their patterns.

Owain dropped to his knees beside the sword. He reached for the hilt, then screamed and yanked back his hand.

"No! I had it. It's mine!"

"Diello," Clevn said, "let the Watchers examine the marks on your wrist."

Diello showed his wrist to the closest Watcher.

"The marks are real," said the Watcher.

Clevn pointed at Diello. "Prove it, Diello."

Diello walked over to the sword, but Owain shoved him away. Crouching, Owain drew Eirian, flinging aside the scabbard. Light flashed from the blade, sparking along its edge. The light encompassed Owain, and he writhed, screaming in agony.

"Help him!" Sheirae called out. "Save him!"

When a guard tried to obey her, Owain slashed the man's chest. The guard fell, and courtiers took flight in all directions.

Tears of pain streamed down Owain's face, but he wouldn't release his grip. His eyes hunted among the faces in the crowd before he locked on Diello.

"You are just like Lwyneth," he said.

Clevn hurried toward Diello, but Owain hit him with mage fire. Clevn staggered, gasping. The queen's guards were flying to her side as Chorl shielded her with a *cloigwylie*. Vassou gave Cynthe and Amalina the same protection before he shepherded Amalina behind one of the columns.

Penrith hovered in the air. "Father, please stop!"

General Rhodri drew his dagger, but Owain felled him with a burst of mage fire.

Cynthe flew at Penrith, grabbing her small bow. Spinning around in the air, Cynthe shot one of her arrows at Owain, but it couldn't penetrate his *cloigwylie*.

"Diello!" Cynthe yelled. "Look out!"

Diello heard Eirian whistle through the air as he dodged the blow.

"Boy!" Clevn called, and tossed Diello his own mage staff.

Diello raised it to block Owain's next attack.

"Eirian!" Diello cried.

The sword should have cut through the staff, but instead the blade stopped less than a finger's breadth from the wood. Owain looked baffled, then furious. He raised the blade again and swung harder. Again, Eirian stopped just shy of striking the staff.

The staff's carved symbols were shining now. Diello felt its unfamiliar magic, twice as powerful as anything his own staff had ever channeled.

I'm holding Clevn's power, Diello thought. *If I want, I can blast Owain to ashes and avenge Mamee and Pa.*

He lifted the staff, aiming its tip at Owain, but then he realized that Owain's powers were pushing at him, compelling him to attack.

Use the staff, Owain's thoughts pounded at his. *Use the staff, you stupid boy. It's more than you can handle. Let it destroy you!*

Diello lowered the staff. "No."

Cynthe landed at his back, holding the bow drawn and ready.

"This Faelin boy is afraid to use real magic," Owain said.

Owain threw a blazing ball at Diello. Diello realized that if he ducked, the mage fire would hit Cynthe. He wasn't sure her *cloigwylie* was strong enough to protect her.

Diello swung up the staff and unleashed its power. It deflected Owain's fire back at him, but the wood splintered.

Owain ducked, staring at him, then lifted Eirian for another swing.

"Give up!" Diello said, dropping the now-useless staff. "The sword won't strike me. You aren't its master. Put it down."

Owain shook his head. His face was pale with strain.

Diello took a cautious step toward his uncle.

"Careful," Clevn murmured.

Diello didn't need the warning. Keeping his movements calm and unhurried, he drew close enough to see Owain trembling.

"Let me have the sword," Diello said.

"No!"

Diello reached out, but his hand was rebuffed by Owain's *cloigwylie*.

"It's not that simple," Owain boasted. "If Eirian will not strike you, I have other means."

Cynthe flew behind the queen and her guards, taking the silver arrow from the servant who held it.

"Diello, now!" she cried. Fitting the arrow to her bowstring, she drew and released it smoothly.

The silver arrow pierced Owain's *cloigwylie*.

Diello grabbed for Eirian's hilt, curling his hand around Owain's.

You, Eirian whispered.

Tendrils of light and power wrapped around Diello's wrist as Eirian's magic flowed into him.

Diello twisted to one side, pulling his uncle off balance. As Owain stumbled, Diello wrested Eirian from his grasp. The sword's grip settled against Diello's palm as though made for his hand. The *chthon* blade shone like molten white fire.

Fight with me, Eirian said. *Let us slay! Let us conquer!*

Eirian's power was stronger than Diello had ever felt before. It sang through his bones, making him throw back his head. He wanted to join Eirian's voice with his own war cries.

But I don't want to go mad like Owain.

"Take Lord Owain away now!" Clevn ordered.

Several guards pounced, wrapping Owain in bands of magic. Levitating him, the guards took Owain out swiftly. Penrith went with them, weeping quietly.

Almost blinded by the sword's radiance, Diello hardly noticed the Watchers positioning themselves in a large circle around him.

"Diello?" Cynthe called.

He didn't bother to answer her. It took all his concentration to withstand Eirian's voice. He realized that the mage-chancellor was now standing at his shoulder.

"Steady, boy," Clevn said. "Control it."

"The scabbard," Diello said.

Cynthe brought it to him.

We will not fight, Diello soothed the sword with his mind, slow and steady. *There is no war. We will be at peace.*

At last he managed to slide the sword into the scabbard.

Its voice faded from Diello's mind. The tendrils of magic loosened on his arm. Diello pulled free.

Cynthe and Clevn stood with him inside the circle of Watchers. Everyone else, including the queen, had retreated to the opposite side of the chamber. Amalina was peeking around the column, and Vassou made sure she didn't leave its safety. Rhodri, getting dazedly to his feet, joined Sheirae.

One of the Watchers stepped toward Diello and extended his hands as though to take the sword.

"Not so fast," Diello said.

"Don't be a fool," Clevn began, but Cynthe tapped the mage-chancellor's sleeve and shook her head.

"Let him speak," she said.

"All this trouble," Diello began, "happened because of Fae greed. You wanted to keep Eirian all to yourselves."

"It has to be guarded," Clevn insisted.

"Yes, but there's so much good it could do," Diello said. "I've seen how much the Tescorsians suffer. The goblins have it even worse."

The courtiers muttered among themselves.

"Silence!" the queen said. "Let Diello speak."

Diello hesitated, glancing at Cynthe. She gave him a nod and stood beside him.

"There's no limit to the good Eirian can do," Cynthe said.

Diello thought of Qod's joy over the young tomtir. "Its magic can help everyone," he said, "if you're willing to share it."

"Then maybe there wouldn't be jealousy among the realms," Cynthe added. "Or war."

"Who are you," the queen asked, "to tell us how to set policy?"

"Didn't Your Majesty exile us so that we would have to find the sword for you?" Diello said, voicing his suspicion. "Don't you care about the dire conditions out there?"

"Your mother has taught you her ideas," Clevn countered.

"My parents taught me to do what's right," Diello replied.

"So you think Eirian should be given to the Antrasins."

"No, I don't."

Clevn looked at the queen before turning back to Diello. "We'll consider what you've said."

"You'll agree!" Diello demanded.

"You must promise to accept our terms," Cynthe said. "Once a year, the Watchers can take Eirian to Tescorsa and guard it there. They can then take it to the Barrens."

"And then to Antrasia," Diello continued, "before it comes back to Embarthi. Every year, it's to be shared this way."

Several people gasped.

"Let my army guard the sword's safety!" Rhodri roared above the noise. "The Black Lion Regiment will see that no harm comes to Eirian or the Watchers."

"And if we don't agree?" Clevn asked.

"I don't have to hand over Eirian, do I?" Diello replied.

Clevn turned to the Watchers. "Do you accept these terms?"

One answered, "We do, if it means Eirian remains under Fae control."

"Your Majesty?" Clevn asked. "What is your will?"

Sheirae stared at Diello. "I agree."

Diello gave Eirian to a Watcher. With extreme care, the Watcher carried it from the chamber, followed by the others.

Clevn grabbed Diello's hands, turning them over to reveal his palms. Neither was burned.

"Master of Eirian indeed," Clevn murmured.

"Oh, Diello!" Cynthe cried, hugging his neck.

Vassou crowded close. "Well done!"

Then Amalina was skipping beside them. "Del! Del!"

Diello scooped up the child, tickling her until she giggled. He looked at his twin. "We've got her back."

Cynthe nodded, her eyes shining. "If only Scree could be here."

"I know."

Sheirae stepped forward. "Approach me," she commanded.

Still carrying Amalina, with Cynthe clutching his arm, Diello faced the queen. Clevn stood beside her now.

"You have done what I thought was impossible," Sheirae said. "I wish to say . . . that is, I cannot adequately express the depth of my— Oh, my dear Lwyneth's children, I am so sorry. Welcome home."

"Then we aren't banished anymore?" Cynthe asked.

The queen gently touched Amalina's curls. "You may stay within the Liedhe Court forever, if you wish. You may have anything you desire."

"Your Majesty," Rhodri said, bowing low, "can you forgive Lwyneth as well?"

Silence fell over the chamber. Diello looked at Cynthe. He could hardly breathe. Cynthe gripped his fingers hard.

Sheirae looked across the faces of her courtiers before she turned to Diello, Cynthe, and Amalina. "Do you know what you're asking, General?"

Rhodri inclined his head. "I do. These Faelin twins have served Embarthi perhaps better than it deserved. The girl is tough, a fighter. She uses a bow almost as well as Your Majesty. Her Gifts are strong. And she is accompanied by a samal wolf. Unlike Penrith, who was never truly suitable to be your successor."

Diello saw that Chorl had walked over to Vassou,

and the two wolves were studying each other cautiously. Glancing Clevn's way, Diello found the mage-chancellor studying *him*.

"The boy has more than proven his abilities," Clevn took over from Rhodri. "He's shown persistence, courage, and compassion beyond his years. This pair is worthy, despite their mixed blood."

The queen seemed about to smile, but she kept her composure. "Let the Liedhe Court hear my decision," she declared. "My daughter, Lwyneth, is forgiven. Her name may once again be spoken. Her children are now my children. Her daughter Cynthe shall be queen after me. Her son, Diello, shall be mage-chancellor after Clevn. And her third child, Amalina, shall be trained in the Mysteries when she is old enough."

The courtiers looked stunned. Then they began to clap and cheer. Cynthe smiled at Diello, her eyes bright with tears.

"Did you hear what she said?" Cynthe asked. "Oh, Diello, think of it!"

Diello had one more request. Handing Amalina to Cynthe, Diello whispered in Clevn's ear.

He wasn't sure what the mage-chancellor would do, but Clevn simply nodded.

"It shall be as you wish, Diello. On the morrow, I'll send General Rhodri's men to find the burial place of Lwyneth and Stephel. They will take your parents' dust to the cloud realm of Dweigana, where they may rest through Eternity."

Cynthe set down Amalina and hugged Diello tightly. "They'll finally be at peace."

"We'll always remember them," Diello said, hugging her back. "And everything they did for us."

"We won't forget Scree either," Cynthe added.

"Qod and Reeshwin, too. Everyone who helped us."

Cynthe rested her hand on Vassou's head, smiling as Amalina began twirling merrily in a circle.

"Everyone," Cynthe agreed.

THE END